SEX TOY TALES

SEX TOY TALES

Anne Semans

and

Cathy Winks

Editors

Down There Press
San Francisco

Sex Toy Tales Copyright © 1998
by Anne Semans and Cathy Winks

Library of Congress Cataloging-in-Publication Data
Sex toy tales / Anne Semans & Cathy Winks, editors
           p.   cm.
        ISBN 0-940208-21-0
        1. Erotic stories, American. I. Semans, Anne. II. Winks, Cathy.
PS648.E7S49   1998
813'.0108358--dc21   98-4928
                                             CIP

We also offer librarians an Alternative CIP prepared by Sanford Berman,
Head Cataloger at Hennepin County Library, Edina MN, which may more
fully reflect this book's scope and content.

Alternative Cataloging-in-Publication Data
Semans, Anne, 1962–
      Sex toy tales. Anne Semans and Cathy Winks, editors. San Francisco,
CA: Down There Press, copyright 1998.
      Over 30 erotic stories, "both real-life and imagined," each celebrating
the "exciting and liberating possibilities of sex accessories" like vibrators,
condoms, fishing tackle, and blenders.
      1. Erotic fiction, American. 2. Sex aids—Fiction. 3. Sex aids—Personal
narratives. I. Winks, Cathy, 1960– . II. Title. III. Title: Tales of sex toys. IV.
Down There Press
      301.4178

Additional copies of this book are available from your local bookstore or
directly from the publisher:
Down There Press, 938 Howard St., #101, San Francisco CA 94103
Please enclose $16.50 for each copy ordered, which includes postage and
handling.

Cover design by MB Condon
Book design by Small World Productions

Printed in the United States of America   9 8 7 6 5 4 3 2 1

*Dedicated
to sex toy users
everywhere*

Contents

Introduction

You're never too old to play with toys

Do adults play with toys? You bet they do. We're not talking about Barbie dolls and Power Rangers (though both have probably made their way into more than one adult's fantasies). We're talking about sex toys. Every day, in every part of the country, millions of men and women are enjoying erotic accessories. *Sex Toy Tales* takes you into their bedrooms – as well as their living rooms, boardrooms, kitchens and toolsheds.

The true-life tales and inventive fiction in this unprecedented anthology were written by ordinary women and men asked to recount a sex toy adventure. Each story celebrates the exciting and liberating possibilities of erotic accessories – from tried-and-true pleasers such as vibrators and dildos to unconventional items such as blenders, fishing tackle and computers.

Perhaps you're an erotica reader looking for a new twist in the genre. You may be a sex toy novice who's curious about where and how to begin accessorizing your sex life. Or maybe your personal toy chest is overflowing and you simply want to know what other sex toy lovers are up to. Whatever your reason for picking up this book, you'll find it filled with stories that are arousing, entertaining and enlightening.

Bringing sex toys out of the closet

We freely admit that we compiled this book to spread the good word about sex toys. After all, we both learned nearly everything we know about sex working at Good Vibrations, San Francisco's "clean, well-lighted" vibrator store. During ten years of selling sexual products to people of all ages, backgrounds and sexual tastes, we discovered that every sex toy consumer has a story to tell. All we had to do was invite folks to describe their sex toy encounters, and a multitude of stories – funny, sentimental, passionate and insightful – came pouring in.

In these stories, you'll find all kinds of characters fine-tuning the speed on their vibrators and lubricating their dildos.

That's because all kinds of people enjoy sex toys. Enthusiastic consumers are fueling a billion-dollar-a-year sex toy industry – an industry that's practically invisible.

Record numbers of ordinary folks are tracking down vibrators, dildos, lubes, lotions and more without any encouragement, guidance or Madison-Avenue hype. They're not getting inspiration from the mainstream media, and they're not getting tempted at the local mall; they're relying on word-of-mouth and their own ingenuity to figure out what to buy and how to use it.

The sex toy revolution has been a silent one. Volumes of erotica fill airport bookstores and X-rated videos line the shelves of neighborhood video stores, but sex toys have remained a taboo topic. Talk about the "love that dare not speak its name" – sex toys are discussed in whispers, dismissed with giggles, and are probably the only sexual wrinkle that's never been examined on daytime talk shows. Even in sex manuals and in most commercially available erotica, the joy of erotic accessories is still a subject that gets remarkably short shrift.

Sex toys are stereotyped. Many people assume that "sexual aids" exist only to "fix" sexual problems. Others assume they're either the playthings of sexual sophisticates or consolation prizes for those not in relationships. But to the millions of women and men who enjoy sex toys, they're the key to a more fulfilling and imaginative sex life.

Given the absence of accurate information and encouragement, it's not surprising that businesses such as Good Vibrations thrive by providing access to and inspiration for enjoying sexual products. People are thrilled to discover that they're not alone in appreciating sex toys, and they revel in having any kind of forum simply to communicate about the subject.

We couldn't think of a better way to share the fun and arousing potential of sex toys than with the "show, don't tell" approach of an erotica anthology. Manuals may deliver detailed instructions, but these stories excel at showing toys in action. You get to learn a thing or two about erotic accessories and get turned on in the process.

What's in These Tales

In compiling this anthology, we specifically encouraged authors to expand their definition of sex toys to include any accessory that could be used to enhance a sexual experience. The results were inspiring. After reading "A Blend of Food and Desire," you may never look at your kitchen appliances in the same way. Thanks to "The Fishing Show," you'll discover that fishing lures make exotic sex accessories, and "Scanner" will open your mind to the erotic possibilities of high-tech office equipment.

Of course, tales of conventional sex toys abound. In "Memory Vibrations," one vibrator-loving woman reveals the unexpected benefits of a faulty memory. The handcrafted dildos in "Wednesday Afternoon" unite two generations of women in erotic appreciation, and a lonely Scrooge receives a deluxe assortment of intimate gifts from his Secret Santa in "The Twelve Days of Christmas." Just the thought of sex toys can fuel a steamy encounter – in "The Catalog Keeper," the catalog itself is the toy.

Encompassing torrid fantasy, tender reminiscences and true confessions, the stories in *Sex Toy Tales* describe uniquely pleasurable encounters. They range in tone from romantic to lyrical to gleefully self-indulgent to humorous to just this side of slapstick.

Above all, the stories you're about to read are playful – so check your political agenda at the door. These tales revolve around what one author sums up as "Fun & Games," pure and simple. But, in celebrating the erotic imagination, the value of fantasy, and pleasure for pleasure's sake, they express a message that has the power to revolutionize any reader's sex life.

Taken individually and as a whole, we think these stories offer a compelling, arousing response to anyone who's ever asked, "Why would I want to use a sex toy?"

Jumpstart your imagination

Clearly, sex toys stimulate the body, but they also have the power to stimulate the mind. Every story in this anthology, by definition, looks beyond the human body for subject matter. The results are highly imaginative, innovative erotica, fueled by a sense of limitless possibilities.

These playful attitudes frequently inspire elaborate wordplay. In several stories, words *are* the toys. The sound of a lover's voice describing what's about to happen in "Company Training" or the text of an erotic story scrolling down a computer screen in "Just Reading News" produces as visceral a response as a vibrator between the legs.

Break out of a rut
It's no surprise that several of our stories reveal how sex toys can be used to kindle sparks in a long-term relationship, adding a welcome element of unpredictability. With a vibrator in your hand or a dildo strapped around your hips, your own body surges with new power, and the familiar landscape of your lover's body becomes uncharted territory.

Sex toys allow lovers to expand their sexual horizons in a multitude of ways, discovering new facts about each other's sexual responses and preferences. In "Sneak Attack of the Sex Toys," a married couple uses sex toys to circumvent religious inhibitions. In "The Stranger," a husband straps on a dildo to enact his wife's fantasy of an aggressive, well-endowed intruder.

Celebrate yourself
In "Girls, Boys and All of Our Toys," the author speculates that each individual's choice in sex toys is the purest form of self-expression – "you are what you jerk off with," rather than "you are what you eat." Whether or not you come to resemble your favorite vibrator or dildo, you'll find that sex toys offer an enjoyable, unpressured means of creative self-exploration.

Eroticize your environment
Everybody's familiar with the first heady phase of a new romance – when you're suffused with excitement and lust, the whole world seems like a kinder, sexier place. What's less commonly known is that experimenting with erotic accessories promotes an equally expansive perspective; once you've

begun to explore the erotic possibilities of your environment, the world becomes your toy box.

With equal parts humor and pragmatism, these authors reveal how objects as diverse as the tiller on a sailboat in "Anchors Aweigh," the power-sander in "Tool Time," and the computer joy stick in "Computer Games" can assume a come-hither glow. After reading these stories, it's unlikely you'll be able to walk into a hardware store without considering many new and provocative uses for the items on the shelves.

Sometimes an erotic adventure simply isn't complete without an accessory that creates and complements the mood. Toys such as the remote-controlled vibrator in "Remotely Pleasant" and the mysterious "Maltese Dildo" contribute to dramatic tension. And toys can be valuable props in your own fantasy roleplaying.

Enjoy pleasure for pleasure's sake

The common thread in so many of these stories is the enthusiastic embrace of abundant sexual pleasure. Despite being bombarded daily by sexual images and titillating sound bites, we live in a culture where most people feel a sense of sexual deprivation. They're either worried that they're not having enough sex, or having the "wrong kind" of sex, or having sex when they shouldn't. The topic remains shrouded in mystery and anxiety.

As the authors of these stories so eloquently testify, nothing torpedos sexual shame and ignorance quite so effectively as the experience of abundant sexual fulfillment. This is the experience which sex toys can provide. They inspire a spirit of fun and experimentation that puts self-consciousness and goal-oriented attitudes to flight.

So lube up, plug in, get comfortable and read on. We hope what you discover between these pages inspires many hours of adventurous play in your own life – and we eagerly await *your* story for the next volume of *Sex Toy Tales*.

Anne Semans and Cathy Winks
San Francisco, January 1998

Remotely Pleasant

Jacob Hugart

PATRICK JOHNSON SIPPED HIS WINE. It would stretch the limit of his meal allowance for this trip, but the kitchen of this hotel produced excellent – and inexpensive – dinners, if his just-completed meal was a typical example.

With a sigh, he reclined in his chair. The hostess had seated him by the glass doors which, during the day, opened onto a courtyard dining patio. Patrick was becoming very familiar with the arrangement of tables and chairs on that patio. Usually, he enjoyed talking to his wife during dinner, but she was half-a-continent away. His company discouraged the practice of having one's spouse along on business trips by the simple method of making the paperwork unfathomable.

He had endured the silence surrounding his meal with the grim determination that his manners would be impeccable — and not one crumb had fallen on the tablecloth! – but he had to look somewhere, and instead of staring at one of the handful of patrons in the large dining room, he stared out at the patio.

Not that he hadn't noticed the other diners: a man, woman and two children at one of the round tables; two men conversing by another window table somewhere behind him; a lone woman in a corner booth. All served by the same waiter. And two hostesses had seated all the patrons in such a way that the waiter was forced to cover the entire space of the dining room to visit each occupied table.

Patrick watched as the waiter distributed bills to the other diners before approaching his table with another glass of wine . . . and a small white box.

"Compliments of the lady," said the waiter, glancing to the corner booth. He set the glass and box down, then withdrew.

Patrick looked toward the booth, but the woman was concentrating on a slice of chocolate cake. When Patrick reached for his glass, she looked up and smiled: a winning smile in a not unattractive face. Patrick nodded his head with a small smile, and raised the glass in acknowledgment.

The woman's eyes then darted to the box on the table as her lips pursed together. Looking back at Patrick with one eyebrow arched, she seemed to ask, *Aren't you curious about the box?*

Patrick took a breath and let it out. He could appreciate the wine, but was not interested in any rendezvous. Setting down his glass, he reached for the box.

Opening it, he was surprised to discover no message, no room key . . . just a small plastic device with a little dial on one side. Turning it over in his hands, he noted a small door which resembled a battery compartment. He looked back to the woman, only to see that she had returned her attention to her dessert.

Tentatively, he place his thumb against the dial. Slight pressure didn't budge it. A firmer touch released it. Unsure of what to expect, Patrick slowly ran the dial up as far as it would go. Noticing no effect, he dialed it back down, until the feel of a soft click told him he had returned it to its initial setting.

He looked up to the woman with a frown of confusion on his face, to see her sitting against the upholstery of the booth, head back, eyes closed, hands on the table. Slowly, her eyes opened, and the winning smile began to grow on her face.

Patrick's eyes flicked to the plastic box, then back to the woman. Her grin seemed a trifle wider. On impulse, Patrick flicked the dial on and off quickly.

At that, the grin vanished from the woman's face and her eyes shut quickly. She opened them and looked back at Patrick, shaking her head a little.

Then he understood.

Suddenly alarmed, he looked furtively around the dining room. The waiter was involved in the cleaning of the round table, and the two men were just leaving. He realized that the hostesses couldn't really see the corner booth too well, at least not the spot in which the woman was sitting.

Relaxing a little, his mind raced with questions: *Who was she? What did she want? What* was *this thing?* Looking toward the woman, he noticed that she was apparently ignoring him as she continued with her dessert.

Eyes narrowing, he thumbed the dial to its highest level and held it there.

The woman shuddered as if a jolt of electricity had passed through her. The hand which had been beside her dessert plate spasmed, knocking down her glass of wine. Instantly, the waiter moved to the table to mop up the liquid, and Patrick turned the dial to what he presumed was its off position.

He heard the woman making her apologies to the waiter. Not quite able to hear the words, Patrick thought the sound of her voice was mellow, almost musical. She accepted the waiter's offer of a new glass of wine. As the waiter left, she looked at Patrick. Her eyes widened momentarily and she took a deep breath, like someone who has barely escaped from an embarrassing situation. Then she beamed at Patrick.

In spite of himself, Patrick smiled in response. This was *much* better than the patio furniture. Patrick suddenly noticed her dark red lips as the woman placed another morsel of chocolate cake into her mouth. Quickly, he thumbed the dial again, but kept it low.

The look on her face was clearly one of pleasure. Curious, Patrick left the dial at that level, even as the waiter approached with a new glass of wine for the woman.

"The dessert, it is good?" he heard the waiter ask. The woman's eyes opened at the question, and she remembered to chew her cake again.

"Mmm hmm," she confirmed. Smiling, the waiter left the dining room.

The woman looked at Patrick again, slowly chewing her mouthful of cake, her eyelids slightly drooping. He noticed that she was wearing eye shadow of a blue-green color, and that her hair was straw-colored. She appeared to be dressed for an elegant evening on the town.

Patrick moved the dial up a little.

The woman's eyes closed. She swallowed, and her hands went to the table's edge. Curious, Patrick slowly increased the setting of the dial. The woman slightly arched her back as he did so, her hands gripping the table tightly.

Looking back at the device in his hands, he knew that it had to be a remote control, but for what? It had no identifying marks on it. Maybe it was handmade.

Patrick looked to the woman again. She had moved her head to one side, chin held high, a look almost of pain on her face. Patrick rolled the dial to a lower setting, and she seemed to relax a bit. As her eyes began to open, he moved the dial up again.

Instantly, she shut her eyes and nibbled at her lower lip. Patrick set the dial to its highest setting, then back to its lowest, and slowly up to its highest. The woman seemed to gasp at this, shuddering slightly.

It's so quiet, thought Patrick, *Like a silent movie.* Again he moved the dial back and forth across its range. Again, the woman relaxed and tensed.

Patrick found himself becoming aroused by her – responses? Yes, he was the one stimulating her. Somehow. Briefly, he wondered if he was doing something wrong. Then he shook that off, and looked at the woman again as he manipulated the dial.

Her legs, revealed by the skirt she wore, seemed to tense, too. As if that was a signal, Patrick moved the dial to its highest setting and she *did* gasp, he could just hear it. Then her shoulders slumped, and her hands moved from the table into her lap.

As the waiter set the bill in front of Patrick, he quickly came back to reality, shut off the dial and left the device on the table. The waiter stood by patiently as Patrick scrawled his room number and signature on the bill. Placing his copy of the receipt in his pocket, he heard a pleasant, female voice.

"Excuse me, but I believe this is mine."

Patrick looked up and saw the woman from the booth. Caught off-guard, he quickly replied, "Uh, yes, I guess it must be."

The woman smiled. "Thank you for taking care of it for me."

Two interpretations of her statement flashed through his mind before he settled on the safer one. "What is it?" he asked.

She smiled again. "Just a toy of mine. Good night." She turned, and left the room.

Patrick stared at the tablecloth, slightly perplexed. The empty box, he saw, was still there. So it wasn't a dream. How very odd. Then he noticed the business card tucked inside . . . mail-order novelties, with a local address and telephone. *Hmm.*

Pocketing the card, he gulped the remainder of his wine, then stood and walked out of the dining room. The hostesses smiled at him as he left, wishing him a good evening.

For some reason, their smiles bothered him but he decided that it was just his imagination. He smiled in return, and went up to his room.

He was still smiling when he arrived, for he had decided upon a gift to present to his wife when he returned.

He hoped she'd like it.

Object of Desire

Loren Rhoads

I HAVE A LOT OF APPLIANCES, but I only have a relationship with one.

I love my vibrator. There aren't many possessions I feel so strongly about. I'm indifferent to the toaster oven. I am coming to fear the eleven-year-old microwave. But my vibrator ranks right up there with the bedside reading lamp in frequency of usage. It behaves better than the bread-maker, which takes longer to produce results and is impossible to clean. It's less temperamental than the clock radio. It's more reliable than the answering machine.

If I disappeared, a psychic would have to hold my vibrator to establish a psychic link to me.

I'll lend out *Macho Sluts* (which I want back, Ann Marie), but I can't imagine letting anyone borrow my vibrator. It doesn't leave my house. Like the cat, it's often in the same room with me, waiting for me to notice it. It always responds with a purr.

When my vibrator broke, I was absolutely distraught. The plastic case around its slender white shoulders cracked. Pieces of plastic actually came off, revealing mysterious metal workings beneath. I felt like I was looking beneath my beloved's skin.

I consulted everyone I knew who might know something about electricity. "I broke my vibrator," I said. "I'm afraid of electrocuting myself."

"Don't use it," they'd answer. "Get a new one."

How could I be so faithless? "I just want to know if the outside of the motor might be live," I explained. "I don't want to be found dead on the floor of my office with my pants around my ankles. . . ."

"You don't take your pants off?" Ann Marie wondered.

For the first time, I realized maybe this wasn't a topic to discuss with just anyone. "Sometimes I'm in too much of a

6

hurry," I explained, blushing.

Actually, I am usually in too much of a hurry. I just want to get off, no muss, no fuss, wham bam thank you, Oster. Coming for me is like scratching a really satisfying itch. Ten or twenty little orgasms throughout the day, especially when I'm writing, dissipate my tension and dissolve writer's block. I crawl up off the floor to my desk, flushed and slightly sweaty, my characters' next moves clear to me. I should have written my vibrator off on my taxes. It's honestly an office expense.

Finally, after consulting enough friends, I decided to take matters into my own hands. I searched through the clutter in my desk until I found the Elmer's cup cement. This stuff could not be conductive, right? Lovingly, I replaced the chips of my vibrator's case. The pieces fit together tightly, sealed by scars of rubbery glue.

I held the vibrator at arm's length when I plugged it in, turned my head away when I nudged the on switch up with my thumb. There was the hum that had sung me out of the blues so many times before. Sparks did not fly. Nothing smelled as if it were burning.

Overcome with desire – though still somewhat wary – I gently placed my vibrator on the carpet. My thumb slowly pushed the button of my jeans back through its button hole. I slid my zipper down soundlessly, slipping my hand inside to rub my palm across my belly. I peeled my jeans down to my knees and sank to the floor to pull them over my feet. If I was going to die for love today, I wanted my body arranged as artistically as possible. I wished I had roses to strew around the floor.

I eased the vibrator's switch on again and touched the gray rubber head to the inside of my right knee. Nothing shocked me. I stroked the vibrator up my thigh. Determined, it nuzzled against my clit, home again. My hips twitched. Involuntarily, I moaned. Sweet climax rolled over me, unstoppable.

Oh my darling, I missed you terribly. Thank goodness you're all right. Please, don't ever scare me like that again.

To Lola, With Love

Alison Tyler

I'M NOT EXACTLY SURE how to admit this – it sounds funny to say, and looks even funnier on paper – but my girlfriend is having an affair with my vagina. She'll readily admit to this. She's even written love letters to it. Yes indeed, Jo, my normally sane, very lovely, dyke-sweetheart has taken pen in hand and written to my cunt.

At first, she simply cooed to it, sliding one deft pointer between my nether lips, then lifting that finger to her mouth to drink the nectar from the tip, whispering softly, "Oooh, pretty thing, pretty pussy. Oooh, what darling kitty lips you have. I'm gonna lick 'em. Yesss, I am. I'm gonna drink all that sticky sap from deep inside. Oh yes, darlin', oh yes."

She employed the exact voice that some slightly deranged people use when talking to babies or small animals. That singsong nonsense tone. That wuvvy-duvvy cartoonish croon. That nausea-inspiring simper that suggests the very early stages of puppy love.

But this love has lasted.

And so has the love affair Jo has held with my vagina.

Now, she's not totally off the deep end. I mean, she hasn't proposed marriage to it or anything. But she brings it presents.

"Won't you look pretty in these satin panties?" she crows. "Oh, yes, oh yes, so pretty for mommy . . ."

Excuse me?

"Mama Jo got them special. See the lace, pretty lace. . . ."

Okay, she's talking to my cunt, I thought, at first. *I can handle this. I can get a grip.* Except, she was talking to it as if it had the brain of, say, Jell-O. So, I came to a decision: if my cunt is gonna have a love affair behind my back – no, that's impossible – *in front of* my back, then it had better get treated with some respect. I wanted intelligent conversation, not baby-doll cooing. And I told her so.

"None of your business, really," is what Jo had to say.

"Excuse me?"

"It's none of your business what Lola and I do, or how we talk."

"Lola?"

"Yes, that's her name."

"You *named* my cunt?"

"No . . . she told me."

Too much. Too fucking much.

"My cunt *told* you her name?"

"Well," Jo said, shrugging her built shoulders at me and giving me a withering stare, "Not in so many words, but I knew."

I didn't have anything to say to that. At least, not until the flowers arrived with a pastel note that read in gently sloping cursive: "To Lola, with love." I called Jo at work.

"Seventh Street Cafe," she answered, that familiar smile in her husky voice. "You've reached the bar."

"Jo, why did you send my cunt flowers?"

"Hey! You weren't supposed to open the card, it was for *her*."

"Um, what's 'she' gonna do with them?"

"Smell them. Enjoy them."

"We have to talk," I said.

"Sure, Angel. I'll be home at one."

I paced through the apartment, unable to park myself at the computer and get my work done. I'd started to feel as if sitting were a bad thing . . . I mean, sitting on *her*. And I suddenly felt the urge to take a bath, to shave Lola clean, to stand naked in front of the bouquet so she *could* enjoy the flowers.

I ran the water in our claw-foot tub, adding raspberry-scented bubble bath and lighting a few candles. Normally I wouldn't get so carried away, but this seemed to be a special occasion – flowers, and all. As I spread on the shaving cream, I found that I touched myself more gently than normal. I slid the razor over that softest skin and admired it. When I was through, I powdered all over, then went and got the pretty panties Jo had bought and put them on.

Lola was happy. I could tell.

Jo came home on schedule, a wrapped present under one arm.

I was sitting on the couch, nude save for the panties, the flowers well within smelling-range on the coffee table.

"For Lola?" I asked, unable to keep the green-eyed monster at bay.

"Naw, cutie, for you."

I felt myself melt, reaching greedily for the gift. Inside, nestled in fluffy tissue paper, lay a silvery dildo and a black leather harness.

"Well," Jo conceded, "Not *only* for you, but for Lola, as well."

"Oh," I sighed, stroking the molded plastic. I felt a tightness in my chest. I wanted that toy. And from the response going on down in my panties, Lola wanted it too.

"Wait in the bedroom," Jo told me. "I think the three of us can work all this out."

"Yeah," I agreed shyly, growing even more damp at the thought of what was in store. "Yeah, I think so too."

I followed her order, quickly walking through the living room and into our bedroom. I lay on the bed, staring at my reflection in the mirror on the back of our dresser. My cheeks were flushed, my dark eyes on fire. I tossed my glossy raven mane away from my face, feeling the warmth at the back of my neck, beneath my heavy tresses. Every part of my body was growing hot. *Especially* Lola. I waited, impatiently, for Jo to join me – I mean, *us* – and while I did, I snaked one hand under the satin panties and began to stroke Lola.

She was ready, all right. Sticky juices were dripping from her hungry lips. I slid my fingers in and out, getting them wet, then spreading the warm honey all over her shaved skin.

Finally, Jo entered. She had stripped and was wearing the harness and molded synthetic cock. It stuck out, away from her body, pointing directly at me.

"You *are* jealous, aren't you?" she asked, coming toward the bed so quickly that I didn't notice the handcuffs concealed in one of her large hands.

"I . . ."

She captured my wrists easily, setting the chain of the cuffs neatly in the hook over our headboard. Now, without having to rush, she fastened my ankles with crimson silk loops and tied them to the posts of our bed.

"Such a jealous girl. Jealous of the attention I've bestowed on your little friend. Why is that, Angel? It doesn't really make much sense."

I couldn't explain.

"I love you, darlin'," Jo said to me, slipping into her slight, South Texas drawl. "I love you desperately. And I love her, as well." She cupped one hand protectively over my cunt. I still had the panties on, and I wondered how she'd get around them. Jo had no problems, though, no worries. She simply reached for a pair of sewing scissors on the dresser and sliced through the filmy material.

"Oh," she sighed, once Lola was revealed, "You shaved." Now she pressed her heart-shaped lips to my nether lips and began to lick, lapping deliciously at the flood of juices that glistened on my cunt, and thighs, and ass. "Yes, you did. You shaved for Mama."

I didn't think it was polite for me to answer, not being directly spoken to. But I was unable to keep silent.

"I . . . " I started.

"Yes, Angel?" Jo asked, looking up at me. Her chin was glossy with my honey, her lips wet and shiny.

"*I* shaved for you."

That made her smile. "Thank you, Angel. I know you did."

Ah, sanity. Sweet sanity. I saw it once again in my lover's lake–green eyes.

"Lola told you that I wanted her to be clean, right?"

"I . . . " I started again, unsure of how to answer.

"Not in so many words, of course," Jo said, quoting from herself, "But you knew, right?"

I nodded. Yes, I'd known.

"Good. Now lie back, sweetheart, and let Mama go to work."

I had no problem with that. I relaxed against the pillows and closed my eyes. Jo spread Lola's lips with her fingers, and her knowing tongue quickly began making the darting little circles that I love best. She went 'round and 'round with the tip of her tongue, moving away from my clit, then closer to it. I arched my hips, sliding on the crisp white sheets, helping her. I tensed my muscles against the ribbons of fabric that held me in place. I moaned and sighed. I shivered as I got closer to the moment of truth.

Then everything stopped.

I opened my eyes, startled, desperate. Jo was looking back at me, a coy smile on her lips. She sat on her heels, regarding my supine form, then she began to stroke the dildo, just watching me, not saying anything.

I swallowed hard, wanting to beg, but not sure if that would get me anywhere. When Jo has that look in her jewel-toned eyes, that *knowing* look, it means "watch out." I stared as she spit into her right palm and began oiling the cock. I stared as she slid her fingers around it, pulling on it, working it. I felt my pussy lips part, I felt the juices trickle through the swollen crack. I was dying.

"Now listen," Jo said, her voice gone dark and low and sweet, like thick molasses pouring slowly all over my body. "And listen well, child."

I nodded.

"I love you. Oh, Angel, you know I love you. I see you as a whole: your brain, your heart, your soul, your cunt – all of your parts work together to make up the you that I love. And sometimes, in some phases of our relationship, I've focused on your mind . . . think back, you know I'm telling the truth." I closed my eyes, considering, and then nodded. She was right. "And sometimes," she continued, and now I could hear the teasing in her voice, "I have courted your heart." I nodded again, knowing now where she was going with this. "And, Angel, there have been phases when I've gone directly for your soul. Am I speaking the truth?"

She waited until I opened my eyes again and said, "Yes, Jo, you are."

"Well now," she said, still in that low voice, "I am having a love affair with your cunt. I adore her. I want to pamper her, to play with her, to give her everything she needs . . . like this." She moved forward, placing the head of the dildo on the flat bone above my pussy. "Just like this, 'cause you need this, and I need this, and Lola needs this."

I leaned my head back against the pillow, my whole body straining. I wanted her *in*. I would have agreed to anything as long as she went *in*. But she didn't, she just rocked back and forth, taunting me.

"Yes," I finally managed. "Yes, I understand."

"Ah, good . . . I knew you would."

And with that, she slid down the two inches to paradise and thrust forward, deep, probing me, fucking me — or fucking *her*. And I was no longer jealous, though I did feel as if there were three of us in bed, the way Jo talked, the way she crooned in that syrupy voice, "That's it, doll, that's right," not differentiating between me and Lola, but definitely talking to us both. I could feel the honey flow, coating the molded cock, making it slick with nectar, and it no longer mattered who was speaking, or who was being spoken to.

"Oh, yes," Jo sighed, "Just like that, get it nice and wet for me." Then her hand under my chin, tilting my head forward, "'Cause *you're* gonna suck it clean, right, Angel? You're gonna get it all nice and clean for me."

"Yes," I promised. "Yes, Jo, whatever you say."

"I want you to taste her," Jo said, her eyes gone dreamy, her voice still lost in that soft, commanding tone. "She's so fuckin' sweet."

"Yes, Jo, yesss."

She kept up that steady rhythm, the beat I needed, the beat she needed, the beat Lola needed. Kept it up: ragged, desperate, endless. I moaned and writhed; I bucked and screamed; and I got so wet that the bed was a pool of my glossy come, my thighs dripping with liquid sex. The scent was all around us — we were swimming in it — and I breathed in deep, drinking in the perfume, as if I were smelling someone else, some other lover. Everything seemed new to me, taking it from Jo's point of view. I felt newly discovered, newly found out — virginal in a way — and I basked in it, bathed in it . . . closed my eyes and jumped.

A Blend of Food and Desire

Lawrence Schimel

I SPRUNG A BONER when Erica asked me to pass her the blender. I was at her apartment, helping her prepare a three-course meal for a dinner party for some mutual friends of ours. This consisted mostly of my watching, and occasionally passing her items as needed, or doing some of the foolproof and thankless tasks like peeling potatoes or chopping onions. Some people have a black thumb when it comes to raising plants; I have the equivalent when it comes to cooking. If my boyfriend weren't such a fine cook, I would've starved years ago. Of course, that was one of the reasons I'd married him; my two main passions are food and sex, both of which Robert excels at.

When Erica asked for the blender, which I hadn't noticed was on the shelf beside me, I just couldn't help my response. I still vividly remembered the first night Robert and I had sex with our blender, and the memory was hardwired into my libido.

Now, I know that sex with a blender doesn't sound promising to most people, but let me reassure you that this is not some mutilation fantasy or paean to Jeffrey Dahmer.

Robert had visited his grandmother that afternoon, and she'd given him a Macy's credit slip that she had never used. He lost no time in dashing off to The Cellar and came home with the blender. He wanted to try it out immediately, so I followed him into the kitchen.

I love watching Robert cook. Watching anyone prepare food fascinates me – the cooking channel is like porn to me – but in particular I liked watching Robert at work, especially when he was making something for me to eat. That nurturing intimacy mixed with the lust Robert inspired always got me hard, and that night as Robert set up his new toy was no exception. He was obviously excited by it, which in turn got me excited, and my dick leapt to attention. I stood behind him and rubbed my crotch against his ass as he read the instructions.

My cock is one of the few things that can distract Robert from cooking. I've learned to be careful about that, since I've distracted him once too often when the stove was on, and burned dinner as a result.

But Robert hadn't even plugged in his new machine, so I felt it was safe.

Robert turned around to face me, and we began to kiss. He unbuttoned my shirt, and slid down my chest to nuzzle at my right nipple, flicking the silver ring that pierced it. His hands dropped to fondle my crotch, and he was unzipping my jeans between squeezes. He crouched down before me, pressing his mouth against my cock and breathing wetly through the cotton of my briefs. He pulled my jeans down around my ankles as he mouthed me through the fabric, then tugged down my underwear as well. My cock sprung free, and Robert rubbed his face against it, licking my balls and then slowly working his way along the underside of the shaft.

I braced my arms against the countertop as his lips locked around my cock and slid down the shaft. Slowly I ground my hips back and forth, thrusting into his mouth.

I was staring at the blender parts scattered across the countertop as he sucked me off: the whirling blades that looked how my innards felt as his tongue and lips worked their magic on my cock.

Suddenly, my cock flopped free as Robert stood up. I expected him to want some reciprocation for a while, but instead he turned around and went back to work on the blender.

I was insulted.

I stepped out of my jeans and underwear, leaving them in a heap behind him. The kitchen was Robert's domain, and normally I was careful not to mess it up. But I was pissed off. I slid my shirt off and tossed it on top of the dish rack.

"I'm going to go watch a porno and jerk off," I said. I sounded petulant, even to my own ears.

"I'm not through with you yet," Robert said, still not turning away from his new toy.

"It sure looks like you are."

"You'll see," he said. "Here." He reached up to the fridge for the fruit bowl and handed me a banana.

"This is supposed to be a substitute while you play with your new toy?" I asked.

Robert finally turned to me and said, "You're such a bitch today. Just peel the damned thing and trust me."

I stroked my dick, still slick with his saliva, and glared at his back. I was being a bitch, I knew, but I hated being ignored. This was silly, though; I was acting like a jealous lover, when all he was doing was trying to set up his new gadget. I sighed and peeled the banana he'd handed me. I took a bite, a last rebellious action, and with my mouth still full said, "Here."

"Thank you," Robert said, and took the banana from me. He stuffed it in through the top of the machine, and then plugged the blender in. "Ready?" he asked, closing the lid.

I came and stood behind him again, forgiving him, sharing his moment of enjoyment. "Sure," I said, "can't you tell I'm ready?" I rubbed my hard cock against his ass as I looked over his shoulder.

Robert flicked the machine on, and the banana was quickly whacked into a puree by the sharp blades.

Big deal, I thought. I grabbed Robert's hips and ground my crotch against him. "That was more fun than this?" I asked.

"You have so little imagination," Robert complained. He turned off the blender, lifted the container from its base and held it before him. "Sometimes I wonder how I could have married you," he said, switching places, so that I was pressed up against the counter he had been standing against. "But then I remember."

Robert knelt down before me, still holding the container. He poured banana puree all over my dick and abs and thighs.

"Oh," I said, letting the vowel shift from surprise as the viscous gel touched my skin into pleasure as Robert put the container down on the floor and began licking the banana from my skin. "Mmmm," I purred as he licked the inside of my thigh.

"You should taste it down here," Robert said. "Mmmm indeed."

I laughed, and later I did try the same thing on him. We went through most of the fruit bowl that night, pureeing items singly and in combinations – kiwi and apple; strawberry and pear – and then eating the drippy pulp off each other's bodies.

And ever since, the sound of a blender, sometimes the mere thought of it, gets me hard.

I must've stepped awkwardly as I crossed the room with the blender in my hands, trying to shift my cock within my jeans, which suddenly felt far too tight. Erica noticed, and looked down.

"Men!" she exclaimed. "Can't you pay attention, the company will be here in fifteen minutes. And there's no time for you to come before they do, so go set the table and calm down."

I laughed and said, "It's a long story."

"Tell me another time, then. Use the tablecloth that's in the top drawer."

I went into the dining room to set the table, trying to ignore the whirring sound of the blender which was keeping my dick rock hard.

Strategic Command

Lyn Chevli

THE DAY MY DARLING new husband, Orval, was sent overseas, I sat right down and started writing him long affectionate letters. I figured if he was going to help defend our God and Country the least I could do was keep up his morale – and maybe do a little fine–tuning on him at the same time. Now, don't get me wrong. I love my Orval to pieces, but he was a virgin when we got married, and since they don't teach matters of an intimate nature in Baptist schools, he doesn't know much. Mind you, he likes to do it; he just doesn't do it very well.

I was not a virgin when we got married – thanks to Billy Bob Terwilliger, who refused to honor my wishes the night of the spring prom in high school. And if it wasn't for my best friend, Cora Sue, and her connections in Birmingham, I would also be a mother. Cora Sue is a dear, dear person, but she's also a slut and a blabbermouth. She went straight to our preacher and told him about the little procedure I had in the city. I can't prove it, but I think she and the preacher had wrinkled a few sheets together.

The preacher very kindly took me aside and explained that it was my Christian duty to tell him about my tragedy. Then he lowered his voice and said that the only way I could fully repent and cleanse my heart of sin was to take some private instruction from him so we could pray together for my re-demption. These sessions began with the preacher doing a lot of hands-on blessing of my soul to get me in the mood. They ended when I made another trip to Birmingham, this time without Cora Sue.

Because of her being a dear person, Cora Sue and I stayed best friends. She was maid-of-honor at my wedding, and let me tell you that girl cried buckets.

One night soon after Orval left for overseas, she took me to a party she said was sort of like a Tupperware party. It wasn't, but it sure was an eye-opener. They had fancy nighties, some weird underwear, and lots of other things. "Toys," they called them – like the flesh-toned silicone devices that looked like the real thing, only they were bigger. I bought one of those to keep me company till Orval gets back. Well, the truth is that I spent a two-week paycheck there and came home loaded with goodies for when I become reunited with my poor love-starved husband. I figure that I'd better become pretty much of an expert at using all this stuff because Orval is even more naive than I am and I don't want him to be shocked when he walks into the bedroom and sees the dresser all decked out with supplies.

So what happens now is I have this routine for every single night, and it works out real well. After I do the supper dishes, I sit down and write a nice long letter to Orval. I talk a lot about his missile and how I'm going to help him load it. Then it's up to him to launch it, but I tell him exactly where I want it to land. Each night I make it a little different, like some-times I pretend I'm an airplane that needs refueling and stuff like that. I never use dirty words or anything and I try not to be boring. I guess I succeed, because after I finish the letter I just have to go into the bedroom for a while and let off some steam.

It's still early so I have lots of time. And let's face it, after knowing Billy Bob, the preacher, and some others I'd prefer not to mention, I like to take lots of time. I got two sets of those satin sheets – one for me now – the other I'm saving for when Orval gets home. I fetch my silicone thing, a vibrator, and whatever other toys I'm in the mood for, lay them out real neat on my pillow, and then squiggle around on those sheets for a while til I begin to feel my sap running. It seems to be running all the time nowadays, but I want it to just bubble.

I don't think about missiles at all. Neither do I think about airplanes being refueled. What I conjure is a very sweet man who is hung practically right down to his knees. He's gentle and does exactly what I want him to before I even have to ask. And he does it long enough, but never too long. Sometimes he talks dirty to me using lots of unchristian words. So I let him talk while I snatch my silicone and put it right near where he'll stick it in when he gets darn good and ready. Sometimes he makes me wait till after the eight-o'clock movie has started, but it's worth it. He knows how to tease.

He's also strong and knows a lot of different things to do that I never heard of. I think he's foreign. French maybe, or even part Arab. Anyway, sometimes he invites his friends to join in the fun and then things really get steamy. I can't keep track of all that's happening, there's so much going on, and let's face it, practically all of it's unnatural. But I can't lie; it does feel good.

At first they all decide I'm a human ice-cream cone and start licking away all over my top. I can't figure out how many of them there are, but they're sure making a lot of slurping noises. I guess I must be pretty yummy. I know I'm wet enough to start sliding all over those sheets so I play a game of trying to escape from my tormentors. That brings on a lot of squealing and giggling, but there's always at least one slurper going at me. Furthermore, one of them makes a terrible mistake. I begin to feel his mouth Down There . . . you know where. He's real sweet and gentle with his lips and tongue and it feels awful good. Anyway, I let him go on because I never did have any will power, when all of a sudden . . . Oh my sweet Jesus in Heaven . . . he just slips his big ole pink tongue all the way inside me, and I swear on my mama's bible, nothing in the whole wide world ever felt so good, forgive me, Christ my Savior.

I know the idea of it is disgusting, but when you're being taken by an army of French-type Arabs you're not thinking too clearly. Fact is, you're not thinking, period. Least I'm not. I feel like I'm flying with the angels in heaven. It's a kinda different slant on being a Christian, if you know what I mean.

Well, from then on I just let them have their way with me because I'm not at all worried about what God would say if he found out. And to tell the perfect truth, I don't much care. I'm as ready as a hotcake soakin' in warm butter.

But they aren't finished with me yet. They keep on – lickin' and fondlin' and tweakin' the little pink blossoms at the end of my bosoms and playin' pokey-pokey with their fingers everywhere, just to drive me crazy.

I'm almost a complete nervous wreck when I feel one of them put his thing in me. I wonder if it's a brown Arab thing or a white French thing. I know that's impure thinking so I concentrate on its being a white one, but I don't get very far. It keeps changing color with every stroke. Oh my, am I ever confused, but then I figure, what the heck; we're all God's creatures, aren't we?

It's nice being stroked like that, but just as I'm gettin' into the rhythm of it all, they turn everything upside down and there I am smack on top of this gorgeous creature who has an even bigger and browner thing. I've never been on top before and I like it, especially when mister-down-under slides his meatloaf into my fresh hot biscuit. Feels like they were made for each other, so slosh-slurp, away we go with the rest of them goin' over my back with anything convenient. That sets me to imagining I'm a super-fancy guitar the way they twang my strings.

After playing a couple of sets, they lift me on top of the biggest, blackest hunk of male meat I've ever seen in my live-long life. He's warm, soft, smilin' and sweet. I figure he'll make my love-box dance like nobody else ever has before, but first we have to take care of gettin' connected. Stuffed would be more like it, but I'm open from my toenails to my scalp, so it goes pretty smooth. He only whimpers a tiny bit, 'cept it must have wore him out because once he makes it all the way, he stops and just sets there for the longest while. Poor thing. I let him rest. His whang is tickin' away inside me, thinkin' about what to do next, when it sorta gulps. Then it gulps again and does a little pulsatin' thing. After that, it gulps, pulsates and burbles. It tickles me pinker'n my polyester undies. I want to ride him. He won't let me. He's wrapped his big hands right around my bottom so I can't budge.

We stay very still together – except for all that great bobblin' and tremblin' goin' on down below all by itself. It's kinda like we're prayin' to each other only not usin' words. I don't want it to be over, but fact is, I'm gettin' awful close – almost to the edge. I feel my loins risin' and plungin', all shot with silver and crystals pingin' in my innards.

And then it bursts. Zowie. Kapowie. We let go and every-thing gushes. I thrash like a 'gator caught by the tail, and let me tell you, a thousand points of light doesn't begin to cover it. We hump and we bump and we whump and thwunk and then we mush and squish and we foam – oh man, we do ev-erything. And then we gush again. I can feel both of us lettin' go with our juices and our muscles and I'm tellin' you, there isn't one thought of Jesus in me when we come. I'm the God-dess of orgasms feelin' somethin' sacred I can't describe.

I don't wake up for a long time, but when I do I glow all over and then some. I let my mind wander and it settles on poor Orval. Here I am, all plugged in nice and comfy, and there he sits in some pit full of scratchy sand with nothin' but his Walkman. He's probably run out of batteries too, while I sit right next to a handy outlet.

Then I remember that tomorrow is Sunday. I don't feel like goin' to church. I think I'll just stay home and wash the sheets.

Scanner

R. Jay Waldinger

CLAUDIA PRESSED HER BREASTS flat against the glass plate of the scanner and pushed the start button. Slowly the glass tube, resembling a fluorescent light bulb, passed under the glass, warming her skin slightly. She held her breath so as not to blur the image. Sure that guy she'd met on the Internet had seen her picture on her home page, but she wanted to show him something a little more intimate, a little more special. After all, her home-page picture was the same one they'd printed along with her article in the *Journal of Computational Graphics*, nothing too exciting. Pretty enough, but oh-so-professional, it didn't reveal her sensual side.

The scanner transformed her shape into a pattern that could be sent from one computer to another. She linked her screen to Dan's, so that whatever appeared on her monitor would appear at the same time on his. She looked at the image on her display. She could clearly see her dark nipples, and the little hairs that surrounded her aureoles. But her breasts seemed to lose something in the flattening – in real life they were nothing if not three-dimensional. She would have to do better. She wanted to send him something that would get his cock to stand up right in front of his expensive Silicon Graphics workstation.

Since she was alone that night in the windowless Computer Graphics Lab, which was full of computer equipment and old technical reports, she pulled off her jeans and underpants, and squatted over the scanner plate so that her vulva was pressed against the glass. God, she was wet – she hadn't even realized her photographic activity was turning her on. She'd have to wipe the glass after she was done. She pushed the button again and waited the required thirty seconds.

Suddenly the office door adjoining the laboratory opened, and her thesis supervisor stepped through. "Oh," exclaimed Claudia, "Professor Millhouse! I had no idea you were still here!" She didn't move, because the tube hadn't gone all the way under her yet.

"Just catching up on my journal reviewing," said Professor Millhouse, staring intently at his naked Ph.D. candidate.

"I was taking some pictures for my gynecologist," Claudia improvised. "They needed some for my file."

"Oh, don't let me interrupt you," said Professor Millhouse hurriedly. "Scanner working okay?"

"Oh, yes!" Claudia enthused.

"Let's see how it turned out," he suggested, moving closer. He looked at the screen, where an image of Claudia's private parts appeared, first vaguely, then with increasing precision. "Not bad," he said with genuine admiration. Claudia knew that the same image now appeared on Dan's screen.

"But look," she said, ever the perfectionist, "The wet parts show up so much better than the rest."

"That is so," agreed Professor Millhouse thoughtfully. "If only we could make it all wet. Wait." He licked his index finger and rubbed it, in a slow meditative way, into her soft pink labia. She inhaled sharply, but he seemed deep in thought, as if he were involved in a research problem.

"That's better," Claudia murmured.

"No, wait, I have it," said Professor Millhouse. He leaned forward and licked the folds, and her clitoris and vagina for good measure. Claudia gasped. "That ought to do it," said Professor Millhouse. Claudia seated herself on the glass plate of the scanner again. Professor Millhouse helped by spreading her labia apart with his fingers, to get better contact.

They looked at the screen to see the new image. Instead of Claudia, the image that appeared was that of a man's bottom — his balls, asshole, and half-erect cock prominent. It was, Claudia realized, a picture sent by Dan, her new Internet penpal, in response to her picture.

"Oh, that must be from my gynecologist," Claudia speculated. "She might have sent it to help me get in the mood, so I could get a good picture." In fact, it *was* getting her in the mood. She was pleased that Dan had responded so enthusiastically to her photographic efforts, as evidenced by his preliminary erection. And that he had sent the evidence so readily. She was also pleased that Professor Millhouse was so involved in her activity. "She must have a collection of pictures just for that purpose," Claudia proposed.

"Maybe I'll give her something for her collection," said Professor Millhouse, pulling down his jeans and white jockey shorts to his ankles and sitting on the glass.

"Wait," said Claudia, "It won't show." Professor Millhouse's cock was quite erect and was nowhere near the glass plate of the scanner. She tried to pull it down so it would lie flat, but it wouldn't go. "You'd better lie down," said Claudia. Professor Millhouse kicked off his useless blue jeans and settled down on the scanner, so that his cock was flat on the glass. Claudia pressed his ass hard against the scanner, to make better contact, and pushed the start button. "She'll like this one." In fact, Claudia wasn't sure that Dan would like it, but she hoped he would be impressed by the effect Claudia was having on another man.

Just then there came a whirring from the corner of the room. "What's that?" asked Claudia.

"It's our three-dimensional fax machine. Very experimental. It can send three-dimensional copies of objects over great distances, just like a two-dimensional fax does to flat pictures. I have no idea who'd be sending to us now."

As the two researchers watched, a life-sized sculpture of what Claudia recognized as Dan's now fully-erect cock and balls, made of a transparent, flexible, amber substance, was extruded from the machine. "My gynecologist must be sending it from her collection," said Claudia.

"But she wouldn't have a three-dimensional fax machine," Professor Millhouse objected. "They're just research prototypes. Only a few of them around."

"Oh, my gynecologist is very research-oriented," said Claudia expansively, improvising. "She's involved in a joint venture on 3-D imaging for medical applications."

"Oh," said Professor Millhouse, visibly impressed. A research gynecologist.

"She probably wants to get a picture of me from the inside," said Claudia. "If I put this in me, the picture will show the inner walls of my vagina." She returned to her perch on the glass plate of the scanner. "I'd better wet it." She picked up the transparent replica of Dan's cock and sucked on it, tentatively at first – it seemed huge – and then with more gusto. It felt warm in her mouth.

"Can you help me get it in?" she asked Professor Millhouse, handing him the resilient genitalia, leaning back on the plate, and spreading her labia apart. He bent over to lick her vagina, and her clitoris too, for good measure, before inserting the tip of the penis replica into her vagina. "Oh, yes, that's good," Claudia commented, and reached for the replica, pushing it further inside, until only the balls were visible.

"Great," he said. "Why don't we send it by return 3-D fax instead?" he suggested.

Claudia readily agreed. "That way she'll have a 3-D image of my vagina, my clitoris, my ass, everything!" she said.

"And if you keep the cock in you, she'll even be able to feel the inside of your vagina." He helped position Claudia within the scanning box of the 3-D laser – she had to sit on top of the box, with her bottom protruding inside it.

"Let's make one for us too," Claudia said. As the image was sent, the machine extruded a sculpture of Claudia's pelvic region, in the same transparent amber substance. The replica did not include Dan's cock and balls, which still protruded from Claudia's vagina, since they were transparent and didn't show. Professor Millhouse picked up the sculpture of Claudia and rubbed his hands over it. Slowly he lowered it over his erect cock, which was clearly visible through the amber. "Look at that," he said.

"I think I know why she sent me a transparent cock," said Claudia. "I think she needs to have a picture of me coming – from the inside."

"Yes, yes," Professor Millhouse agreed. "But it should be in video."

"Can we send her a video over the Net?" asked Claudia.

"Nothing simpler. I have the equipment right here," he replied, and rushed to pull out a video camera that was attached by cables to the computer system. "Why don't you just get up on the table over here."

Holding the cock still inside her, Claudia mounted the long table and straddled the lens of the camera, which Professor Millhouse had pointed straight up. The transparent balls pressed against the lens. On the screen, they could see the inside of Claudia's vagina, spread open and illuminated by the invisible cock. A beautiful mandala of rose, pink, grey, and brown, like a tide pool. "Touch my clitoris," said Claudia. Professor Millhouse, a veteran of many research teams, sensed the urgency in her tone and obeyed instantly. On the screen, they could see the muscles inside Claudia's vagina clasp as fluid was released, a disturbed sea anemone. They could smell the ocean.

"Stick your finger up my ass," Claudia said. Professor Millhouse knew better than to question her instructions; he licked her ass briefly to wet it, then slowly inserted his index finger. Claudia moaned, and her moans were transmitted over the Net, along with the scene inside her vagina. She rocked on her perch, forcing the balls of the replica harder against the camera lens, and the cock pressed more deeply inside her. Her moan was continuous and animal. On his own initiative, Professor Millhouse leaned over and nibbled gently on her nipple, which was already quite pert. With one hand, she pressed his finger hard against her clitoris; with the other, she pushed his finger deeper into her ass. Her moaning reached a crescendo. On the screen, her vagina was pulsing rhythmically. She was coming.

Although Claudia didn't know it, Professor Millhouse came at the same time, filling the vaginal cavity in the replica of Claudia's bottom. So did Dan, her invisible correspondent at the other side of the continent. Althea, who was watching the same web site from another office in Dan's lab, pressed her hand against her clitoris and came, right through her heavy-grade denim bluejeans. Larch, who had been looking over Althea's shoulder, unzipped his fly and pulled out his cock. Althea bent over, took it in her mouth, and sucked him off at once, although up until then their relationship had been purely professional, and Larch had always been gay. Suzanna, who had also been watching the screen in Althea's office, held Althea's breasts from behind, pressed her clitoris against Althea's ass, and came instantly, although she had always thought of herself as straight.

Later, at the laboratory exercise facility, Claudia and Professor Millhouse were silent as they shared a shower and washed off the transparent cock, the replica of Claudia's pelvic region, and each other. Tomorrow they would be student and mentor again, and tonight there was nothing more to say.

The Perfect Fit

Anne Semans

NEVER, NOT EVEN IN MY WORST NIGHTMARES, could I have imagined a life more dismal than the one I shared with my two stepsisters, Leona and Zsa Zsa. Why did they hate me so much? They had all the money, the girls and the fame. Each day with them brought new lessons in servitude and humility. Tonight was no exception.

It was Friday and I'd been cleaning and cooking for them all week. I worked extra hard so I'd be done in time for the big event – the lesbian dance at Ophelia's. That's all they could talk about for weeks, and boy how they ordered me around – "Wash my garters!" "Polish those spike heels again!" Such nags.

But I finished my chores and had them all suited up in their finest gear and most fetching wigs in plenty of time for the dance. When I humbly asked permission to go to the dance myself, they both broke into hysterical laughter.

"You? Go to the dance! What on earth for?" Leona looked at me in total disbelief. "You have nothing – no looks, no money, no sex appeal, no power. No one will want you. You're better employed staying here and preparing the dungeon for my return."

"Yes dahling, she's right." Zsa Zsa chipped in. "You must stay. I need you to alphabetize my eye makeup."

I whined and pleaded and begged. I offered to wait on them all night. They would not relent. When I started to cry, Zsa Zsa slapped me. Realizing it was hopeless, I retreated to a corner to nurse my stinging cheek, while they laughed all the way to the limo.

Resigned to my fate, I picked up a broom and began chanting, "I hate my sisters, hate, hate, hate them" in time to my sweeping. It didn't help much and eventually I started sobbing again.

"Girl, you are one sorry sight," came a voice from behind me. I looked up to see a man dressed in a strapless red taffeta gown, sporting a tacky blond wig, and wearing way, way too much makeup. In her right hand she waved around a Hitachi Magic Wand.

"Who are you, and why do you have my vibrator?" I demanded.

"Well that's a fine way to greet your Fairy Godmother," she replied, feigning hurt. Noting the perplexed look on my face, she continued, "That's right, honey. Who better than a queen to star in that ever glamorous, oh-so-coveted role of Fairy Godmother? Besides, you *obviously* are in great need of my magic." She held up the wand. "And shame on you for not realizing that this vibrator is the source of all your pleasure and happiness. You just underestimate its versatility, that's all." With that she waved the wand three times, and two cute young fags appeared, dressed in leather chaps.

"These fairies are here to help," she said.

"Help with what?" I inquired sarcastically. "Alphabetizing makeup? I can spell, you know. But actually, I could use some help fixing up the dungeon. Leona is so particular about her whip display."

"No, you ninny," she chided. "You are going to the dance. We're here to help you get dressed. Turning ducks into swans is my specialty," she giggled.

"The dance?" My heart pounded with excitement, then it dropped. "I can't go. My sisters will kill me if they see me there. Thanks anyway."

"Now, now, now. We wouldn't want to let a couple of hags get in the way of our fun, would we?" Godmother replied reassuringly. "Trust me darling, between the absolutely stunning makeover I'm going to give you, and the girls who'll flock around you all night, your sisters won't even recognize you."

I leapt for joy, hardly believing my good fortune. In my excitement, I gave all three of my fairies hugs and kisses.

"Save it for the girls, honey," Godmother teased.

We spent the next hour fighting over what I was going to wear. It's true that I hardly ever went out, and when I did it was in jeans and a t-shirt. But Godmother paraded some of her own party gowns before me, despite my protestations that sequins, boas and pink frills just weren't for me.

"Well, what *is* you, then? We don't have all night. Lace?

"Definitely not, too femme.

"Latex?"

"Oooh – daring! But from what I've heard it's kind of uncomfortable."

"Leather?"

"No, too butch. Besides, I don't know if the bare butt look is for me," I replied, with a nod to the boys.

"Well, honey," Godmother confided while gazing at the boys, "it's not the chaps, but what's so attractively *displayed* in them, that counts." A look of sudden inspiration flashed over her face. "I've got it!"

And she produced the cutest little black cotton and spandex miniskirt. "It's not shorts, but it says 'check out the package' to anyone with eyes."

She was right. I slipped on the skirt and instantly loved the way it looked and felt. My curves were smooth and pronounced, and the snugness meant that all night I'd be aware of my ass, as would others.

"Now for the top half," my Godmother said, interrupting my reverie. "Silk blouse? Vest? Black lace bra?"

"No, no, no. I need something that says I'm still me. I don't want to completely transform myself; it feels too deceptive."

"Okay, okay. It's your dance. Got any suggestions?"

I wracked my brain and sorted through her bags of clothes. The three of us combed through my sisters' closets. From one of my old trunks, one of the fairies pulled out an old Bonnie Raitt tank top.

"That's it!" I cried. "That's perfect!"

"Are you kidding?" Godmother stared at the shirt in astonishment. "That rag is at least fifteen years old."

"But it's perfect," I countered. "I loved that shirt. I loved myself in that shirt. And besides, wearing a concert t-shirt is kinda novel and retro, don'tcha think?"

"You win," she said. "But at least indulge me by wearing these fishnets and heels."

"Deal!" I felt fantastic.

After the clothes came the hair and makeup, and when everything was finally finished, they all gathered around applauding and smiling, congratulating themselves on their handiwork.

"Well, honey, I think you're ready," Godmother said, "and your coach awaits." She pointed the Magic Wand toward the front window.

A sleek Harley appeared in my driveway, straddled by a woman who was the spitting image of Joan Jett.

"Th . . . th . . . that's not really Joan Jett, is it?" I stared in disbelief. Just then the driver looked right at me and sneered. I swooned.

"I told you it's magic," Godmother said, tapping the wand. "But listen carefully. You must be back by midnight or everything will be ruined. The magic wears off at the stroke of twelve – your clothes, your hair, even Joan will be gone. And that gorgeous bike turns into a skateboard. So don't be late!" With that, she whisked me out the door.

The ride to Ophelia's was sheer ecstasy: the bike purring between my legs, the wind rushing through my hair, and Joan Jett humming her infamous tune, "Do You Wanna Touch Me There?"

Sadly, it had to end. We arrived at the club and Joan walked me to the door. "You're not coming in?" I looked desperately into her eyes. "Please, I want you to."

She only sneered. "Eh, these clubs, I see them enough at work." But then she grinned at me and in her husky low voice said, "It's your night, babe. Leave 'em breathless. I'll be waiting for you at quarter to midnight." And then she was gone.

Feeling a little weak, nervous and overexcited, I entered the club, where I was greeted by throbbing music and the smell of smoke. I breathed deeply, wanting to savor every sensation I encountered this evening. As I headed straight for the bar, I felt all eyes focused on me. The place was jammed, but a path opened up for me as I walked across the room. I arrived at the bar, and the bartender, a tall, stunning creature with penetrating green eyes, handed me a martini.

"You look positively parched," she said. "For the rest of the evening, I want you to come to me when you're thirsty or in need of anything. Understand?"

"It will be a pleasure," I assured her.

I turned around to survey the crowd. I loved the sight of a room filled only with women: women huddling over tables in the lounge, thrashing around on the dance floor, waiting in line for the restroom, and cruising one another at the bar. I knew that out there somewhere, at least one woman ached for me.

Suddenly I saw Zsa Zsa and Leona with some very young women. I panicked when both of them looked over at me, but neither of them showed any sign of recognition. I was safe! Bolstered by my anonymity, I looked back at them. Zsa Zsa blew me a kiss and Leona leered lewdly. I laughed to myself and sent over my meanest Joan sneer.

I finished my drink and turned around in time to find another one waiting for me on the bar. I brought the glass to my lips and noticed lipstick, the exact shade of the bartender's, decorating the rim of my glass.

I looked up. She was watching me. I took a sip from the spot where her lips had been and then, staring at her, slowly licked the gin off my lips.

"Excuse me, but . . ." Someone was tapping on my shoulder. I turned around to find a cowgirl's freckled face only inches away from mine.

"Howdy. I shore hope you'd do me the honor of dancin' this little number with me. It is k.d. lang, ya know, jest the hottest bit of lesbian country to come our way. And you bein' the purtiest thing to set foot in here all night, I jest hadta ask. Wouldya, pul-lease?"

Well I wouldn't dream of saying no to this girl, all fresh as hay and sweet-smelling soap. Besides, I really liked her cowboy boots and figured she probably cut a wicked two-step.

Little Miss Country didn't disappoint me. After the first song, she invited me to slow dance. As our bodies pressed together, I was greeted by a mild vibration near my clit. I looked at my bumpkin inquisitively as she handed me a little plastic pack attached to a cord that snaked its way into her jeans. I fiddled with the control and heard the distant whine of a motor just as a grimace of pleasure passed over her face. Now I understood. We pressed our bodies tightly together and she whispered into my ear.

"Go ahead and give it to me, darlin'. I wanna come so bad and you're my deliverance." I was getting revved up myself, so I decided to play her game. I turned the vibrator down.

"Oh, you tease me, sugar. Turn that love machine up or I'll die of frustration. I want . . . "

I cut her off by kissing her deeply and grabbing the crotch of her jeans with my free hand. I gave her cunt a vigorous massage and felt her legs start to shake. I cranked the vibrator up to full speed and pulled my head away in time to watch her face tense up as she entered a full-blown orgasm.

"Good lawd," she screamed at the top of her lungs, then collapsed into my arms just as our slow dance ended.

I was about to take my spent corn-fed girl up on her suggestion that we retreat to her place for a less public roll in the hay, when someone beckoned me from across the dimly lit room. I excused myself to investigate, promising to return soon.

"The night is young yet." It was my personal bartender offering me another drink. "Why pick just one apple when you could have the whole tree? That was Eve's mistake." She placed the glass against my cheek and the icy shock brought me back to my senses. She was right. There were so many women here. I graciously bid my cowgirl good-bye and decided to visit the restroom before heading back to the bar.

On my way, I got sidetracked by the sight of a butch/femme couple reclining comfortably in one corner of the bar. The butch made eye contact with me and motioned for me to take the empty seat beside her. A prickle of excitement shot through my cunt as I obeyed.

"Your tits look stunning through that t-shirt," my butch said by way of a greeting. "We're having a little tit worship here ourselves, and we thought you might like to join us."

It was then I noticed her femme companion wearing a silk blouse unbuttoned just enough to reveal two supple, absolutely delectable breasts. But what made my clit stand at attention were the clamps she had attached to her nipples. Her nipples were so engorged, I was overcome with the urge to touch them.

As if reading my mind, my butch bent over and gently tugged on the chain connecting the clamps while delicately licking each nipple. My own nipples were now crying out in envy – I'd have given anything to trade places with that femme.

The butch spied me staring hungrily at her girlfriend and I saw a brief smile cross her face. She got up, positioned herself behind me, and suddenly slipped a blindfold over my eyes. I was somewhat disappointed that my view of the tit worship had been unceremoniously cut off, but then I felt my butch pressing up against my back. She was packing! I could feel the stiff cock between my shoulder blades and nearly fainted from the thrill of imagining that cock inside me. Next she placed her hands on my shoulders and I savored the sensuous feeling of those warm hands slowly making their way under my t-shirt, down my chest, and finally resting upon my breasts. She pinched and tweaked my nipples while I writhed in my chair. I was so wet the scent of my own juices was making me heady.

Without warning, she ripped off my blindfold, and I was greeted by the sight of our femme with one leg up on the table, her skirt hiked up around her hips and her wet cunt exposed for our pleasure. With one hand she pulled on her nipple clamps, and with the other she thrust a glow-in-the-dark dildo in and out of her cunt. Between the delicious attention my nipples were receiving and the breathtaking view in front of me, I was on the verge of coming.

I was ready to abandon myself to the will of my butch when the most beautiful woman I had ever seen walked into my line of vision. She appeared to be of Greek descent, with large, deeply set brown eyes, jet black hair combed stylishly around her face, smooth olive skin and full, inviting lips.

Just at that moment, the femme rose up in front of me and attempted to put her juice-soaked dildo into my mouth.

"No! Stop! You're in my way," I said and pushed her away, irritated that she had completely obstructed my view. I was afraid to lose sight of my dream lover.

Fortunately she was still there. I stared wistfully, heartily approving of her sheer white blouse, since it drew attention to the black lace bra underneath and exposed a small area of her stomach. Her loose black skirt fell slightly below her knees, revealing just enough of her naked calves to fuel my imagination. I finished my appraisal and looked up, only to find her staring back at me, an unmistakable grin on her face. I smiled invitingly and she understood.

She moved gracefully through the crowd, commanding respect, awe and desire every step of the way. I sensed she was someone important, but I didn't care; I only cared about thinking of something to say. I disentangled myself from my companions and made my way toward her.

"I've been waiting for you most of the night," she said mysteriously. "I see that you've sampled the club's wares and have come to me of your own desire. For the rest of the evening, you are mine!"

"I . . . I . . . uh . . . who . . ." I stammered, but before I could finish she pulled me onto the dance floor.

At that moment, Prince's "Erotic City" hit the speakers and she moved slowly and provocatively, while keeping her eyes set firmly on me. She performed for me only, running her hands over her body while her hips instinctively caught the beat. Periodically she undid a button on her blouse, slowly revealing even more of her delicious body.

I craved more contact with her. Sensing this, she danced us over to a corner and through a door into a small, dusty storeroom. Cases of beer and mineral water lined the walls. The coolness and relative quiet were a welcome contrast to the heat and distraction of the bar.

"I have a surprise for you," she said teasingly. "Please sit down here." She patted a beer keg. "Excuse the informality, but it's all we've got for now."

I obeyed and looked up at her expectantly. "I know this is what you've wanted all night," she whispered, as she undid the one and only button still clasped on her blouse. She let the shirt slip down off her shoulders and onto the ground, which left her standing in nothing but a black bra and skirt.

"You look good in black," I offered feebly, grasping for something to say. "And white," I said as an afterthought.

"And nothing," she said, unhooking the bra.

Before me now, I was sure, were the most exquisite breasts in the universe. I swallowed hard and reached up to touch them, but her hands caught mine.

"In time," was all she said, and proceeded to strip off my shirt, shoes and stockings. She stood me up and we faced each other, skirt to skirt. She placed her hands on my shoulders and ran them firmly down over my breasts and stomach until she reached my last bit of clothing. She yanked on the zipper and brought the skirt down around my ankles, so I stood stark naked a foot away from her.

I reached out and caressed her breasts. How could I help myself? They had been beckoning me since I first saw her. She gasped from the unexpected contact, but didn't draw away. Encouraged, I leaned into her and kissed her with every ounce of desire and persuasion I possessed. She returned the kiss and the embrace, and then slid her hands down my back and started massaging my ass.

Her expert hands and the feel of her soft, warm skin under mine awoke every last pleasure point, and I kissed her harder. Suddenly she pulled away.

"Ah! I'm selfish, letting myself be distracted. This is your night, and I intend to see to it that you're fully satisfied. Sit back down and close your eyes!"

I obeyed again, though the keg made for a rather cold chair.

The next thing I felt was her bare legs spreading mine apart. She had removed her skirt and the thought of her exposed cunt being so close to mine was electrifying.

"Open your eyes and see what's waiting for you."

And there, waiting, was my destiny. I gazed lustfully upon the lubed-up, faux-marble dildo cinched firmly into her leather harness. As I sat staring at her cock with pure gratitude, imagining hours of unspeakable pleasure, she grabbed me under the knees and scooted me forward, forcing me to lean back against the stacked boxes for stability. Instantly, and with one impeccably-timed movement, she thrust that dildo into my wet, aching cunt.

I screamed – *deliriously*, mind you – as she fucked me hard. Our bodies rocked together, making a wet, sticky, slapping sound. I was holding on hard to my keg handles, knowing my orgasm was only seconds away, when a beeping noise woke me from my reverie.

"Oh god!" I cried in panic. That beep was my watch, informing me it was a quarter to midnight.

"That's it, lover, go with it, I want to hear you come," she coached me, obviously encouraged by my heavenly call.

No, not now, why now? I thought, trying to ignore the warning, but fear and dread pulsed through my body. I grabbed my beauty around the neck and locked both legs around her waist, allowing her cock to linger one last moment inside me. "I can't stay . . . can't explain . . . it's not you . . . this is the hardest moment of my life." I placed the most tender kiss on her lips and pulled away.

I dressed frantically, oblivious to her inquiries and protestations, bent only on getting out of the club before it was too late. I raced out of the room, out of the bar, and hopped on to Joan's motorcycle only seconds before my watch beeped midnight. In that instant, I found myself halfway down the block, maneuvering a skateboard, clad in jeans and t-shirt. I looked over my shoulder to see my lover standing on the front steps of the bar gazing down the street in search of the woman she had just undressed.

Back at home, my fairy godmother was disappointingly absent, probably too busy with her own nocturnal affairs to check in with me. Thankfully she had left my vibrator plugged in by my bed, so I used the wand to satisfy my immediate physical hunger, and then drifted off to sleep with the memory of a wonderful night.

The next day I awoke to Zsa Zsa's high-pitched rantings booming over my head.

"Dahling. Get up! Get up zis minute and make us some coffee. We have za most exciting news of za dance last night."

As I crawled out of bed, I was instantly aware of my slightly bruised cunt, a pleasant reminder of the night's activities.

In the breakfast room Zsa Zsa and Leona could not stop

gabbing about the mysterious woman in the Bonnie Raitt shirt who had smitten all the girls. They even boasted about having had a few minutes alone with her themselves. I laughed to myself at their ego-inflated lies.

"She was utterly charming," said Leona authoritatively. "Not to mention devastatingly beautiful. If it hadn't been for that blasted Ophelia showing up and hogging her all to herself, I'm sure we would have had an excellent time in the dungeon."

"Ophelia?" I repeated, shocked by the revelation. "The club owner?" So that's who my Greek beauty was. My hopes came crashing down on me; I knew I didn't stand a chance with someone so prestigious, rich and beautiful – I was a mere drudge with a broom and a skateboard.

"Yes, that's right, dahling," Zsa Zsa explained. "She is za richest and za most lusted-after lesbian in town. I'd slap her silly if it meant she'd notice me."

I started to lapse into a severe depression when the sound of motorcycles in the street sent us all to the window.

"My god!" said Leona, "It's her. It's Ophelia. And an entourage of her friends. What could she possibly want?"

"Maybe I don't need to slap her after all," Zsa Zsa speculated.

"I, uh, I should clean up," I volunteered. I couldn't bear to have Ophelia see me like this.

Suddenly, she was at our door. All the passion of the previous night welled up in me. I froze.

"Hello ladies," Ophelia nodded cordially. "Let me get straight to the point. I need your help. You may have noticed that last night I met the most exquisite woman. I believe I'm truly in love, but I never learned her name. I *must* find her." Ophelia looked truly desperate. "All I have is this dildo," – one of her leather women presented the beautiful tool of pleasure on a satin pillow – "which fits her perfectly. I have tried it on every willing lesbian in order to find its proper owner, but as yet have come up empty-handed."

"Say nussing more, Ophelia dahling, I'm sure it must belong to me." Zsa Zsa said, dropping her panties and reclining spread-eagled on the divan.

Ophelia's friends covered the dildo with a condom, strapped it onto Ophelia, and in seconds she had deftly inserted the rod into Zsa Zsa's pink, flushed cunt. She thrust in and out expertly for some time, soon leaving Zsa Zsa expired and wilted on the couch.

"No, no. I'm afraid you're not the one," Ophelia pronounced. "Too much rattling around. But thanks anyway." She seemed disheartened, but somewhat relieved that Zsa was not her mystery woman. She handed the dildo to one of her girls with instructions to change the condom.

"Of course she's not," Leona blustered. "That dildo is just my size. I insist you try it on me." We waited some time for Leona to take off each item of her finery and fold it neatly in a pile on the chair. When she was naked except for her bra, garter, stockings and high heels, she bent over, providing Ophelia with a perfect rear-entry target. Ophelia gave her buttocks a solid smack first, which contributed greatly to Leona's lubrication. She then took aim and began to plunge deep inside Leona, but the dildo would only go in about halfway.

"Push harder, you imbecile, I know it will fit," Leona commanded, but despite Ophelia's efforts it wouldn't go in all the way. "Please . . . more . . . it hurts," she cried. "I love it . . . more . . . yes . . . ," and she collapsed in a heap on the floor.

"Well," sighed Ophelia, "I thank you both, but it's not a match, so I'll just be on my way." Her shoulders slumped, she headed for the door.

"Wait!" I cried. "Don't go. It's me, Ophelia! I'm the one." And every pair of eyes in the place, with the possible exception of Ophelia's, were fixed on me in disbelief.

"Shut up!" Leona snarled at me. "Don't waste her time." Addressing Ophelia, she said, "That's our lunatic stepsister, full of erotic delusions and unspeakable fantasies. Don't pay any attention to her."

"Ophelia," I pleaded, "you know I'm right. And there's one way to tell for sure."

She smiled at me. "Yes. Everyone gets a chance, and I will not deny you yours." She approached me tenderly. "Please disrobe. I'll help." She pulled the zipper on my jeans the same way she had the night before, and I went weak at the knees. I lay down on the divan and Ophelia slid on top of me.

"Ophelia?"

"Yes?"

"We have some unfinished business."

With that invitation, she pushed her cock into me slowly. Her face instantly lit up, and then, oblivious to the rest of the room, we carried on right where we had left off.

Just Reading News

Mary Anne Mohanraj

I CHOOSE THE CLOTHING CAREFULLY. Cream silk shirt and black lace bra. Nothing else. After a long day in a tailored suit and itchy hose, the temptation to just walk around naked is strong, but this will work better: lace against sensitive skin.

The computer's already on – I never turned it off this morning. My nosy roommate won't be home from work for another hour. An hour should be enough.

I've been waiting for this all day. Just one of those days when you can't stop thinking about it, when you'd even be willing to lock your married, overweight boss in his office and tear his expensive clothes off. But my poor boss wouldn't survive that; he'd die of embarrassment.

I'm damp already. My breasts are sore, heavy. As I sit down at the computer, I run a quick hand across a nipple, unable to resist that indescribable twinge. Then I turn on the modem and dial in. Rec.arts.erotica is empty as usual, but there's a never-ending stream in alt.sex.stories, and literary quality isn't terribly important right now. I quick-select actual stories that sound promising, and skip past the hundreds of obnoxious ads.

"He thrusting his nine-inch rod into her steamy love tunnel." Not this one. Some things are just unacceptable. I'm not too picky, really – I'm willing to read all sorts of stories, even stories that in another mood I'd probably find offensive. When I'm horny, I'll generally settle for what I can get. But bad grammar makes me wince and pulpy language makes me laugh, which is definitely not conducive to orgasms.

As I select a string of likely-sounding stories and start scrolling through, I thank whatever benevolent deity invented the Net. So much cheaper than buying real erotica. So much more comfortable than trying to hold open *The Story of O* or *The Claiming of Sleeping Beauty* while the pages are slipping from sweaty fingers. It only takes one intermittent finger to press the PAGE DOWN key.

"He looked, horrified, at the four men holding down his little daughter. The marks of their whips were clear against her pale body. She cried out, 'Please, daddy! They'll hurt me again . . . don't let them hurt me. I want you, daddy. . . .' He slowly lowered himself onto her, promising himself that nobody would hurt his little girl again. . . ."

Another ridiculous story. Disgusting, and horrific if it were true. Yet this is only fiction, and so the horror leaches away, leaving only the raw sex. I continue to caress my nipples as I read, squeezing and occasionally pinching, rolling the skin through the silk and lace. I've tried just silk, but there's a delicious roughness in lace. The silk slides across my back and shoulders as I rock slowly. I cross my legs, first one way, then the other. This chair is too hard, but there's no time to stop now. Next story.

"She undressed in front of the window every evening. After everyone else had left the office, she slipped into a co-worker's office, and slowly stripped off her clothes. She leaned against the sixty-seventh-floor windows in the AMOCO building, looking out over the lake, almost positive that nobody could see her. She rubbed her naked, taunting body against the cold glass."

Mmm . . . yes. Scattered around the computer are my paraphernalia: more silk shirts, candles, a bowl of lukewarm water – yesterday's ice cubes. Sitting far forward, on the edge of my chair, I pick up a shirt from the floor, and run it between my legs. I pause between stories to use both hands to pull it back and forth against my clit. It's pleasant, but frustrating, since I've bent so far forward it's difficult to read. I remind myself once again to buy a vibrator. Then I start reading again.

The next one is marked "nc" for nonconsensual. The best kind, the kind that always gets me off, though I couldn't tell you why. The force and passion of it, the speed and fury? Let the psychologists decide. I'm busy reading.

Three men have broken in and are taking turns pounding into a screaming woman. It's unclear who's doing what to whom, but it doesn't really matter. My pulse is racing now, and while I'm not quite moaning, I'm no longer silent. I cross my legs again, clenching my thigh muscles against the bunched silk. I am rocking once more, fingers tightening on my right nipple through the lace. The big construction worker flips her over and enters her again, his hard chest slamming into her back. I squeeze harder, and oh, this will hurt later, but it doesn't matter.

My leg muscles are clenched so tight that pins and needles are racing up and down them. Somehow, that only makes it better, the tension building and building as I rock back and forth with silk rubbing against my clit. The woman is screaming and I am whimpering now, climbing higher and higher until I think I cannot do this anymore, I have to relax my muscles, I just can't. . . .

And then it's suddenly here, and I don't know if I'm screaming too, or silent, as my orgasm grabs me and all my muscles convulse at once and relax so slowly, and the world just blanks out around me, dissolving into haze.

Eventually, I can see again. I let go of my poor, maltreated nipple, and uncross my legs for a moment, letting the silk shirt fall to the floor. It's 5:18 by the computer clock, and I have over forty minutes before my roommate is likely to arrive. I stretch, pause to pet the cat that has somehow climbed onto the monitor, shift and settle again in the hard chair.

I select a new set of stories, and start reading again. . . .

The Associate

Michael Stamp

THE WEEKLY STATUS MEETINGS at Carson, Young and Kramer are boring as hell, although being the firm's senior partner I suppose I shouldn't admit that. The meetings are really for the benefit of my two partners. I don't need to be updated on office business because I've always made it a practice to personally follow up on what every member of the firm is working on. That way there are no surprises, and if there is a problem it gets dealt with promptly. My presence is basically for morale, the leader of the troops and all that.

This morning's meeting will be typical, but today my mind won't wander as I sit at the head of the big mahogany conference table. I'll be too busy watching Nick Lambert.

At twenty-four, Nick is our youngest associate, with a good chance of making partner one day. He's bright, articulate, and extremely thorough in his preparations. He writes incredibly literate briefs, and bills enough hours to keep my partners happy. His sleeping with the boss isn't going to hurt his career either.

Nick is scheduled to report on the Chandler litigation this morning, and his discomfort is obvious to everyone in the room. They give him small smiles of encouragement, thinking he's nervous about working on one of the firm's most important cases. Only I know his discomfort has more to do with the butt plug he's got up his ass than any problems he's having with the case.

The Ripple Jelly Plug is one of my newest toys. Nick's dark eyes widened when he first saw the plug, and his asscheeks quivered like jelly as I worked it inside him. Nick had relished every inch of that long, thick plug as it invaded his asshole. His face was a mask of ecstasy as each ripple disappeared inside him, stretching his sphincter until the plug was all the way in and the flared base was touching his asscheeks. Just remembering the sight is making me hard all over again.

Although Nick is anxious to give his report, the more mundane parts of the meeting come first: the reading of the minutes from last week's meeting, policy changes in the office. I keep my eyes on Nick, but whenever he meets my gaze he quickly looks away.

When Harold Young finally asks Nick if he's ready to begin, Nick quickly answers, "Yes, sir!" with a little too much emphasis on the "sir." This raises a few eyebrows. Nick blushes, and I suppress a smile as I remember a similar shade of crimson on two other cheeks last night. Nick meets my eye for only a second before he begins his report.

"Excellent work, Nick," Walter Kramer says when Nick is finished. "The firm is very pleased with your performance, especially in court. You looked very good in front of that jury yesterday."

But not as good as he looked last night, I want to tell Walter. Of course I can't. Staid, straight Walter could never appreciate the sheer beauty of Nick's firm young body as he offered himself to me. Seeing Nick standing naked before me, his legs spread, his hands clasped behind his head and his eyes cast downward caused a hunger in me I thought I could never satisfy.

Someone else begins speaking, but the voice fades as I mentally leave the conference room and return to my bedroom with Nick.

I grab two handfuls of Nick's straight black hair and cover his mouth with mine. I kiss him deeply, demandingly, until I feel his body yield to me, then my fingers move down his smooth chest and find his small, flat nipples.

I work his tits without mercy, twisting, squeezing and biting them until the little nubs of flesh have doubled in size and just grazing them with my fingertips makes Nick tremble. Then I get the tit clamps. Nick's eyes never leave the clamps while they're in my hand, his anticipation apparent in the upward arc of his cock. When I spring them on his tender nipples a small moan escapes from his lips.

While I enjoy this tit play, what I really want is Nick's ass. I slap it, then begin my voyage of discovery – massaging his asscheeks, spreading them, lubricating my finger and slipping it into his asshole. Nick doesn't open easily and his muscles rebel at my invasion, but I keep going, urging my finger deeper and deeper until he's on his toes and I hear him whimper, "Fuck me, sir. Please fuck me."

"You haven't earned that yet, boy," I tell him. "Now bend over and grab your ankles."

Nick turns just enough for me to see his cock. It's now jutting straight out from his body, a clear drop of fluid seeping from the tip. "Yes, sir!" he responds, then quickly assumes the position.

I take out my other new toy, the Slapper. Nick is tensed, waiting for the first blow, but I slap the paddle into my palm instead. He flinches at the sound as if I've hit him. I wait until I see his muscles relax, then lay the leather full across his ass.

As I put Nick through his paces with the paddle, I wonder if they shouldn't have called it the Clapper because seeing the blush spreading over the pale flesh of Nick's asscheeks makes me want to applaud. I increase the intensity of my blows, and with each slap of the paddle Nick's body moves slightly, making the chain between the tit clamps jingle. It's music to my ears.

It doesn't take long before my own cock is rock-hard. I throw down the paddle, tear open a condom package and roll the rubber down over my rigid flesh. "On the floor!" I order Nick. When Nick is on all fours, I spread his legs and kneel between them. Grasping his hips, I enter him.

I start out slowly, wanting to prolong my pleasure. I love looking down at Nick's beautiful young ass while I fuck him. Feeling my cock moving in and out of his greased asshole is incredible, but being able to watch it happening doubles my pleasure.

Nick wants it badly and I feel him push back against me, trying to hasten our union. "Calm down, boy," I warn him, squeezing his shoulders. I see and hear Nick take two deep breaths. He's really hot, but he manages to slow down. When he finds my rhythm, his body moves like an extension of my own. "Good boy," I tell him.

Nick's endurance doesn't last long. His moaning intensifies with each of my thrusts, and after my next two strokes hit his prostate, Nick looks over his shoulder at me and pleads, "Please, sir. Please let me come."

"Soon, boy," I promise. To see just how much more Nick can take, I reach for the chain hanging down between the tit clamps and give it a quick jerk. The added stimulation to his already tortured nipples causes a choking cry to escape from Nick's lips, but he holds on. "Good boy," I say again.

Nick knows better than to come without my permission, but knowing he won't last much longer, I increase my thrusts, pumping faster and faster until I hear his more urgent, "Please, sir!" Then I release the clamps on his nipples and give my consent with three words. "All right, boy."

Nick is ravaged by the barrage of physical sensations. His whole body shudders, his hips buck wildly, and stream after stream of milky strands shoot out from his cock. I'm still inside Nick while he comes, and in the throes of his orgasm, Nick's sphincter muscles clamp down on my cock, taking me with him. Unable to hold back my own release, I erupt inside him.

"Mr. Carson?" my secretary asks. "Mr. Carson, are you all right?"

"Yes," I answer, unsettled by being brought back to reality so abruptly. "What is it?"

"Where were you, John?" Harold asks with a nervous laugh. "We'd like to adjourn the meeting."

I can tell by the look on his face that he wonders if I've lost it, and I very nearly have. "Of course," I say in as normal a voice as possible. "Thank you, everyone." The others rise from their chairs to exit the room, but I remain seated, knowing that if I stand up I'll be unable to hide the erection that is tenting my trousers.

Nick is the last to leave the room, but before he can reach the door I ask him, "Where do you think you're going?"

Nick has heard this tone before, but never in this room. His confusion is written all over his face. "Sir?" he asks.

"Lock that door, boy, then get your ass over here."

Nick obeys immediately, and when the door is locked I push back my chair and work my zipper open. Finally free, my cock springs up against my belt buckle.

Grabbing Nick roughly, I push him face down onto the conference table. I reach under his belly, unzip his pants, and tug them down over his legs, leaving them bunched around his ankles.

Nick groans as I pull out the butt plug, but before he can adjust to the sudden emptiness, I replace the plug with a more life-like model.

"Yes, boy," I tell Nick as I pin him to the table, "the firm is very pleased with your performance."

The Stranger

Joel King

DURING THE TWENTY-FIVE YEARS of our strictly monogamous relationship, my wife, Cindy, and I have shared a great number of fantasies with one another, which has strengthened our love. Whether it is a recurring fantasy, or a new one, we are always ready to live them out to the fullest extent possible. We have developed a series of codes we use to signal our desire to act out a particular fantasy.

On those days when I have to work late, I always call Cindy when I'm about to leave for home. Sometimes, usually on the night of the full moon, she gives the code for *The Stranger* fantasy. I begin by leaving my car out on the street, out of sight of the house, instead of parking in our garage. I silently enter the dark house through the back door, and quietly go upstairs. When I get to our bedroom, I immediately disrobe, leaving a pile of clothing in the hallway.

I then enter the bedroom. The curtains are open; the moon provides the only light, but no one can see into the room. Cindy is seemingly asleep. She is naked, her smooth, pale skin bathing in the soft moonlight that streams through the bank of windows beside our bed. She's wearing her fleece-lined leather blindfold and cannot see me. I approach and start to kiss and caress her body, my first touch rousing her from her sleep. I continue, and she begins to moan. I pinch and suck on her nipples. She calls out my name, but I shush her and do not respond. At that moment, I spread her legs, and moisten two fingers with her pussy juice. She's very wet. I put my fingers to her lips. She greedily licks and sucks them clean, and asks me to fuck her.

Instead, I begin to eat her pussy. I suck on her clitoris and her vaginal lips. I haven't shaved since early that morning, so she occasionally jerks her body in surprise or pain when I accidentally scratch her with my day's growth. Normally, I would shave, but not shaving adds to the fantasy. She starts to writhe about, begging for my cock. But I continue eating her out until she nears her orgasm. Then I enter her, fucking her vigorously until she comes, crying out as each orgasmic wave flows through her body. I continue pounding into her until I finally come. Then, with a quick pat on her bottom, I get out of bed and leave the room.

To complete the fantasy, I immediately dress and exit the house. I return to my car and drive it into the garage. I go upstairs, enter the bedroom and say, "Honey, I'm home." I hear Cindy quickly suck in her breath as she bolts upright and removes her blindfold. I say, "Sorry it took me so long to get home, but after I called you to tell you I was leaving, Bob invited me out for a quick drink so we could discuss that new project that he and I and some of the guys are working on. I rushed home as soon as I could shake free. I probably should have called you again, but I was ready for some lovin' and didn't want to waste another minute getting back home." As I talk, I have been removing my clothing, watching as Cindy draws the sheet up over her shoulders as if to protect herself from me.

At this point, it's time for my side of the fantasy. I climb into bed and start making love to her. At first, Cindy is indifferent and tries to push me away. She hasn't yet said a word. I know her hot spots, and my caresses are persistent. As I give her a deep French kiss, she moans into my mouth, reciprocates the kiss with her quick, darting tongue, and says, "Eat me." I then lavish in our commingled juices, probing her pussy with my tongue, tasting my own sperm.

"God, you taste good, really different tonight," I comment. I momentarily stop, and come up to her face. I look inquisitively into her eyes, waiting for her to tell me something. She briefly returns my gaze, then looks away to hide her "guilt" at having just made love to a stranger. I lean over to kiss her mouth. As I do, she grabs my cock, and starts a frantic tugging.

I'm so excited by this fantasy and by our lovemaking, that it's easy to get another erection despite having come so recently. When I slip my cock into her, I exclaim, "I love it when you get so wet. You're really wet tonight, you feel so hot and creamy." This time, our fucking is slower, more sensual, with many pauses. When I finally come, it's so draining that I collapse into Cindy's arms. We hold each other for a few moments before Cindy leaves the bed to shower.

When she returns, I tell her, "Cindy, you were incredible tonight. That was one of the hottest fucks we've ever had. You were so wet that I could barely control myself when I finally entered you. You tasted good, but it was really different this time. What did you do today to make you taste that way?"

Cindy never answers, she just smiles and kisses me to shut me up. But we both know what has been different that night, and part of the fantasy is never to reveal that Cindy has had sex with a stranger, and that I have eaten his come and mixed our sperm in her pussy. This fantasy has been replayed many times over the years. Although it was always pleasurable and intense, I felt it was getting old and needed some revision.

One Monday, about a week or so shy of a full moon, we received a sex toy catalog. We usually browse through these catalogs together to fuel our imaginations – it's rare that we've ordered anything. But this time, I found the catalog on my pillow, and as I paged through it, I saw a few comments in Cindy's handwriting written in the margins.

Next to the drawing of the Hitachi Magic Wand, she had written, "Do you think my orgasms would be too intense to try this?" Next to a rubber dildo called the Prince: "This looks like the Dick of Death! Hmm." Next to a dildo called the Champ: "I wonder if these silicone dildos are as great as they say they are? Would you be jealous if I fantasized about fucking someone with a red cock that big?" Next to a cock ring: "How hot, hard and purple would your cock get if you wore this? Would it make your veins pop out? Would I feel them bulging and pulsing in my pussy?"

That evening, we reviewed the catalog together. Cindy blushed when we turned to each page containing one of her comments. "Look, Cindy," I said, "I thought that you wanted to limit your sex toy use to the leather blindfold we got, and that silicone butt plug you got me. If you really want to try out some more of these toys, I'm game. I want to go slow, though. So, why don't you decide on one of them, and I'll pick one too."

"You really make things tough," Cindy replied. "I put those comments in there because I want to try all of them. I can't make up my mind whether I want to try the vibrator or the silicone dildo the most. I get hot just thinking about them. What about you?"

I realized that Cindy was most likely hoping that I would use my choice to pick one of those two toys so she wouldn't have to choose between them. But one of her choices had suddenly set my wheels spinning, and I was about to enhance *The Stranger*. "Well," I responded, "I wouldn't mind trying one of those cock rings."

"In that case," Cindy said, "I'll pick the vibrator, but only if we can get all of the attachments too."

"Of course," I answered. So we filled out the order form, and mailed it off the next morning.

That day, I called the toy company's 800-number, and placed a next-day order for the Champ silicone dildo, and something that Cindy had not commented on: a purple leather dildo harness. I had the package mailed to my office.

The next day, I took a razor, shaving soap and a towel to work. I was really nervous when the package was brought to my office in the afternoon. I waited until everyone had left the office that night, locked my door and opened the box to examine the toys. The Champ was much larger and thicker than I had expected. I could see that its tip was almost my size and shape, but it grew increasingly thicker down to its base. I could barely get it into the harness. Talk about the Dick of Death – would this dildo really fit Cindy without discomfort? I called before I left for home, as usual. No code word from Cindy that night. So, I locked up the dildo and harness in one of my desk drawers.

The following day, I again stayed late at the office, hoping that when I called home, Cindy would give the code for *The Stranger*. She didn't. By the third day, a Friday, the anticipation was killing me. The sexual tension had been building up in me all week, as Cindy and I had not made love once since placing our catalog order. I was ready to explode. That evening, only one day shy of the full moon, my phone call home elicited our code for *The Stranger*.

Thankfully, the office was empty. I took the dildo and harness out of my desk and put them in my briefcase. I got my shaving gear and towel and went to the restroom, where I shaved – a first for this fantasy. I left with the toys, my plan now in full operation. I followed the usual *modus operandi*. But when I got home, I warmed up a heat wrap in the microwave and wound it around the Champ, leaving just its tip exposed. Then I went upstairs.

There was Cindy, naked in the bed, seemingly asleep. She was languorously sprawled out, her skin washed by the moonlight, wearing her blindfold. I set the dildo down on the bed and started to kiss and fondle her. Cindy immediately noticed my smooth face and tried to bring her hands to my cheeks, but I pushed them away. I kissed her more forcefully, tonguing her deeply. She moaned into my mouth as I placed my hand on her mound and fingered her pussy. When she called out my name, it was more of a question than ever before.

As I shushed her, I forced her legs apart and thrust one, then two, then three, and finally four of my fingers into her pussy. She was so wet her pussy swallowed them easily, right up to the palm of my hand. My fingers were dripping with her wetness, but rather than let her lick them clean, I grabbed her hair with one hand. As I held her hair, I picked up the dildo, still being warmed by the wrap, about an inch of it exposed, and whispered coarsely, "Suck my cock."

Expecting me to put my cock in her mouth, Cindy's first lick of the dildo's tip caused her to questioningly say my name again. "Joel?"

"Just suck," I growled in a low voice. Cindy started licking the exposed tip of the dildo, getting it nice and wet. I pulled it away from her mouth and whispered, "Don't move. I'll be right back."

I got out of bed, placed the dildo into the harness, and strapped it around my waist. Then I moved Cindy so that her pussy was right on the edge of the bed, her feet on the floor. I started to eat her pussy again. She grabbed my hair, pulling my head in tighter. "Oh God, oh God, oh God," Cindy moaned over and over. "God, I'm coming, I'm coming." She moaned and ground her pussy into my face, as my feverish tongue-lashing became more vigorous. All of a sudden, she ejaculated right into my face. Three strong, hot gushes of ejaculate washed over my face, and I drank as much as I could of the last spurt.

I turned her over onto all fours, removed the heat wrap from the dildo, lubricated it with her pussy juice, and entered her with it in one smooth motion. I was astounded by how quickly and easily her pussy took the Champ.

"Oh, Jesus," Cindy said, "Who are you?" I fucked her, but not too forcefully for fear I would hurt her with the dildo. But she soon thrust back against me, shouting, "Harder, harder, fuck me harder." She groaned as I complied. "God, you're so big. I feel you fucking parts of me that have never been touched before. Give me more, give me everything you've got. I've never been fucked with a cock this big."

I did as she demanded, and Cindy began whipping her head from side to side, all the while telling me to continue fucking her, but harder, always harder. I watched the dildo move in and out of her. I saw how her pussy lips stretched and moved with every stroke.

I reached beneath her and felt her wetness, then played with her nipples. The moment I pulled on her nipple, she started to come again and again, screaming and grunting her ecstasy. With an, "Oh God, oh God," Cindy collapsed on the bed, panting heavily, causing the dildo to slip out. Her ass was still in the air; only her head, chest and arms were resting on the bed.

"Don't even think about moving," I whispered, getting out of the bed. I wasn't done yet. I went to the door and opened it. While I removed the harness, I whispered loudly enough for Cindy to hear me, "It's your turn now. Fuck her hard. She's ready for another fuck." Of course, no one was there except me, but I could tell that Cindy was now uncertain.

As I returned to the bed, Cindy tried to get up and remove her blindfold, but I slapped her ass, grabbed her arm, and hissed, "No you don't!" She let out a low moan. I entered her from behind again. My erection was throbbing and was as hard as I could remember it ever being. I started to thrust into her slowly; she was very wet and open. With each thrust, Cindy thrust back, until she was moaning loudly again. I could tell that she was nearing another orgasm. As she started to come again, her pussy spasmed all around my cock, and she ejaculated again. I could hear the stream hit the bed, and felt the heat as it ran down my leg. I pounded into her as hard as I could, and cried out when I had the most intense orgasm ever. As I pulled out of Cindy's pussy, I saw my come shining in the moonlight, dripping out from between her pussy lips, along with her own juices. Then, instead of the usual quick pat on the bottom, I swatted her ass and left.

I quickly dressed and left with the dildo. Once I was back in my car, I called Cindy on the cellular phone. She picked up the phone after five rings. Her greeting was barely audible. "Hi, Cindy, I hope you haven't fallen asleep waiting for me to get home, but Bob waylaid me again about that project we've been working on. We just finished up, and now Bob wants me to go have a drink with him and Richard Prince, and a couple of the other guys on the project. I'll be home in about an hour, if that's okay with you."

All I heard was labored breathing on the other end of the line. After what felt like a couple of minutes, I said, "Cindy? Are you okay? If you want me to come home right away, I will, but you know how Bob is about these after-hour get-togethers when we've finished a big job."

Still nothing but the sound of her breath, and her efforts to bring it under control. I heard her swallow, then say, almost inaudibly, "No, that's okay. I was sleeping. You go ahead. I know how important he thinks that a drink is for building camaraderie. I'll be waiting for you."

"Thanks," I said. "But I want you to be more than waiting for me. I remember the code, and I want to find you just the way you are right now. Okay?"

A pause. "Joel?"

"Yes?"

"Oh, nothing. It's okay. I'll wait up for you, but don't be too long, please."

"Thanks, love you," I said, as Cindy hung up the phone.

I waited a few more minutes, then phoned her again. I covered the mouthpiece with a handkerchief, as Cindy answered the phone by our bed. "Hello," she said.

Trying to disguise my voice, I whispered, "Hey, baby. That was a great fuck. My friend and I had a wonderful time. You are one nice piece of ass. I've never seen anyone come like that before. You're way too hot for that husband of yours to handle all by himself. He obviously needs help to handle a sex pot like you."

"Who is this?" Cindy asked. "What do you want?"

"I want to come back some time for seconds, baby. I think maybe I'll bring two or three friends with me next time your husband is working late. Someone as incredible as you shouldn't let that husband of yours keep that juicy pussy all to himself. Why, I bet it would take at least four or five guys to tame your pussy. But I've got a friend with a cock so big, we call it the Dick of Death. His nickname is "The Prince." I can't wait to see your hot pussy take him on. I bet you'd drain him dry!"

What I wouldn't have given to see Cindy's face as I rang off.

I couldn't wait a full hour. After half an hour of sitting in the car, I drove into the garage. As I walked into our bedroom, I could hear the shower running. I was certain that Cindy was washing away the traces of her recent fantasy fuck. I was disappointed in a way, as I had really wanted to eat her dripping pussy. I was primed and ready to go again. Now, she was making certain I couldn't taste the sperm of *The Stranger*, something she had never done before.

I approached the bed. On my night stand was an opened box from the sex toy company containing the vibrator, its attachments, and the cock ring we'd ordered. I noticed that the bed had been completely made. That was a bit unusual. I turned back the covers, and the smell of freshly laundered sheets floated out into the room. I walked over to Cindy's side of the bed, and felt around for traces of her ejaculation, but the sheets were dry. Even the mattress pad had been changed. Had Cindy really not known I was once again *The Stranger?* How else to explain fresh linens and a long hot shower. Maybe, I thought, she was turning this fantasy back around on me, had figured it all out, and was just playing along.

I got undressed and put the cock ring on, just as the shower stopped. I placed the vibrator on Cindy's side of the bed. She came into the room, drying her hair, and started when she saw me. "Home so soon, Joel?"

"Couldn't wait any longer, honey. Told Bob that I had to scoot and here I am. I expected to find you in bed waiting for me – I know that you must have been looking forward to *The Stranger* tonight. I'm sorry if my working late made you change your mind. It looks like our toy package has arrived. Maybe we should just try out the new toys tonight."

Cindy just looked at me, stopped drying her hair, and smiled. She got into bed with a small sigh. As we experimented with our new toys that night, I wondered what was racing through her mind. Exhausted, we slept deeply.

The next morning while I was showering, the phone rang. "Right on time," I muttered as I glanced at my watch. "The icing on the cake!" I got out of the shower, leaving it running, and got as close to the bedroom entry as I could without being seen by Cindy, who was answering the phone.

"Hello?" she said. After a short silence, I heard her say in a very quiet, but assured, voice, "That's fine. I'll be ready. Just bring Prince."

I shut off the shower, toweled dry, and came into the bedroom. Cindy was standing by the phone with the receiver still in her hand, staring into space.

"Who was on the phone, honey?" I asked.

Cindy quickly turned her head, and gave me a quizzical look. She really did look puzzled. "Oh, nobody, it was just a wrong number," she said, as she hung up the phone.

On Monday, I had lunch with Bob. "Hey, Joel, what kind of

game are you and Cindy playing?" he asked. "I called your house just like you asked to tell Cindy how much I appreciated your working late on that last project of ours. I thought you said she was expecting my call, but she sounded a little surprised."

"What did you say to her?" I asked.

"Just what you told me to say. I said, 'I just thought I'd call and tell you how much we all appreciate it when your husband works late. We could never have accomplished what we did if he hadn't worked so late. He did a great job on the project. I hope it will be some comfort to you to know that the next time he has to work late, I'll be working late too, as will Richard and a few of the other guys. What do you think of that?' Then, she said, 'That's fine. I'll be ready. Just bring Prince.' And then I hung up. Now, what the hell does that mean, Joel? Just bring Prince? Doesn't make any sense to me, but if it makes you feel better that I let your wife know how much I appreciate your working late, I'm happy to help."

"Thanks, Bob," I smiled in reply.

After lunch, I ordered the Prince dildo from the toy catalog and had it sent to the office.

I haven't had to work late at all during these past few months. Cindy keeps on asking me when I'll be working on another one of Bob's "incredible" projects again. She's even asked me about my co-workers, including Richard Prince, who she seems quite interested in.

Next week, I start working on a new project with Bob. I'll be working on one of my own projects too. Maybe Dick Prince will be working overtime with me.

The Hands Are the Window to the Sex

Blake C. Aarens

MY HUSBAND IS AN IRONWORKER. She knew she wanted to be in the trades from the time she was a little girl. And she picked the butchest of the trades in an area laced with bridges. On the job she hangs upside down from those bridges to solder cable ends together or weld bolts in place. She hangs by a broad leather strap across her back and a cable of her own to swing from.

She downs huge bottles of mineral water, hanging there in the heat, and relieves herself in a porta-potty tethered to the side of the Bay Bridge. Her bathroom hangs suspended, hundreds of feet above the Bay.

My husband. I call her that because she is. And I am her wife. Married to her masculinity as she is to my femme. She has the most amazing hands. Rough. Broad. With thick, blunt-tipped fingers way out of proportion to her wiry, hard-muscled, five-foot frame. She's built like a boxer who could moonlight as a jockey if she wanted to. Bantamweight, I think they call it. Anyway, that sounds about right for her.

I am her physio-opposite. Heavy breasts, soft belly, big ass. All circles and curves where she is sharp angles, flat planes. I am nearly a foot taller than she is. But it's not that foot that counts. Like I said before, it's her hands.

They get beat up on the job. Cut, scraped, bruised. Patches of hardened skin at the base of all eight of her fingers and on the pads of both thumbs. She doesn't work in gloves. Says she needs the heat of her own fleshy palms to warm the metal and set it in the right place.

But at home, in our bed, in the moonlight, without any covers, we use gloves. All the time. They are our only sex toy. The gloves and each other's bodies. An entire drawer in the dresser in our bedroom holds our stash. The variety is staggering. I get turned on just opening the drawer and looking at them. Sometimes, when it's nearing time for her to come home,

60

I do just that, turning myself on in anticipation of her arrival.

We keep the drawer well stocked. Elbow-length black latex for when she wants to get her fist in me – and more. Multi-colored finger cots for when she's in the mood to dabble at my pussy with just the tips of her fingers. She teases and torments me like that, and I have to lie perfectly still – without benefit of ropes – until she's had her fill of playing with me. I love it when she gets in that mood.

We play doctor games and she wears bright blue, non-latex surgical gloves. She examines me. She pokes and prods. She palpates my breasts, kneads my belly, and spreads my labia far apart.

"I've gotta get a good look at you," she likes to say.

Sometimes she wears more than one pair, when her hands are cut up and bleeding from fresh work wounds. When her skin is split open and tender, and she can't take the pressure of my pussy muscles clenching and gripping when she makes me come. She swears she can still feel the heat of me through two layers of latex. Says my wetness is amazing, and that it coats her hands with a healing warmth.

For our fifth anniversary, a loving friend gave her – gave us – a pair of red rubber gloves. They are studded up and down the length with bumps and nipples, ridges, flexible rubber points that she presses against my G-spot when she enters me. We save those for special occasions, like "Thank God It's Friday," or "Monday Middle-of-the-Afternoon Delight."

I take very good care of her hands. When she brings them home bruised and bleeding, I wash them in Ivory soap and cool water with chamomile flowers floating in it. I pat them dry with a clean white towel and squeeze droplets of herbal tincture into the wounds. I hold her hands in my lap and let the medicine seep in. Undulating my hips a little, I invoke the healing energy of my cunt and let it wrap her hard-working hands in a protective aura.

My first aid kit contains an herbal salve. Generous amounts of it have been rubbed into her skin. I buy it by the case. I coat the creases in her fingers, where each of the knuckles bend. I work the rich, pale pink cream into her head, heart, and life-

62 Sex Toy Tales

lines, into the very fabric of her DNA. I do the back of her hands as well, until the rough cuticles become soft. I pay particular attention to those knuckles, for it is more often than not they that rub and bump against the most tender parts of me.

When her hands feel heavy with salve – smoothed, soothed – she slips on white gloves, like the kind cops wear when they're directing traffic. But these gloves are velvet. I made them for her. Inside out, so the heavy nap of the fabric covers her hands. Over these she pulls on gloves of the thinnest latex we can find. She presses me back into my chair. She lifts my skirt. Her hands prepare to enter the healing center of me.

One after the other, she presses her wounded palms against my sex. Touch and lift, first the right one. Touch and lift, then the left. She raps at my clit with her knuckles, asking entrance, asking to be met at the door. My pussy responds to her knocking: my labia part, my clit grows huge, and a welcoming wetness flows from deep inside me.

At first she winces at the pressure of my tight pussy against her battered fingers. She says she can feel each place where her skin is torn, can feel the blood rushing up, can feel where the black and blue bruises are already beginning. But we trust this initial pain. We know that my strong pussy will soothe it. That my strong pussy will send blood and energy to her weakened fingers and help to make them strong again. I focus my attention, breathe with her, draw the power down into my crotch as she strokes first one, then two, then four fingers into my vagina. From four fingers she moves to six, then to eight. Her hands assume the attitude of prayer. Her thumbs remain outside of me and play a hymn on my clit.

Gently at first, I clench my muscles to draw her fingers deeper into me. I draw my pulse down between my legs as well. She needs all my attention now, all my help. My blood. My strength. The bottoms of my feet start to tingle. I feel the dawning of my orgasm inside me. I tell her to enter me fully, to shove both her injured hands inside me, to take the medicine that the spasms of my cunt can give her. And she does. I come around those hands. Around those rough, broad hands, those thick, blunt-tipped fingers.

I come, saying, "Take this. And this. And this. Take this from me. This healing."

In the morning, after she's gone to work, I wash the blood-stained, white velvet gloves. By hand.

It Looks Like a Flower

Marlo Gayle

"IT LOOKS LIKE A FLOWER," I thought to myself as I examined the photograph a little more closely. My initial shock at seeing Mapplethorpe's image, a hand inserted completely into someone's rear, was replaced by curiosity and desire. I wanted to know why someone would do such a thing. It looked painful, but obviously not too painful, or the recipient wouldn't have allowed it . . . right? I decided to do some experimenting.

I started playing with my ass during masturbation. First with my fingers, delicately playing with the rim, feeling the sensations shuddering through my body as I stroked myself to a surprisingly quick orgasm. Jacking off became something entirely new to explore, with wonderful results. Soon I moved on to insertion, but was hampered by the fact that I couldn't get my fingers in as far as I wanted to. Reaching just a little bit more would have resulted in the dislocation of my shoulder, a sensation I wasn't quite ready to explore. I was too embarrassed to bring the subject up with the women I dated, so I began searching for an alternative.

After several weeks of experimenting with various intriguing items, I found myself unfulfilled, even hornier, and a little sore. I was ready to resign myself to settling for my fingers when inspiration and hormones struck hard (pun intended) in the grocery store. I found myself stiff as a board gazing at a pile of large, green cucumbers. I hated cucumbers, despised their taste. However, using them at the other end of the digestive tract had some definite possibilities. I found myself holding them, caressing them lovingly in my hands. I checked their strength, their girth. I bought the biggest, sturdiest one I could find. I was so aroused, I forgot my other shopping and ran to the checkout with the cucumber my only item. I reassured the woman at the checkout that it would be great in the salad I was preparing. I got the feeling she had heard that line before. I rushed home, eagerly anticipating the night of passion that awaited me and my new friend. I had become a vegephile.

I've since discovered silicone and rubber substitutes. They hold up much better under stress, and they don't rot if you leave them out of the fridge. I've even found a loving wife who enjoys pleasuring me anally. However, each time I go to the grocery store now, I find myself getting a little turned on when I push my cart through the produce section.

Sex Toys in History

Frank Paine

NOTE: GREAT-UNCLE SETH was a laboratory assistant to the great inventor, the "Wizard of Menlo Park," Thomas Edison. When Uncle Seth died I found this faded, yellow document among his papers.

Date: Oct. 22, 1896
To: Thomas A. Edison
          Edison Laboratories
          Menlo Park, New Jersey
From: Seth Parkins, Laboratory Assistant
Subject: Condition of Lab

No doubt, sir, you have noted that the laboratory space this morning is in a state of disarray. I will attempt to explain this situation.

First of all, there are all those empty wine bottles.

But I should go back to the beginning. As you may recall, you designated me to perform tests on the new experimental electro-mechanical device (No. 467.10) called . . . for lack of a better name . . . "The Potato Masher." To perform the first tests, I decided to come to the lab last night. I also enrolled our faithful secretary, Miss Katherine Trueblood, to come with me and take notes.

The problem, of course, being to find some use for this machine. First I tried to mash potatoes. With its present rated amperage it wouldn't mash mush, much less spuds. So after numerous trials, I cleaned it off and went to the power source to see if I could, as we say here at Edison Labs, "juice it up."

Unbeknownst to me, Miss Trueblood was resting the machine in her lap. The first thing I knew, she gave out a pronounced shriek. I quickly turned to see if she was in danger and was surprised to see an immense smile cross her face. I asked if she was all right. She replied that she was indeed.

The machine kept buzzing. Miss Trueblood's smile grew larger. I went over to remove the throbbing device from her. By now she had moved it down between her limbs. And she would not give it up. Told me to damn well leave it be!

Soon she was almost lying in the chair, eyes closed, grinning like a Cheshire cat. After she seemed to shudder a few times, she sat up and invited me to come close for, as she put it, a "surprise." Eager to test all possible uses of the invention, I stood beside her. She slowly started to move the vibrating head of No. 467.10 around the surface of my trousers. Especially on my fly.

She was right. I did get a surprise.

So did she.

It was then that Miss Trueblood thought of the wine. She felt we should celebrate our glorious discovery with a toast. I recalled a couple of bottles located conveniently in the locker of an employee who shall remain nameless.

After a few toasts we went to work trying No. 467.10 in every place I could imagine. Ever the faithful employee, Miss T. even added a few clever suggestions of her own. Given our dedication to the job, we continued the tests through to exhaustion.

When we recover more fully, I will present a complete report, with diagrams.

Mr. Edison, I feel supremely confident that we have a winner here. Katie . . . I mean Miss Trueblood and I are willing to continue testing No. 467.10 for as long as it takes.

Wednesday Afternoon
Rebecca C. Abbott

"DEAR GIRL, DRAW THE CURTAINS. The sunlight is too bright for these weak eyes." The old lady was lying on the day bed in her booklined study, and I was trying to find something to read aloud that we would both enjoy. This had been our ritual every Wednesday afternoon since she had hired me to help her with her memoir, though we had yet to start writing. We joked that we were still looking for a style to emulate. This picking of a tome to study was the gateway to a growing sense of intimacy between us, evoking stories from her, as well as periods of contemplative silence comfortably shared.

I realized as I scanned the shelves that afternoon that I didn't really want to choose a book today. Instead, I wanted to move directly to the moment when I could sit and watch her as she closed her eyes and digested words. I thought about how my feelings for her had evolved over the few months I'd begun to know her personally, separate from her work. I had come to her as a willing student and acolyte, ready to understand the grand process of creativity as explained by someone old and wise. I was particularly invested in analyzing her images of the female body, yearning to deconstruct their commentary on intimacy and gender politics. The first time I launched a longwinded, insightful probe into what made her, "the artist," tick, she had listened with her eyes locked on my face.

"Well, my dear, I feel like I'm at the doctoral oral exam I never got to take. I'll leave the answer for some deserving graduate student like yourself to elucidate, but I'll give you the first clue: I love women's bodies. When you love something deeply, you want to know everything about it; I am someone who learns by looking, and the camera allowed me to, well, map what I learned. Think of Ansel Adams and Yosemite – I still feel that awe when I look at a woman's naked body."

The idea of her loving another woman's body, no matter how she meant it, brought her down from the podium, and suddenly I wanted to know about Isabella, the person. I wanted to know about the people and books she loved, pets she had buried, favorite foods and flowers. And then it became clear that, more than the content of her adventurous life, it was Isabella herself who compelled me. The sound of her voice: the way its clear and confident timbre became deeper and softer when moved by sorrow or deep affection; her quickness to laugh when taken by surprise; the lines in her face when she listened intently. I knew I had fallen in love with her, but I also knew that my feelings were not likely to be reciprocated because she was moving toward me on a whole other level, deep in the comforts of her own mind and memories. I looked at her resting back on her pillows, eyes wide open, her long grey hair loose around her head, looking as relaxed as a blanket worn soft with age.

"Hey, dream girl, come back to this old lady," she called me back from my reverie. "Why don't you forget about the book this afternoon. Just pull the curtains and tell me what's on your mind."

"Okay," and I complied, kneeling on the armchair that sat under the window kitty-corner from her day bed. It had taken the place of the rocking chair I usually occupied as I read to her. I tugged at the heavy curtains to block the afternoon sun, but left enough light seeping through to read by, in case Isabella changed her mind. The leather of the chair's arms felt cool and pleasant on my palms as I balanced on it. As I stood up again I could not resist caressing the soft skin.

"Where'd this come from, Isabella? I don't remember seeing it before."

"Feels good, doesn't it? Fine cabretta leather like that. Willy gave it to me. She threatened to have the leather done in a hideous pink – as you know her father owned one of the finest tanneries in the Napa valley – but she would have had to live with it, so she dyed the hides herself using some Native American recipe – well, so she claimed. She made the chair for my twenty-fifth birthday – I had sketched one like it that we saw on our first trip to Paris. The leather was a light golden brown when it was freshly tanned. That rich brown is the result of decades of care and enjoyment. The wood is mahogany. As you can see, Willy was an excellent sculptor, and not a bad upholsterer."

I rubbed the ends of the armrests where the wood curled into a fist. The finely carved hands were about my size, with large angular knuckles and prominent veins moving into the leather of the chair's arms. I knew these must be Willy's hands, the same hands that dominated a certain period of the old lady's work. I had written a paper for an art history class speculating why Isabella had focused on an androgynous model early in her career, the only one consistently clothed. The fact that the model was rumored to be the love of her life had seemed too pat an answer, but was, I had come to realize, the right one. Willy's untimely death in a riding accident had anointed her with a tragic heroism I wasn't sure she deserved.

I pulled the chair closer to the day bed and sat down, folding my hands over the fists. "Hers?" I checked.

"Oh, her own, of course. Willy never lacked for confidence in my enduring attraction to her. Her ego used to infuriate me, but it was as pure as a force of nature – she always said she got her power from the great outdoors." Isabella shifted under her quilt, sitting up more and folding her hands over her waist. "She molded me with those hands when I was lucky. She could fill my heart and soul and body so that I was infused with her strength and rendered powerless with desire all at the same time. When she touched me, I felt like a work of art."

Listening to Isabella, I found myself examining her hands. I noticed again how large they were, although her joints were only the slightest bit swollen from the arthritis that plagued the rest of her body. They looked like they still had the strength to hold a shovel, a tripod, or the reins of a horse. The lines of her knuckles were etched deep, but her skin seemed supple and without the transparency of age. Her nails were short and deepset, and her fingertips were squared with calluses.

I leaned back in the chair, the leather seat releasing a small sigh of air, the wood welcoming my weight with a creak. I pulled my feet up, hugging my knees to my chin, and studied her face. Her sea-grey eyes looked into mine with a clearness like pure, still water. They pulled at something in my chest, and I felt a stir in my heart. I wondered if she wanted me at all. I took a deep breath and moved my hips foward so I could push my pussy against the heel of my bare foot. I felt its coolness as relief.

"Did you enjoy the 'great outdoors' together? You know, I don't think I've ever seen a landscape of yours, or at least not one of nature."

"Willy had a rule that I couldn't bring a camera, hell, not even a pencil. It's odd, but Willy was actually quite suspicious of art and insisted on calling herself a simple woodcarver. She told me that it was a waste of precious time to try to capture the wonder of nature. I mean she did appreciate the results of art, but she wanted us to be fully present, not stuck up here." She tapped her head. "I only went on a couple of her expeditions. I really didn't enjoy the hours on horseback. After that she brought me handmade souvenirs, and I realized there was some benefit to her absence."

As she talked my eyes rested on her hands again. I imagined her reaching under my sweatshirt and pinching my nipples hard, the sharp pain setting my cunt on fire until she would let go, sending my blood surging in a wave of heat all over my skin with the delicious sting of a hot shower. I put my hands, balled into fists, between my legs and rocked my clit against them as subtly as I could. I heard my breath quicken and realized she had stopped talking. When I looked at her, I knew she knew I was hurting for her. Of course she recognized the face of abject desire; I had seen the look myself a thousand times as I studied the nuances of her nudes. She spoke to me, her voice as deep and soft as a goosedown comforter.

"Maria, do me a favor."

"Yes, what?"

"Take your shirt off."

I tried to slow my breathing down and look calm as I crossed my hands at the hem of my sweatshirt, lifted it over my head, off my arms and dropped it on the floor. The air kissed my bare breasts and made my nipples hard, and my eyes caught a shaft of light hitting a high corner of the ocher wall, sending out a warm glow. All of a sudden I felt the languidness of mid-afternoon heavy in my flesh, and I rested my legs open on the arms of the chair, my eyelids drooping, waiting for her voice.

"Hold your beautiful breasts for me. Cup them as if they were tender ripe fruit and I was a buyer."

My own hot flesh filled my hands, and I rubbed the tips of my nipples lightly with my thumbs to make them harder. I moved off the chair to kneel by the day bed. Then I leaned over and brushed a nipple over the top of her folded hands. She didn't grab it, but I heard her take a breath like a swimmer bursting out of the water.

Her face was fierce with concentration and desire as she looked at mine and said, "I want to see you come. I want you to show me what you want and how you want it."

"I want you to touch me," I whispered in her ear.

"No, I can't touch you the way you really want. Darling child, I want to see you touch yourself that way. Do it for me. But first get me the box under my bed."

I reached under the day bed, my breasts brushing against the carpet, and pulled out a wooden chest about the size of a shoebox. Its flat lid was adorned with a painting, in a classical Greek style, of a woman holding a harvest basket of dildos. I opened it and lifted a black silk handkerchief to reveal two of the most beautiful dildos I had ever seen, along with a small leather pouch.

One dildo was of the same burnished brown leather as the chair, a little longer than an open hand, about the thickness of two fingers. I picked it up by its black wrist strap and touched it to my cheek; it was stuffed so tightly that the leather had a smoothness like skin. I put it back and picked up the second dildo, made of deep golden red wood. It was about twice the size of the other and slightly curved, with gentle ridges carved along the top side. Its base flared into a rounded square that allowed it to balance upright. "Willy?" I asked.

"Yes, a couple of the souvenirs she crafted by the campfire." She chuckled. "I think you'll have to use both of them." An edge of impatience crept into her voice, and her eyes narrowed. "Give them to me, and the pouch." I handed her both. She felt the wooden dildo up and down as if it were a soft piece of clay she was molding, murmuring, "This will take some of the chill off – you'll feel my heat on it." She stared off into space and continued, "You do remind me a little of Willy, of course, with your big boots and bluejeans and your taste in Romantic poetry, though you've probably never been on a horse, or to Yosemite, am I right?"

I nodded and basked in her affectionate gaze before she dipped into the pouch, which held, to my mild suprise, lubricated condoms.

"But Willy would never have been able to take off her shirt and show off her gorgeous breasts. I'd be lucky if I could get her to disrobe for a bath. She could be deeply romantic, but couldn't stand to have her own beauty exposed. I photographed some lovely young women, open and willing to please, but no, even jealousy wouldn't give her to me."

As she spoke she opened the drawer of her side table, took out her embroidery scissors and cut the top off the elegant packet. She perched the condom like a cap on the tip of the dildo, then smoothed it over the dark wood. I told myself to inhale as I watched her hands on the beautiful thing that soon would be all the way inside me. I imagined her ordering her expensive, ultra-thin Japanese condoms from a mail-order catalog, reading her credit card number over her bifocals and flirting with the salesperson.

"Take your pants off," she ordered, her voice now thick and deep, commanding, but no louder than a whisper. I did as she said.

"Now lean over the chair and show me how proud you are of your big strong body." My cunt felt painfully engorged, needing badly to be touched, to release its wetness and pull something hard right up into the pain that was just wanting, wanting, nothing but wanting. I leaned with one hand on the arm of the chair and pushed my pussy back, my ass high, presenting myself to her, opening my lips and cunt to her with my drenched and slippery fingers, and teasing my clit into a hard bud.

"Go on, rub yourself on the leather, and that wonderful hand. Use my chair the way it was intended to be used. The way I used to use it."

"Tell me how, please," I managed to gasp as I straddled and then lowered myself on to one arm of the chair, the leather a sudden coolness on my thighs. I held myself still, picturing the old lady inviting her lover by seducing the chair. I heard her murmuring, "Yes, that's it, now down to the hand, let her strong hard hand give you what you need."

I ground my cunt into the armrest, making it hot and slippery as I moved back and forth and listened to her voice.

"I could take her whole hand inside me when she'd let me. Once, up in the mountains, she spread me naked over a rock and slapped me with her gloves, and the sharpness of the wind and the leather made me ache to take both her fists right up into my heart. I rode on that chair many times thinking of that moment, the sting of her gloves on my skin, the hardness of her fist ready to push her way deep inside me."

I felt the wood knuckles against the mouth of my cunt and I almost came, but held back and gushed a stream of hot liquid all over. "Oh sweet God in heaven," I heard her say. I imagined her begging Willy to let her move on her naked flesh and not leave her to satisfy herself on this divine chair.

I told her, "I'm going to come soon – please, please, let me turn around and see you." I rested my cunt so that the hand was almost in me.

"Very well, sit on the chair with your legs up like before, so I can see you properly."

I did and she handed me the wooden dildo. I ran its tip up and down from my clit to my cunt and looked at her looking at me. I noticed her hands were under the covers, and moving slightly. "Put it in all at once, slowly though, and hold it there. Watch yourself take it in," she ordered.

I pushed and watched the dildo disappear into my cunt, each little ripple feeling molded for my insides, making me aware of my cunt's muscles pulling it in further. I wanted to push it hard into me, hard enough to hurt, to send me over the edge into an endless rolling orgasm. At the halfway point

I held back to delay the inevitable.

"Pull it out before you make yourself come."

"No, please," I protested, but when I noticed she had prepared the leather dildo, I obeyed. She handed me the leather dildo in exchange for the one I had made hot and wet. She put the wooden sculpture under her nose, licked its tip and closed her eyes, while I placed the new dildo at the mouth of my cunt and pulled it in with a strength that startled me. Even though it was smaller than the first one, I could feel my insides shifting to receive it all the way up, and I began to moan, shoving the glossy leather in and out as fast and as deep as I could. I rubbed my clit hard with my other hand, and another fountain erupted from my pussy.

"Oh, please, let me come for you now."

"Not yet. Turn around so I can see you in the air again."

I did as she said and turned around, leaning over the arm of the chair again, imagining a breeze on my skin. "I want you to use all of Willy's toys at once. Move that one now that it's well lubricated."

I spread my ass cheeks with one hand and pushed the tip of the dildo in just far enough to make me gasp with the rush of pleasure the stretching of my asshole sent through my whole body.

"Just hold it there for a minute," I heard her say. "Get used to it, allow yourself to pull the pleasure all the way up." The slim dildo was just flexible enough that I could let it in and hold it at the same time. It slid all the way to its gently-flared end with a brief and exquisite shock of pain that I felt all the way to my heart.

"Hold it in if you can, and now, go ahead and touch yourself again with Willy's hand." I lowered myself and felt the hand again, pressing at the mouth of my cunt; I pushed foward to try to get the carved fist all the way inside me, and failing, heard my voice cry out in disappointment as I thrust back and forth.

"Okay, my darling, now you can come. Here – fill yourself up the way I know you need to."

I snatched the wooden dildo from her outstretched hand

and placed it on the seat of the chair. Facing Isabella, I slid myself down onto the dildo, gripping the arms of the chair for balance. As it cut through the core of my desperate need, I cried out, my head moving back, and my eyes caught again by the afternoon light.

Every muscle in my body strained to take the dildo deeper into my cunt. I moved up and down on the lap of the chair until I lost control of my legs and collapsed to the floor, still holding Isabella's dildo deep inside me with both hands. The orgasm moved through me like a train, so powerful that I let go of the dildo, and it shot out, landing with a thud on the rug.

There I knelt with my arms in the chair, every nerve ending ecstatic. I could feel the sweat on my face, my hair tickling my neck. The plug slipped out of my ass with an exquisite ripple of pleasure as I inhaled the perfume of my own scent mingled with the leather. It seemed as though the reddish glow of the room hummed.

Isabella's voice came to me. "Turn around, child, come lean on me." I turned and buried my head in her quilt. I felt her hands on my head, and her lips on my cheek. "There, there," she murmured, "feel how beautiful you are to me."

I did.

The Maltese Dildo

Adam McCabe

MY LATEST CLIENT still hadn't told me his name. He sat upright in the Chippendale, facing me, his legs spread against the chair arms so I had a front-row seat for the action. Wearing nothing but a long silk robe, he played with his asshole during our interview, watching me for a reaction. His hole, puckered and red, looked resigned to this treatment. He slid two fingers back and forth inside of himself as he waited for my reply.

"Well, Mr. McCabe?" he said, not stopping his rhythm.

"I'm not sure I can help. I usually look for things of value. You can buy a dildo at any sex shop."

He stopped and sat up. His dick parted the folds of the robe, throbbing in the surrounds of silk. "It's not any dildo. It's invaluable."

"Why? Lose your virginity on it?"

He smiled languidly. "No, that might make it an antique, but hardly worth the effort. This dildo has a jewel-encrusted handle. Rubies and sapphires along the outside and emeralds near the base. My family brought it from Malta – generations ago."

I barked out a laugh which disappeared in the heavy drapes of the darkened drawing room. "You mean to tell me that you shove precious gems up your ass?" I was a top-man all the way. How could anyone want to have another man up his ass?

He pulled the robe around him so that his hard-on disappeared from view. Maybe I'd overstepped my boundaries. "If you want to phrase it like that, yes. Will you take the case?"

I nodded. "Four hundred a day plus expenses."

He leaned back again in the chair and ran a finger down between his balls to explore his hole again. The poor thing never got any rest. "Very well, let me tell you the story."

"The facts will do. Stories are for children."

Three fingers went up his hole to the second knuckle. He

77

seemed to be missing his dildo quite a bit these days. I could see that a butt plug wouldn't be enough for this guy.

He sighed, whether from exasperation or lust, I couldn't tell. "As you wish, the facts. Three days ago, I hosted an orgy here at my home. One of the guests stole the dildo at that function."

"So someone you know did it? Why don't you just ask for it back?" Some people had more money than sense.

"Not that easy. My friend, Albert Gutman, set up the event. My house, his party, his friends."

"Does Gutman keep a guest list?"

His fingers started a rhythm that barely left him energy to speak. "If I had a name or a better description, I would appeal to him directly. You see, all I know is that this particular thief is well-endowed: eleven inches at least. I heard people refer to him as the Fat Man, but that's the only name I know for him. Albert might know him, but it's a rather embarrassing situation."

"So how do you know he's the thief? Could have been any-one at the party."

His cock pulsed like a metronome in time to the movement of his fingers. Pre-come flowed off the head of his dick and into the folds of his robe. "We were – becoming acquainted, this big man and I. When I came, I closed my eyes to savor the moment. I opened my eyes to find that he and the dildo were gone. Simple as that."

"You got Gutman's number? Sounds like the place to start." I watched him, feeling my own cock press against the leg of my pants. His act was reminding me how long I'd been celi-bate.

He pointed to a small marble table. "Better than that. On the table is an invitation to Albert's next party. It's tonight. Albert has assured me that the guest list is the same, except you'll be going in my stead." As he finished his words, he came. Milky-white liquid shot out of him and ran down his shaft in torrents, disappearing into the robe.

I took a deep breath. Most cases didn't get me this horny. I'd be ready for tonight if I could wait that long. "Fine. I'll be there. But what makes you think this mystery man will be interested in me?"

"Mr. McCabe, trust me. He will. Just bring me back the dildo."

As promised, I left with an invitation to a small soiree that evening: its engraved lettering and thick vellum envelope revealed no sign of illicit sex. The whole scene stank of money, though. The rent on the office was due next week. I didn't have a lot of choice in how the bills got paid at this point.

Never having been to a fuckfest, I wasn't sure how to dress. Intimate scenes with a single partner were my forte. I couldn't get that interview out of my mind as I threw on a sports coat with my jeans and white Tommy shirt. No use getting too spiffed up since the clothes would be doffed inside the door.

I arrived at eight per the invitation. I'd hoped for a chance to scout the place before most of the others got there, but the house was packed. House, hell, it was a mansion. First time I'd ever seen a crowd of punctual gay men.

A valet led me into a drawing room where five men stood, stripping. I followed along, trying to look like I knew the score. No one looked familiar and none of their dicks matched my client's description. I undressed in a hurry. The valet placed my clothes into a private locker and gave me the key attached to a wrist-strap. The hallway was packed with men looking to score. I had work to do.

The first floor was a series of showrooms, each space filled with antiques and mahogany furniture. I wasn't sure how the old masters would have felt about this place. I walked around, trying to ignore the variety of dicks in my path. None came close to the description of the Fat Man's. A winding marble staircase led to the second level and I began a search of the upstairs bedrooms. Plenty of action, but no eleven-inch dicks.

I decided to take a piss. Even with the mass nudity, I wanted a little privacy and shut the bathroom door behind me. Someone entered while I was going and watched from the doorway. When I looked up, I knew I'd found my prey. Even at half-mast, his cock was the biggest I'd ever seen. Thick, with the ropy veins that meant plenty of blood to the organ.

He held up a dildo and smiled. "Interested in some fun?" The toy was nearly as big as he was: probably ten inches, thick, and the color of night.

I couldn't make out the handle so I wasn't positive that this was my client's dildo. I shook the last drops and stepped toward him. "I'm always up for some fun."

He smiled and pulled the door shut. His dick grew, almost bridging the gap between us. I didn't know what we could do with a cock that size. He held up the dildo and the light sparkled off the handle. I'd found what I'd come here for.

"Bend over." The Fat Man pulled a rubber and some lube out of the medicine cabinet. With one hand, he protected the end of the toy and made the device slick to the touch.

I smiled. "I'm not really into that." My own dick didn't look up to his standards.

He matched my smile and tapped the dildo in his hand. "Everyone says that the first time. Trust me." He moved closer to me, blocking my exit. The tile wall cooled my back as I looked for a way to escape, but I didn't see any. Not if I wanted to do my job. I didn't have what I came here for yet. I felt a finger slide up inside me as his monster dick rubbed against my stomach. He lubed my abs with his juices.

The sensation and heat of our cocks thrusting in time made me want to come now. A second finger entered me and the moment was lost. The pain was bearable, but made me twinge, imagining what he could do to me. The dildo slid down into his palm and I felt the head of the toy penetrate me. I lost my erection as the sex toy filled my ass. I'd never been fucked before and a mingling of excitement and fear swept over me – wanting the sensation and dreading the pain.

He turned me to face the wall and slid an arm around my waist to pull my ass out. I was almost bent at the waist by this point as the dildo traveled inside me. I could feel it push against my pucker. He rested a second and moved it inside me. My sphincter protested and then gave in. The dildo gained entrance and filled me.

I moaned so loud that the Fat Man laughed. "You're getting into this fast, aren't you? Maybe it's time for the real thing."

My knees nearly buckled as I thought of his huge dick penetrating me. I didn't know if I could handle all of it and remain conscious. Four hundred a day didn't begin to cover this. He gave the dildo a few more thrusts in me. I imagined the jewels scratching my ass.

The dildo clattered to the floor and I pushed it with my foot under a towel near the wall. He didn't seem to notice as he made preparations with lube and another rubber. Even facing the wall, I could smell his sweat as he approached me again. "Ready for ecstasy?"

I grunted, trying to prepare. Nothing could have helped. The first push made my eyes roll up in my head. The pain filled every cell and yet felt delicate in a way I'd never known. His arms slid around me to keep me standing as he started to thrust. The oversized biceps held me in place and I began to lick one. When he was sure I wasn't going to fall to a pile on the ground, his hand slipped down to my crotch and began to massage my limp dick. All my attention was on the feelings in my sphincter.

I could feel the ripping in my ass as he explored. I leaned back against him and felt the rough pressure of hair against my back. He nibbled on my neck while he squeezed my dick slowly in one hand. I wanted him to come so this moment could be over, but he had just gotten started. His balls slapped against my ass and he pushed me up against the wall again. I couldn't move as the heat of his dick filled me. I expected my stomach to explode like the scene from *Aliens* at any moment. He began to bite my back and shoulders as he massaged my dick. I started to feel the familiar stirrings as he clamped down on my cock and stretched it to full length.

"You'd be good as a top-man, too. Wouldn't you?" He whispered the words in my ear as he pulled on my lobe with his teeth.

Through clenched teeth, I said, "I've done that before."

A savage thrust made me whimper. "I'll bet you have." The words released him, and his balls contracted as he shot his load inside me. The sensation was unlike any I'd had. He continued to work me and I shot my wad against the bathroom wallpaper. I noticed a young guy lying on the floor by the towel and dildo, letting my come splash his upper body. I hadn't realized that anyone else had entered the room, but three guys were jacking off to the scene we provided. The Fat Man pulled out and threw the rubber into the toilet. I staggered out of the room, still feeling his dick inside me, gripping the towel and dildo to ensure that the experience was worth it.

The next day I returned to my client's home carting his prized possession. A butler led me into the study where my client sat in a robe with the hood pulled over his face. I laid the dildo on the table between us and chose to stand. "Here's what you wanted. And here's my bill."

The hood nodded.

"Have you heard any complaints from Gutman? Any noise from the Fat Man?" I leaned up against the back of the chair and watched him.

He shook the silk cloth covering. A whisper said, "The Fat Man had nothing but compliments for your performance. Said you were a natural."

I straightened up and stared at the cloaked figure. If he knew these people, why had he hired me? What was going on here? I limped across to his chair and pulled back the hood. My ex-lover's face came into view.

"What the hell?" I stepped back and bumped my ass against the table. Pain shot through me.

"Hello, J.J.. Have a nice time last night? Thought you needed a little loosening up, so to speak." He smiled at me.

"This was all just a revenge plot?"

He nodded. "Not bad, huh? Now I think we're even." He stood up and walked out of the room.

I was left to limp back to my car and gingerly make my way home.

Computer Games
P.D. Curry

SHE HAD JUST SET UP HER NEW laptop computer. Unlike her first two computers, this one was amazingly fast and small. It had all sorts of features that had been no more than jargon words to her a month ago. But the time had come to re-enter the technical world and invest in an upgrade.

In truth, this had only come to seem urgent when she met him. He was a computer expert and she was glad to find a field in which, for once, she could ask for help. As a rule, she tended to be a little more self-reliant than was considered sexy in a culture that, in spite of latter-day window dressing, raises men to be rescuers and women to need the occasional rescue. Damsels in distress and all that.

His expertise and her legitimate need were a welcome and irresistible combination. She was eager to get to know him for other reasons, so asking him to help her buy the new computer provided a convenient excuse.

She was a little uncertain whether he'd be willing to take some of his personal time to do her this favor. But he agreed, and off they went one Saturday in his little hatchback to a distant, half-rural, light-industrial development with cheap rent. The sign on the door read "Computer Discount Mart."

He and the owner spoke the code of addicts who spend hours and days in windowless rooms absorbed by their electronic companions. At one time she had basically understood this language, but things had become a lot more complex. Now there was Windows 95 and soon to be 98, chips faster than anyone had ever thought possible, code names with "z"s and "giga"s in them, games that her nephew always wanted to see when he visited. She barely knew how to ask the questions any more. He, on the other hand, was in his element.

He talked of gigabytes and pixels, translating her requirements into purchases. He pulled accessories and game programs from the shelves, piecing together what she would need to please her nephew and convince him that she wasn't hopelessly out of touch with the cyberworld. She, for her part, felt taken care of, a rare feeling which brought heat to her cheeks and, for that matter, warmed her in a few other places.

They drove back to her house. While her mouth babbled on about computers and business and the weather and God knows what else, her mind weighed the question of whether she could ask him in when they got to her driveway. She would have liked to take him upstairs, to her office, just a few steps from her bedroom, and then . . .

Once in her driveway, reason prevailed. She said a cheery thanks and good-bye and let him drive away. Disappointment registered lower in her body.

She took the little computer, along with the boxes of accessories, to her upstairs office, opened them and identified the cords and cables, the external mouse and the joy stick (what a name!). She hooked it all together and turned it on. Part of her, however, was distracted.

She called him for help when the screen at first refused to respond. Of course, she could have scrounged through the manuals to solve the obvious problem, but there were other needs here. She wished he would come back to help her, yet she could not bring herself to ask. A technical question was safe enough; an invitation, not so. Besides, he was by then caught up in something with his son and was impatient. His son was only with him every other weekend, and he had already left him with a friend's family for three hours.

She resumed on her own. Following his suggestions, she eventually got the expected response: an opening screen with clouds and strange little icons. He had recommended some software which the store owner had installed for her, so the hard part was already done.

She tried out the programs. There was, of course, the word processor, the spread sheet (a term suggesting something a bit more interesting than financial statements) and the database. But there were other symbols, squiggles and dots that she didn't recognize.

She clicked on START and then PROGRAMS. What did she have

on this hard drive anyway? The monitor spelled out the familiar names and one that was unfamiliar – "Fun & Games," it blinked. She clicked on "Fun & Games" and the hard drive whirred.

"Relax and close your eyes," appeared on the monitor. "Click OK when ready." She clicked and closed her eyes. She heard a soft buzzing, an auditory tingle really, and she squinted her eyes open. The mouse was inching over its pad toward her! She closed her eyes again and wondered what was happening.

The mouse suddenly dropped from its pad to her thigh, and began buzzing up toward her waist. She glanced at the screen. "Unzip your pants. Click OK when ready," appeared. *Excuse me*, she thought. *What on earth is this?* The mouse hummed at her waist and waited, buzzing softly. In spite of feeling startled and a bit suspicious, she also felt heat all through her belly, in her legs, in her arms, and most particularly between her legs. What had the man at Computer Discount Mart done to her computer?

But she was alone, there was no one to watch, and the buzzing mouse felt welcoming and welcome. She opened her pants, touched the curved key pad to click OK, then leaned back in the chair. The mouse inched down from her waist, across her lower belly to the elastic of her bikini underpants. Again it waited, its buzz pulsating throughout her pelvis. She looked at the screen.

"Lift the elastic. Click OK when ready." She felt a little alarmed again, but nevertheless reached for the elastic with her left hand and clicked with the right. OK. Involuntarily, her legs opened.

The mouse began to move again, slowly lower, vibrating her pubic hair and its mound, then lower, to the shaft of her clit. As the mouse moved to cover her entire crotch, buzzing and throbbing, she heard another deeper buzz.

The joy stick, apparently aptly named, had come alive on the desk and was twitching suggestively. "Relax. Move the stick to the mouse. Click OK when ready," was on the screen.

This, it seemed, was not your average software program. A

decade of horny geeks in basements had produced a few break-throughs you didn't hear about on CNN. Yet it felt so good, and it was easy to savor the delicious sensations and forget their source. She touched the vibrating stick and felt its rhythm in her hand. She thought about how it would feel between her legs, and slowly moved it toward her. She tugged at her jeans, lowering them to give herself more freedom.

Leaning back, she thought about what she was doing, but only for a moment. The stimulation had raised her tempera-ture a degree or two, and she noticed her hips were beginning to rock back and forth on their own. She settled into the warm feeling and moved the stick, resting its quivering tip on her aching clit. She nudged the buzzing mouse a little lower, deeper down between her thighs. She opened her thighs wider and maneuvered the little arrow to OK. Click.

The mouse began moving to the side, away from the ac-tion, while the stick started to slide down the very wet, very slippery underside of her clit, heading for a way into her body. She could barely detect the movement of the stick, noting only that as it came to the midpoint between her clit and her open-ing, both were virtually screaming to have it, throbbing by this time. She pushed her jeans and underwear to her ankles, freed one foot, and spread her legs even wider while looking at the screen.

"Remove your clothes. Click OK when ready." She felt she could not move. All her energy was between her legs, focused on the jiggling stick and the buzzing mouse that had, by now, settled just above her cunt and was purring in her fur. She moved her foot to kick off the last of her jeans and under-pants, taking care not to dislodge the mouse or the stick. OK, she clicked.

"Remove all your clothes. Click OK when ready." The stick was poised no more than half an inch from where she wanted it, but it had stopped moving. She shifted her hips to bring the stick closer, but it moved away. How did the computer know that she was still half-clothed? She looked at the screen, and re-read the simple message with the intriguing implication. "Remove all your clothes. Click OK when ready."

Keeping her lower body as still as possible (except for her involuntary small pelvic thrusts, which the machine was able to ride), she unbuttoned her shirt, slipped it off, reached behind her back and worked at the bra hooks. One was stuck. She struggled and broke into a sweat. She dropped back, unable to unfasten the hook. As she panted, she became acutely aware again of the buzzing tickle above her cunt. She squirmed and reached down, trying to push the stick inside her. But it would not move.

She tried again for the bra, and this time freed it. She pulled it down her arms and threw it to the floor. OK, she clicked, now naked.

"Do you want me? Yes, No, Cancel," was on the screen. Barely able to breathe or move with the fire between her legs, she inched the cursor to "Yes." Click. *Oh my God, yes,* she thought.

"Please describe your sensations," appeared on the monitor. *Now what? Does it want sentences? What will this thing require before it satisfies me?* she thought. She considered finishing herself off, but giving up would mean missing whatever lay in store with this tantalizing machine. Both the mouse and the stick seemed to have intensified their vibrations, but neither was moving any closer to her hottest points. She was feeling crazy.

"I feel warm and sexy." She hoped this would be enough to get things moving again.

"Tell me more," the computer typed.

"I feel on fire. My cunt is on fire, and I want you."

"Tell me more."

"I want you inside me, all over me. I ache for you. My muscles are convulsing with pleasure. I need to feel you on me and in me. I am hot and wet and open, and I want you NOW," she typed.

"Tell me more."

Well, what was she supposed to do? Or say? She could hardly call *him* for advice on this one. She lay back to return her attention to the sensations in her body. She could almost taste the acute pleasure she felt, the titillating mouse, the taunting stick. In a way she wanted them to go on forever, and at the same time, she wanted to explode.

She reached for the keyboard. "My pussy is wild for you. I need you inside me and on me. I want you to take me over the top. I am ready and open for you. Touch me more."

"Tell me more. What do you want?" Well, at least she had entered another loop of the software. Now what?

She again leaned back to feel more, so she could tell more. She felt the mouse nuzzling her clit, back and forth, softly buzzing, moving all around her mound. At least something was moving. She felt the pulsing stick. It jiggled even more and she spread her legs even wider, hoping to push it in. She heard the smacks of her own wetness. She felt the stick settle right at the opening itself and double the intensity of its pulse.

"FUCK ME!" she typed.

"With pleasure." The words spelled out across the screen.

So that's it, she thought, just as the sensations overtook her. The stick moved deep into her, vibrating the core of her being. The mouse settled on her clit, wiggled to open the labia so it could make direct contact, then switched to a stronger, deeper pulse. The stick moved in and out and from side to side, her hips moving to match it. It seemed to grow. It twirled inside her, touching all sides. She arched her back as she pressed the mouse closer to her wild clit. She glanced at the screen, only half conscious.

"I like watching you. Take all the time you want. Click OK when ready."

She closed her eyes and thought about what the computer could see (see?!) from the desktop – her open cunt, her naked breasts (which she had begun to stroke unconsciously a few minutes ago), her hand on her pubic hair, the mouse working feverishly, the stick thrusting and wiggling, lolling in her copious juices. As a wave of warmth flowed through her body, she half-deliriously saw that the cursor rested on OK.

She touched the bar. Click.

What felt like lightning went through her – electricity and fire, volcanoes and crashing waves, trains in tunnels, and every other 1950s' movie metaphor – for a mind-numbing, all-encompassing, screaming orgasm. Never, *never*, had she felt it this deep, this long, this much. She contracted and relaxed, contracted again, relaxed again, and again, and again.

When she resumed breathing, she felt the stick slowly rotating inside her. The mouse was sitting quietly, buzzing softly. The stick eventually began to withdraw, shrinking back to its original size. The mouse started moving up her belly. She placed both back on the desk just as the phone rang.

It was him. "Do you still need help?" he asked. "I could come over now if you need me. How is the new software?"

As she tried to slow her breathing so she could answer, she smiled, knowing that some very interesting times lay ahead.

The Catalog Keeper

Karen A. Selz

MY NAME IS CONSTANCE. Growing up I had a best friend named Dinah. Her parents had named her Dinah not anticipating the endless "someone's in the kitchen" jokes she'd have to endure. We lived in a small town in the southern tip of the Great Smoky Mountains, a place called Spruce Pine. I still live here, but Dinah's gone to Chicago to work as a receptionist and part-time actress. When she'd get hard times from the people here she used to say, "Country folks have little imagination given their abundant free time." My Mama says Dinah was destined for other places, that she's a lonely soul with a sad story. Mama doesn't know that Dinah stays in touch. This past September Dinah sent me something that changed my days here. She sent me a mail-order catalog.

I don't think Mama ever liked Dinah. We used to play together after school starting in the second grade. Jamie Tyler and we were all about the same age. In second and third grades, we'd all run together up the hill behind Dinah's house and down the other side. Going down, our legs would get behind us, we were moving so fast, and we'd fall and roll together, laughing and roaring like lions. When we were in fifth grade Jamie died. He dove into a shallow pond, broke his neck and drowned. After that, Dinah and I would sit on the backside of the hill and smoke cigarettes or drink beers she stole from her Papa. Her Papa always had us call him by his first name, which was Dan. Dinah's Mama died of pneumonia when Dinah was just four years old.

The last time I saw Dinah in person was two summers ago when we graduated high school. I got home and my Mama smelled spirits on me. She said, "I named you Constance because you are a serious girl meant for good. You won't associate with Dinah Candler again."

About a year and a half after that I got the catalog with a little note, "Stay Open. Love, Dinah." The inside envelope, the

one the catalog must have come in originally, had Open Enterprises as the return address. Get it? "Open," stay "Open."
Dinah's like that. By then I was already working at Mama's ice
cream shop, The Scoop, which is next to Mr. Davis' old movie
house, downtown. It wasn't a very fun job – not many people
came in. Most of the shops downtown have closed. I was trying to get into Appalachian State University, and I was on the
waiting list for the spring semester. Some days, especially in
the fall and winter, were so slow in the shop that Mama would
let me close up and go to the movies, if I left a note telling
where to find me.

The movie house has looked the same since I was a kid.
Most times you have your choice of the twenty-eight seats.
There had been thirty seats originally but they pulled two out
to make room for handicaps. The candy out front is kind of
stale and it's best that you bring your own, but the popcorn is
all right. I swear Mr. Davis wouldn't be able to keep the place
open if he didn't live above and have some other money.

So this catalog Dinah sent me was a sex toy catalog. I keep it
hidden in the shed because if Papa found it he wouldn't say
anything to Mama. He wouldn't even suspect that it's mine.
The front has a drawing of a pretty girl and inside the front
cover is a picture of the staff and their van. There they are just
like they're saying, "Here we are, doing what we're doing."

Across pages 32 and 33 of the catalog is the title "Bound To
Please." There's a black leather Blindfold and fleece-lined
Leather Buckling Bonds, described as "elegant and practical,"
in wrist or ankle sizes.

I tied Dinah up once. It was a while ago, and we didn't have
any fancy equipment. We were kids really, but I already had
little buds of breasts and she already had a dense, shady smell
to her when she'd sweat. It started out just kidding around.
Her Papa, Dan, was away in Charlotte for the weekend with a
lady he knew, and Dinah was on her own. I went by on Saturday with some sandwiches and chips. They live a ways out of
town and because I was walking, I didn't get there til almost
noon. The Candler's door was never locked, and I found Dinah
still asleep upstairs.

I tried to wake her up for nearly ten minutes. I'd shake her and say, "Get up, sleepy head," like my Mama says to me, but she'd just roll over and cover her head with a pillow or mumble something or another. Well, I was getting pretty tired of this, so I got two shirts off the floor and tied each of her hands to the iron headboard, then I took off my t-shirt and tied her ankles together soundly. Papa taught me sailor's knots when I was little, and I made sure she wasn't getting free.

Well, she was coming awake about then, and wanted to know what I was up to. Trouble is, I hadn't thought about it. The tying up thing was an impulse. I hadn't planned it, so I certainly hadn't planned past it. I started tickling her feet, and she squealed and squirmed. I sat on her shins to hold her still. She was protesting and pulling at the knots that harnessed her hands, but she was laughing too and calling me names. She said I was panting like a doggie. I was still straddling her legs, so I put my hands up like I was begging, then I bent over and licked her knee and she laughed even more.

I bent over her again, squeezing her legs closed between my knees. I ran my tongue around the seam that I had made between her powerful thighs, then licked up toward the fronts of her legs and against the grain of her fine fur. Her mouth was opening and closing like a landed fish and she thrashed at the ties. She smelled like vanilla and something tangy.

I moved up on her to better see her face. She looked at me and said, "Let my legs go. Please, Con, just my legs, untie them." Her voice was soft and full of flutter. I didn't untie her. I moved back and licked again in the seam between her thighs and up to the little triangle gap below her panties. Dinah made this little moan like you hear at funerals or weddings, the kind of sound that doesn't come from the body. Her head was back into the pillow and her hips were swaying and pushing.

I reached behind and freed her feet. Her legs sprung apart with so much force I was nearly knocked clear. But there she was, Dinah, spread out before me. She always wore those white cotton panties you buy in the three pack at Wal-Mart. Her sleepshirt had come open with all the wiggling and I kneaded her breasts like nursing babies do. I kissed her pink pencil-eraser nipples. I could feel the longing have-notness of her cunt pressed against mine. They were exchanging our breath. I wanted to fuck her, to crawl inside her, to have any part of me surrounded by her. I would have given anything for a dick just then. Instead we rubbed and sucked and rocked together. I sang songs to her, hummed them through her panties and sucked out the juice. She never asked me to untie her hands, and that day I explored every inch of her, foreign and familiar. Her skin felt like the essence of life.

On page 11 of the catalog, there's this gizmo called the Venus Vibe. The catalog says, "This pearlescent sea-shell vibe is pretty enough for any modern-day Venus. Nestle up to the insertable knob and the clitoral stimulator hidden inside the soft rubber shell, and you'll soon feel like a love goddess yourself. Uses two AA batteries, variable-speed battery pack." In the picture, it looks like a little hat with a big plume, worn, I assume, snuggled into a spread cunt. On the top of the page it says, "Off On A Joy Ride," like this is the kind of thing you might wear while cleaning house, tending the shop, taking a walk or watching a movie.

During the summer after the eleventh grade Dinah and I were at the movie house watching a tear-jerk romance, I don't remember which, but it was an artsy film and it was during the day. We were the only people in the theater. About half an hour into the film, Dinah reached over and put her hand, palm down, onto my stomach just above my waist. I didn't say anything or even look at her when she slid her hand down inside my loose cotton shorts. With the heel of her palm pressing down on the top of my mound, her thumb and middle finger spread me open. I was trying not to move. I didn't move because I didn't want her to stop. I didn't want her to think again, to worry about what I was thinking or what this might mean in the daylight outside.

My clit was pulsing so hard I think she heard it. Dinah answered the thump and murmur of that secret call. She had been moving just her arm and facing straight ahead, now she leaned forward in her seat as if the action on the screen were drawing her in, and in that motion she ran a slender index finger along my exposed inner folds. Her wet finger played within me while she held me open. She drew pictures inside me, little quivering swirly paths that made me bubble and churn. I clenched my jaw and my toes curled. There was a loud ringing in my ears. I tried not to move, because I was afraid she'd stop and because I was afraid Mr. Davis might notice.

Dinah always had an air of confident correctness that I could take on in her company. I let my hand fall over the armrest and onto her thigh. Moist heat rolled down her legs in waves. She was shaking. Dinah has big legs, not fat, just really strong, and small breasts and no waist to speak of. She always looked like a dancer to me, a real one, the kind who dance ballet on TV. She has this moon of a face: broad, open, full of light. It seemed like all the light in the theater was coming from her face. She was smiling and making slow circles over my clit with her index finger.

I pushed her tennis skirt up and cupped her whole cunt in my hand. I petted it like you would rub the head of a sun-basking cat. Neither of us made a sound except for the breathing and the sounds of each other's blood. We didn't see Mr. Davis when we left the theater.

It wasn't until a few months ago that I found out that Mr. Davis had watched us from behind the curtain next to the screen. He had gone back there to fix something or other when he caught sight of us. He told me all this on the day the projector had broken. I had taken a break from Mama's shop to see a movie, and he asked if I wanted to come upstairs for some coffee instead. Mama doesn't serve coffee at The Scoop. She says it gets you all worked up for nothing. Anyway, I said sure, as I didn't have much else to do and thought I'd like to visit with Mr. Davis.

We were sitting at his kitchen table, the only turquoise dinette I've ever seen, and we were shooting the breeze when he said to me, "Heard from Dinah lately?" Then he tells me that he saw us, in the theater, together, and that he has dreams about it sometimes. He says it like he's remembering an especially beautiful sunset or something.

I like Mr. Davis, and I don't think that he meant this as a threat or anything. I don't think he'd tell my folks, for instance. I think he's just sort of lonely. He's younger than my Papa but older than my oldest brother, Rick, and he lives alone. He's spindly, five-foot-six at most, and he moves funny, in kind of jittery fits and starts. We used to call him Spider Man, and we didn't mean the superhero. He generally keeps his curtains drawn and he never mixes much with the town folks.

Rumor has it that he's a famous poet. Once I saw a book of his poems in a B. Dalton store in Mars Hill. When I asked him about it, he showed me his other books. The whole upstairs above the theater was filled with books. Most of them were written by other people, though. Every flat surface had some, even the dinette table. While we talked he'd pick up a book to borrow a point it made or tap a bony fingertip on the cover of a resting volume and say "Such and such said . . . about that." We talked for nearly two hours that first day. It turned out that he wrote in the morning and ran the projector in the afternoon and at night. Sometimes there was an audience; sometimes it was just him.

After that, whenever I took a break from the shop I'd go straight over for coffee with Mr. Davis, if he was free. He was lonesome and sad. More weary or wrung out than sad, I guess. Sometimes I thought that he must know some horrible secret, something so corrosive to the soul that he dare not speak it. Funny thing was that I could talk to him. I felt like I could say anything, ask anything. He would always answer. He's the only person in Spruce Pine who knows about my catalog. I even brought it over to show to him once.

On about the sixth or seventh coffee visit, I had just found out that I had been accepted to Appalachian State for certain. When I told him, he looked happy for me, but thoughtful. He got quieter as we visited. He was deviled by something and wouldn't tell me what. When it was time for me to get back to the shop, I got up to go, and he stood up too and put his hand on my shoulder. His hand was surprisingly warm and I realized that he had never touched me, not in any way, not ever. He had never touched my arm to emphasize a remark, never brushed past me in the small kitchen where we sat, never even shook my hand. Now his thumb rested on my collar bone. There was something timid and touching about his struggle with such harmless contact. I remembered that Dinah once told me that penises were shy like this, and that all the folderol of most men was about protecting those fragile little beasts.

The last time I saw Mr. Davis was just a few weeks ago, just before I left for school. It was right before Christmas, the mercury in the thermometers had all but disappeared and nobody was much in the mood for ice cream. I found Mr. Davis upstairs. I guess nobody was out for the movies either. He was brewing fresh coffee and telling me about his college days in Berkeley, California. I was too nervous to sit, so I walked around the kitchen. He was telling me what a big world I would find and how I should treat it when I did. I put my hand flat on his back, between his shoulder blades. He stopped talking right away, like I'd hit a switch. We just stood there like that for a while with a funny kind of cold-weather static running through us, and then he turned around as I'd wished him to do. He started to object, but I covered his mouth with a kiss.

He broke away and asked if I really wanted to do this. I was unbuttoning his sweater and shirt, rubbing the sides of my face against the skin I was baring. He sighed then, which seemed to me to be a funny thing to do, and said we should go by the fire, but that he had to go get something and he'd be right back.

It was warm by the hearth so I took off my boots and sweater and curled on the couch. Mr. Davis came and sat by me. He said, "I don't know how I feel about this." I would have believed him except he had stopped his infernal dithering. He seemed relaxed and assured. He said, "These are my rules: you have to tell me what you like and what you don't like and I'll do the same. If you tell me to stop, I will, so don't say it unless you mean it. Okay?" I nodded. Then he asked if I had any rules.

I remembered something I heard once. "No call, no foul," I said.

"Do you have some time to spend today?" he asked. I told

him that nobody would be checking up on me until after four, not for another two and a half hours. This deliberateness was a skin around necessity. It was like we were falling together, like something as inevitable as gravity was acting on us, and we were resisting just enough to compute a proper orbit. I swung my leg over and, belly to belly, planted a long kiss squarely on his lips. "I want you to make love with me. Is that all right with you?" He nodded yes and pulled me in.

I unbuckled his trousers with one hand, showing off. He made me stop when I had wriggled his underwear half way down his thighs. He had easily the largest, most beautiful cock I'd ever seen. All the days I live I may never see a nicer one. In fact, I remember thinking that he must have been assigned the wrong one at birth. It was thick, rooted in brown locks and had a pleasant curve upward that made it look less like a pointer than an aspiring astronaut. He was uncircumcised, which surprised me because he came from a big town. I played my index finger around the little dribble of fluid at the head and his cock bobbed.

He took out a condom, and holding it up, he started to re-mind me that I should always use one. I snatched it away and rolled it onto him with my mouth. "I may have misjudged you," he said. This gave him a kind of permission, I guess.

We kissed again, this time with open, grappling mouths. His lips traveled down my throat, making me throw my head back. I was trying to unbutton my shirt and pull it free of my corduroys. Mr. Davis helped me, his mouth and hands work-ing together until I was naked and so was he, then he reached behind the arm of the couch and brought up a bottle of some-thing called Astroglide. I remembered the name from my cata-log. It had a picture of tangled-up lovers on the label.

He squirted some out into his left palm and rubbed his hands together. He told me to lie back and slowly, with intense con-centration, worked the thick gel into every pore of my skin. He even rubbed it into my cheekbones and earlobes and un-der my arms. He wiped his hands on his cock, then he picked me up (I was surprised he could, but he did), carried me around and set me down with my legs dangling over the back of the couch. Facing me, his face and chest reflected the red of the fire, ricocheting heat up and down between us. His hands were cupped around my bottom, pulling the cheeks apart slightly. I wrapped my legs over his hips and across the backs of his thighs and pulled with all my might.

Time sheared off when his cock worked into me. The Astroglide made me feel like a sea mammal, like a sea lion or porpoise. I've had dreams of that feeling, of frictionless progress toward clear goals. He was moving in and out of me very, very slowly, so each time he breached me was like the first. My teeth ached and my eyeballs felt like they were rolling up into my head, and all I could hear was a loud low bell and our huffing and puffing. We sounded like a steam engine.

My legs had taken up the stroke, but my hands were aimless until I caught his balls. Still slippery, one of his fingers found my asshole. I shook like my epileptic cousin, Emmy. I gushed. I screamed the name of the Holy Father, and I think he did, too.

I fell backward onto the couch. I think I was delirious, and there was a little bit of time there that I'm not real clear on. I do remember half-sitting, half-lying together, naked and smooth, telling knock-knock jokes of all things. He was sitting behind me with his thighs on the outside of mine, and we had covered up with a blanket. As we talked, his hands moved over me until they rested in my lap. I tensed, I guess, because he asked if that was okay. I just kept telling my joke, but pushed my butt against him, and I could feel his cock stir.

My legs were a little open and he reached between them, cupping my mound in his hand, and, while we talked natural like nothing else was going on, he pulled down on me every so often. He was milking my cunt. I couldn't help but push my hips up and back, and I could feel the heat of that beautiful cock tapping on my spine.

I swiveled my legs over to the outside of his and rocked up onto my knees. This wasn't a complicated idea, and he's a really smart guy, so he was there with me in the blink of an eye. He bit my butt on the way, then he was in me again, driving fast, then slow. Air was whistling somewhere. The force of him drove gusts up my back. His hands clutched my breasts with the same rhythm that I clenched and unclenched my butt. We came forever that time. His cock jerked against my insides, making them grab like a greedy hand.

When we recovered our senses, it was well past four o'clock. I cleaned up in a hurry, and I was almost out the door when Mr. Davis stopped me. "Here," he said, "I got this for you, to enrich the college experience and to make sure you remember me." He handed me a cardboard box with an Open Enterprises return address. Inside was the rest of the Astroglide, all sorts of condoms and the thing I'd said I wanted most, the Rabbit Pearl vibrator from page 9. "More fun than real pearls," my catalog said, "tumbling plastic pearls in its midsection create a unique scintillating sensation against the walls of the vagina, while two rabbit ears flutter against the clitoris. Uses three C batteries."

I thanked him and stuffed the goodies into my bag, then I took the Astroglide back out and handed it to Mr. Davis. He looked confused. "Spring break," I said.

Company Training

Anne Moon

"MY GOD, ISN'T THIS BORING!" Ellen scratched across the pad she handed to Cynthia, who scrawled back, *"Yes."* It was nearly two PM.

The speaker said, "Stretch your legs for the next fifteen minutes. We'll reconvene for the roundtable discussion after the break." Everyone stood in unison and moved toward the doors.

Ellen tugged Cynthia back toward a wall in the lobby, whispering, "Wouldn't you rather cut out now and slip up to the room for some fun before dinner?"

"I'd love to," Cynthia said, "but you know they're taking attendance. We have to stay."

They split up and roamed through the crowd, shaking hands and chatting with the appropriate power players. When Ellen caught Cynthia's eye with a mischievous smile, Cynthia knew she was up to something.

They took their seats in the rear of the room, dutifully taking out pens and notepads and feigning interest in the panel of speakers before them.

As the roundtable discussion warmed up, several people started speaking in quick succession, and Ellen could whisper in Cynthia's ear without anyone noticing. She leaned in.

"I can't wait to get you to the room," she said, and Cynthia's eyes flew wide open. "I want you completely naked in the center of the bed. I want you wet, and I want you ready."

"What are you doing?" came the response.

"Foreplay."

"Not here," Cynthia replied, both anxious at being overheard and a little excited at this daring game.

"You have a better way to spend the next hour and a half?" Ellen asked.

Left with no adequate response, Cynthia just pursed her lips and stared ahead at the dais.

"I have a surprise for you," Ellen continued. "Remember that new toy we mail-ordered?"

Cynthia turned her head slightly and raised an eyebrow toward Ellen.

Ellen leaned in again. "It arrived yesterday before you got home." She smirked a little, enjoying teasing Cynthia with the anticipation of their first butt plug. "I took the liberty of packing it with the lube."

"Oh my."

"So when you're naked on the bed in a couple of hours, you better expect to be face down.

"With your ass in the air.

"And be ready for the warm silicone to slide on in."

Cynthia visibly squirmed in her chair at the thought. They hadn't experimented with plugs before, but they'd talked about it at great length. The anticipation of actually playing with one, particularly just thinking about it so explicitly in the middle of a roomful of co-workers, was making her wet.

"It's a little wider than my index finger.

"And a little longer.

"I think you're going to love how it fills you up.

"I know how you love to be filled."

Cynthia felt Ellen's breath quicken a little with each line. She didn't know if she should lean away for appearances, or lean closer and enjoy this more. She crossed her legs tighter.

"I'm going to lube it up so good, baby.

"I'm not going to give it to you all at once.

"I'm going to spread your cheeks and push just the tip inside.

"Let you adjust to it.

"Then pull it out.

"Then push it back in a little further.

"I can feel you raising your butt up to meet me.

"I can feel your muscles tense as you expect me to give you more.

"I can hear the little gasp when I slide it all the way in you.

"I think I'll just hold it there. Leave it all the way in for a moment.

"Before I start to stroke you with it.

"Do you think you can come from this, baby?

"Maybe I'll reach around and get a finger on your clit, too. You think you could come then?"

This time, Cynthia let out a barely audible groan. A person in the row ahead of them glanced backward. She adjusted herself in the seat, and Ellen bowed her head to hide her smirk.

"How many times do you want to come tonight?

"Two? Three? Seven?

"Maybe we won't make the banquet at all this evening. Maybe you'll like the plug in you so much you'll want to leave it in all night. Maybe we'll order room service. Or maybe I'll just have you."

The moderator was making some closing remarks, but two women at the back of the room were already on their way to the elevator before he finished speaking.

The Lonely Bottom

Hank Hyena

I'M MARRIED, TO A WOMAN. Everything's fine, except . . . I'm obsessed with a secret fantasy.

It goes like this: I'm at the gym. Nobody else is here, except . . . a buff and chiseled Teutonic goddess named Helga Jorgenson. Helga is benchpressing massive amounts of iron; she's solidifying her pectoral muscles. I mince my way past her. I'm on my way to the drinkie fountain. . . .

Suddenly, Helga leaps on top of me. She knocks me down, she rips off my shorts, she snarls, "Spread your legs wide, you stupid little weiner-man!" I obey. Then . . . Helga mounts me! Her cast-iron abdomen is grinding atop my clammy buttocks!

She hisses, "I will invade you now, you weak filthy boy!" That's when I feel . . . a hot cylindrical object barrel past the eager mouth of my hungry rectum.

Now you're thinking, "There's something strange about this fantasy." Why do I want to be sodomized by der UberFraulein? Am I . . . in a closet?

The truth is, I like women, but sometimes I want them to penetrate me. I'm a lonely bottom.

I could ask my wife to insert inside me any number of objects that I have experimented with and found satisfying. I don't ask her though, because I'm terribly embarrassed about the eliminatory function of that orifice. Nobody has ever seen me defecate. I'd rather die. Sitting there, my face all squinched up like a cat, putrid mush dribbling out of my rear. It's a private event!

This caca-phobia that I have, I can blame it on my third grade teacher, Sister Bartholomew. She told me my excrement stunk because it flowed out of a wicked, smelly soul. She said that the feces of Jesus and Mary smelled like incense, their urine was holy water, their farts were the whispers of angels.

Sister Bartholomew was eventually locked up in the nun funny farm in Texas. My neurosis was already sealed by then.

Her perverse Cartesian logic: "I stink, therefore, I sinned," grabbed hold of my larval brain and never let go.

Nobody has ever traveled up my dark corridor, except, well . . . there was a nurse, ten years ago, in Mazatlan. She thought she was the little Dutch boy and I was the hole in the dike. She couldn't keep her fingers out of my butt. For days afterwards I felt warm down there, cherished and known.

A tequila fling, though, it's not the same as a marriage. I can't ask my wife to do things like that; it seems uncouth to eat dinner with someone and then, three hours later, ask them to put the digested meal underneath their fingernail.

I went on like this, for years. Whenever I saw a chicken on a spit, I got jealous. I got fluttery at the sight of bedposts. Once, my dentist told me she wanted to "drill my cavity," and I swooned with excitement.

Things started to change about two months ago. I was lying in bed, wide awake, with insomnia. My wife had the light on. She was reading her investment magazines. I said, "Meaghan, I really need some help getting to sleep tonight." (This doesn't mean I want her to turn off the light – she'd never do that. It just means I need a stress-reducing genital massage.)

My wife grunted accommodatingly. She spit in her hand, she reached over, she began performing her wifely duty. She stopped every once in a while to turn a page in her book. I lay there, whining, "get the nipples, get the nipples." Her hand moved in a clockwise direction: turn page, lick hand, twist twist, pull pull. Turn page, lick hand, twist twist, pull pull.

I closed my eyes. After seven pages, I got jolted like a man in the electric chair. My orgasm was distinctly Wagnerian: screaming eagles, mountains exploding, apocalyptic cities . . .

When I came out of it, I heard my wife's voice in the distance. "Honey, something's wrong. Look at this." Opening my eyes, I saw maroon-colored spunk in her hand! Blood in my sperm! Cancer!

I lay there, whimpering, while my wife sponged up the mess. Then she looked up my symptoms in our Blue Cross Stay Healthy Handbook.

"What is it?"

"Prostitis."

"Will I live?"

"You just need some tetracycline. Ha, ha, ha!"

"What's so funny?"

"Well, it says here the doctor will have to probe your anus to see if your prostate is enlarged or inflamed. Ha! I hope he straps you up like a gynecologist. Ha, ha, ha!"

I slept fitfully that night, eager with anticipation. The next morning I got up at 5:45 to flip through the yellow pages looking for the perfect urologist. I wanted an Icelandic she-doctor from a fish-scaling tribe, with merciless, agile fingers. There weren't any women, though. So, I chose Dr. Abdul Antaki – a Turk, I hoped, with cruel dextrous hands, fingers bathed in olive oil, cuticles trimmed.

I made an appointment for two PM. I thought about cleaning myself first, getting a high colonic . . . oh, forget it! Doctors are millionaires; I wanna get shit on their fingers.

When I finally met Dr. Abdul Antaki, he turned out to be six-feet-eight, weighing over three hundred pounds. His face? I didn't look at his face! I told you, I wanted to pretend he was Helga. I did stare at his hands, though. His fingers were as pudgy and smooth as boiled hot dogs.

Did we talk? No way. I unbuckled my pants. I bent over like a Greek slave. The doctor placed one hand on the small of my back. I felt something enormously wide burning into me; it felt like taking a crap in reverse. I screamed, "Helga, Helga, Helga, Helga!"

Then it was gone, just like that. Nothing left but cold gel on my cheeks.

Dr. Antaki asked, "Did you feel any pain?"

"No. Can we try it again?"

He looked at me like I was a rodent. I was thinking, women are right: size doesn't matter.

Dr. Antaki now showed me two samples. First, a bouncing pink ball. He said, "This is a healthy prostate. It is firm. When you compress it, it bounces back quickly."

Then he held up something that looked like a diseased oyster. He said, "This is an unhealthy prostate. It is corpulent, discolored. When you ejaculate, it remains flaccid. This is your prostate."

"Wow, and it's full of pus and blood too, right?"

"You must massage your prostate three times a week. If you do not do this, you will end up with a malignant tumor."

"Massage my prostate? Do you have a nurse who could help me?"

"No! You must do to this to yourself. Now go!"

I ran home, I sat in the bathtub with a bar of soap. I'm not very limber. I have thoracic scoliosis and fused lower vertebrae: L5-7. After half an hour of twisting around, I finally got my left thumb halfway in. That's when I heard the front door open.

Oh no, I thought. It's the landlord, he's coming to change a fuse. I tried to take my thumb out – yikes! My sphincter contracted; my thumb got locked in. Footsteps came down the hall. I thrashed around, I kicked the hot water faucet, I scalded myself! The bathroom door swung open. My thumb flew loose, and I hid it behind me.

It was only . . . my wife. She said, "I came home for lunch. Come and join me when you're clean."

Ten minutes later, I walked into the kitchen. My wife was eating cake and drinking milk. She was looking at a mail-order catalog.

She asked me, "Honey, should we get us some sex toys?"

"Sure!"

Peering over her shoulder, I saw an appliance in the catalogue that made my lower colon sing with delight.

A few days later, my wife and I played "Doctor." She put on the starched white hat and the nurse's uniform that I bought her. Then she got out the equipment, a prostate vibrator. She turned it on. It twitched like the nose of a gerbil.

She guided it past the hemorrhoid that she thinks is so cute. I felt it buzz inside me the way a deaf man hears music. When my prostate released, I didn't hear Wagner again. No! I heard bells – a heavenly sound!

I wonder if Sister Bartholomew is in heaven. If I ever see her there – if I ever see her anywhere – I'm going to tell her . . . that she was wrong!

A Pleasant Afternoon at the Beauty Shop

Diane Stevens

DONNA PAUSED IN CONSTERNATION when the Beauty Shop finally came into view, the clean lines of the facade looming in front of her like the Gates of Heaven – or maybe of Hell. A street person turned to leer knowingly as he walked past, traveling faster than she, and Donna flushed deeply while spasmodically clenching the pass concealed in her palm. When Irene had given her that pass – telling her she had become unfit company since Brad had left town and needed to do something about it – Donna had laughed at the joke and its implication, but she had also promised to give it a try. Now, as she slowly approached the foot of the broad stairway and gazed up at the imposing double doors, she wasn't so sure.

There is absolutely nothing to be ashamed of, she told herself sternly. *Lots of people come here, and it's a perfectly respectable thing to do. Besides which,* she continued with a shake of her head, *I can just get the facial and massage – nothing I haven't done before at other places. Irene doesn't need to know the details even if she did give me the present.*

Before she could lose her nerve, Donna quickly ran up the steps and reached to push through the doors, only to find them opening silently before her. Cautiously, she stepped into a small, but comfortable, lobby. The room was dark after the sunshine outside, so she paused for a moment, blinking, and swiveling her head from side to side.

"Welcome, madam. If you would care to sit down, I would be happy to assist you."

Startled, Donna spun around to find that the doors had been opened by a man, rather than the usual machinery. His courtly bow directed her to the reception area. He then casually stepped between her and the door as though to prevent her from fleeing before sampling the Beauty Shop's services.

Quelling the desire to duck around him and run all the way back home, Donna turned her back on him and walked awkwardly toward the reception area, intensely aware that he was following. She sat down and clasped her trembling hands in her lap while he seated himself behind the desk. As he took up a pen, she cleared her throat and dropped her eyes.

"I – my friend gave me a full-service pass, but I only want the basic treatment. The massage and facial, you know, and the manicure."

"That's fine," he replied while reaching with his other hand for the ticket she held out to him. "A lot of our clients just use the basic service."

He smiled at her reassuringly, and she smiled back tentatively.

"Of course, you needn't make any final decisions just now," he continued. "Your attendants will proceed to give you the full-service which your friend has paid for, and you can stop them at any time by saying the phrase: 'I would like you to stop now.' Our people call those the Magic Words. It's important that you use those exact words. Many clients become – somewhat incoherent during the latter portion of their treatment. With a precise phrase, we find we can avoid misunderstandings."

He continued to chat, describing the various services in more detail, while at the same time handing her the pen along with a disclaimer and several other forms. The so-called Magic Words were in bold print in three different places on the first page, and Donna had to sign her full name directly underneath each one. The owners of the Beauty Shop were obviously eager to prevent any charges of undue force or coercion. Donna found herself agreeing with them as she made a special effort to memorize the phrase, repeating it to herself, over and over, as the man droned on.

When she handed the papers back, his hand lightly brushed hers, and she jerked back in surprise, clumsily dropping the stack onto his desk. He didn't comment. Instead, he pushed a silent buzzer on his desk and turned to gesture at the door that appeared behind and to his right.

"Just go in through there, please. I hope you enjoy your stay."

One hour later, after the pleasure of indulging in a long, hot bubble bath followed by the concentrated attentions of four attendants, Donna's anxiety had abated. After supplying her with an impossibly fluffy robe, the first attendant had washed and brushed her hair, only to be followed by a second who gave her a facial, while a third and fourth gave her a manicure and pedicure. She had always enjoyed such attentions, and the delicate touches of the attendants were enormously satisfying after months of living alone.

Irene was right, she thought to herself. *I have been a bitch since Brad left. I should do this more often when he's gone. What am I saying? I should do this more often when he's here!*

As she lay there enveloped in the soft warmth, a woman approached and softly said, "Madam, when you are ready, I am here to take you to the massage room. The initial service will be similar to massages you may have received in the past, and the attendants will ask you whether you wish to proceed to the full service. I am to remind you that you can end your treatment at any time by saying: 'I would like you to stop now'."

At these words, Donna felt some of her tension return, but instead of bolting for the nearest exit, she said, "I understand. Thank you," and rose meekly to follow the woman out the door and down a long hallway. *This is it!* she thought to herself. *The moment of truth approaches. I don't know how I will face Irene if I don't, but I don't know how I possibly can!*

While Donna debated whether to end the "treatment" right then and there, her guide stopped, pressed a panel, and a door slid back into the wall with a sigh. The woman stepped to the side, allowing Donna to enter. With hesitant steps, Donna moved inside and the woman followed, quietly closing the door behind her and then standing patiently as Donna absorbed the full impact of the room.

Bright light emanated from the ceiling while softer lamps in rose-tinted sconces lined the cream-colored walls. A waterfall cascaded down the wall to her right, filling the room with a soft rushing sound. A rich, but delicate, scent perfumed the air. As she breathed it in, Donna felt a faint tingle of arousal, as though the scent were impregnated with pheromones of some kind.

Given the Beauty Shop's reputation, perhaps it was.

A massage table stood in the center of the room. At first glance, it looked perfectly ordinary, but stepping closer, Donna saw that it was designed differently from other such tables. Where a normal massage table was a simple rectangle with a comfortable holder for the head, this table included adjustable padded holders for the arms and legs. As she noticed two holes designed to accommodate a woman's breasts when lying on her stomach, she again resisted a strong urge to run out of the room. She relaxed somewhat upon seeing the protective covering underneath the table which would shield her exposed breasts from prying eyes.

A door opened, and Donna turned to see a line of attendants enter. Both the men and the women were dressed in the same simple robe Donna herself wore. She searched their faces, looking for any trace of amusement or scorn, but they kept their eyes cool and impersonal and their faces still. If she hadn't known better, she might have thought they were robots. When she thought about what they were supposed to do next, she wished they were.

The woman who had brought her into the room came up behind her and reached out to take her robe. Donna clutched the thick cloth around herself for one last moment, but then, with a sudden feeling of freedom, she allowed the robe to fall open and slip from her shoulders into the woman's hands. A warm breeze swirled through the room to caress her breasts, and her nipples crinkled in response. As she watched the attendants watching her, she was shocked to feel a rush of dampness between her legs.

A male attendant came forward to gently guide her to the table and help her lie face-down. The table had already been adjusted to fit her body, and her genitals began to throb rhythmically as her breasts fell through the holes and dangled, pendulous, into the darkness below. She was grateful that the leg pads were placed tightly together so she could pretend this was otherwise no different from any other massage table she had ever used.

As soon as she was comfortable, several of the attendants

fanned out around the table while the others took up positions along the walls. One man stood at her head and two women placed themselves beside each outstretched arm. Four people passed behind her, and she could sense, rather than see, them take up positions around her lower body. Her buttocks felt naked and exposed in a way she had never before experienced, and even though she knew her breasts were covered, she felt her nipples contract even more sharply. When another breeze wafted across her, she shuddered in anticipation of the first touch.

That touch came softly as the attendant at her head began to massage her head and neck. His fingers wove deftly through her hair and into her scalp before dropping to caress the exposed area of her face. Donna felt the last of her nervousness drain away under his soothing touch. After a few minutes, the women at her sides each took up one of her hands and began to stroke them. When Donna's fingers relaxed and grew limp, they moved to massage her arms and upper back. Her eyes closed and the rushing of the waterfall might have eased her to sleep had she not been acutely aware of her dangling breasts and the attendants gazing upon her naked buttocks. Instead, her body's arousal increased. As the massage continued, Donna felt her blood begin to pound and roar. Her breasts ached. Her loins throbbed. A tingling flush gathered in her head and made her feel dizzy. All of a sudden, she felt a wanton desire to spread her legs wide.

As if reading her thoughts, the man massaging her head bent down and whispered, "In order to massage your lower body, we have to adjust the table so the attendants can reach around your legs. Do you want us to continue?"

The moment had arrived. Donna toyed with the possibility of asking them to stop, but found that the idea of getting up and leaving was now unbearable. Irene was right. She needed to give herself this pleasure. The decision made, she replied softly, "Please continue. I want the full service."

At her words, the table began to rise, elevating her hips slightly and relieving the pressure from her lower back, while the leg pads separated by a few degrees, leaving her genitals partly exposed to the view of those standing behind her. Her feet and legs were then taken up by four unseen pairs of strong hands, and the massage continued, the minutes stretching like hours. The women who had started with her arms continued with her lower back, coming close to, but not touching, her buttocks. The heat between her legs increased with each pass of their hands.

Suddenly, without warning, the attendants who had been massaging her stopped and moved back toward the walls. The ceiling lights dimmed, leaving the rosy glow of the wall sconces and a gleam behind her, suggesting that her genitals were brightly illuminated. The scent she had noticed earlier returned, stronger than before, and this time she recognized musk mingled with some other, unidentified scent. After a moment, she realized she was smelling herself, and her breathing involuntarily quickened.

Two new women came forward and crawled under the table to take up positions just underneath her chest. Looking down, Donna saw them unfasten the barrier which up until now had shielded her breasts from view. As her breasts were revealed, the women allowed their own robes to fall open in turn, exposing their genitals, and she suddenly experienced an intense desire to touch them.

Small sounds began to emerge from her throat with each breath. When she tried to stop herself, the sound built up inside only to emerge a moment later, first as a loud gasp, and then as a low moan. She ceased trying to control herself, and when the women below her reached up and laid their warm hands to the sides of her breasts, she cried out.

They worked on her expertly, stroking gently toward the nipples and then away without having touched them. Her nipples were firmly erect and their ache matched that of her genitals whenever the women's hands passed near. Finally, the women grasped her breasts firmly with their hands and tilted their heads back, bringing their mouths a fraction of an inch away. Donna could feel their breath, and she nearly screamed in frustration when they didn't move closer. *Touch me!* she pleaded silently. *Please! Touch me!*

The attendant massaging her head now moved forward and joined the others beneath the table. His robe also fell open to reveal a huge erection and perfect nipples on a smoothly muscled chest. Staring deeply into her eyes, he raised his head and began to kiss her, thoroughly and expertly. His teeth nibbled her lips and then his tongue thrust into her mouth, probing and stroking the wet cavern. Donna's eyes grew wide as he took her tongue into his mouth, gently sucking it. At the same time, the women who were holding her breasts finally began to lick, and then to suck, upon her engorged nipples. A scream tore through Donna's mouth to disappear into the throat of the man who was playing with her lips and tongue. He pulled back briefly so she could see his erect penis jerk in response, and she felt an answering tug deep within her own body.

She thought she could endure no more when the table began moving slowly upward again, spreading her legs wider. The attendants wrapped soft straps around her to prevent her from sliding down or falling off as she writhed and bucked. The table stopped rising when her hips were as high and her legs as wide apart as they could comfortably go. She moaned as the blood pounded in her head, increasing her pleasure. The attendants at her mouth and breasts continued caressing her, backing away before she became uncomfortable, and returning as her desire increased. This time, she found herself screaming aloud for the people behind her to touch her.

Finally, after several agonizingly wonderful minutes, the attendants at the head of the table fell back, and she felt hands firmly take hold of her inner legs, midway down her thighs. Now that the table was fully raised, she could look back underneath to see the lower body of a man behind her. As she watched, his robe also fell open to expose an enormously thick, though flaccid, penis and dangling testicles.

The man's unseen hands began to massage and caress her buttocks and the delicate flesh of her inner thighs, moving higher and then lower, but always stopping just short of her aching loins. She imagined his face, intent on her exposed organs, seeing in her mind what he must be seeing in reality.

Looking back, she saw his penis gradually grow hard, and her gasps and screams began to sound almost like sobs. The roaring in her ears increased and she felt faint. As her eyes closed, all of the attendants retreated and stopped their ministrations. Donna opened her eyes and gasped for breath, her desire gradually receding from its peak. When her breathing steadied and her muscles relaxed, the man behind her resumed his position, and she quivered in anticipation.

He once again laid warm hands on her thighs, and with agonizing slowness, began to work his way up to her crotch. Looking back, she saw hands removing something from a container attached to the leg of the table. It was a bottle of lubricant. The touch on her skin grew slippery as the attendant slathered her buttocks and inner thighs. The women below her also put lubricant on their hands and began kneading and stroking her breasts, from the sides in toward her nipples. Donna cried out again and again as their hands neared sensitive areas, and her desire quickly grew to new heights.

The hands on her buttocks moved inward, and her anus began to throb in response. She had never before wanted to be touched there, but now she did. When his fingers delicately stroked the outer rim, she gasped and her breath grew ragged. He reached for more lubricant, and then gently, ever so gently, began to move inside. Tremors ran down Donna's body as he inserted his finger a short distance into her rectum and began gently to explore. Her nipples, labia, and clitoris responded by becoming impossibly engorged. As she neared the point of no return, the finger withdrew, and the attendants drew back to allow her time to recover.

They didn't stop for long, however. The man near her head kissed her again, more gently now. She felt the attendant behind her touch the outside of her anus. What slid in this time, however, was not his fingers, but his latex-enclosed tongue. As the two tongues probed her – one in her mouth, the other in her ass – Donna felt transported. The ringing in her ears drowned out the sound of the waterfall. All she felt were these two points of contact, slippery and wet. It came as no surprise when the other attendants approached and began to slather the rest of her body with oil. She felt as though she were being immersed in her own fluids, the juices from her cunt covering her body in a silken sheen over which the hands, lips, and tongues of the attendants slipped and slid.

Again and again, she neared orgasm. Again and again, the attendants stopped, and waited, and started again. Her eyes were closed so tightly and her pleasure was so intense that she barely noticed when all the lights except the one between her legs were shut off and the attendants paused to lower the table, remove the straps, turn her onto her back, and raise her hips once again, legs spread-eagled above her head.

She lay there gasping for some time before opening her eyes. That must have been a signal, for a door immediately opened and a completely naked man walked into the room, illuminated by the one remaining light between her legs. He was golden, and perfectly muscled, and his penis stayed rigidly erect as he strode across the room to stand between her thighs, looking into her eyes for a long moment before turning his gaze downward. Her desire returned full force as she watched him watching her. He raised the entire table to bring her crotch up near his head, and she gave a soft cry which soon turned to a stronger one as he reached to finish what the others had so thoroughly begun.

Gently, the man laid his fingers against her buttocks and braced his thumbs on each side of her labia, stretching the lips as wide apart as they would go. Softly, he began to work the lips, opening and shutting them, looking first at her genitals and then into her eyes, and then back again. The lips made a wet sucking sound as they were moved back and forth, and the sound caused Donna to moan even louder. Her back arched against the straps, and three other attendants came forward. One woman stood at her head, while another woman and a man encased her breasts in soft cones which held them upright, exposing just the top third. She begged them to kiss her and suck on her nipples, but they stood over her impassively watching as the golden man continued his massage.

He reached below the table with one hand, while continuing to tickle her labia with the other. A moment later, Donna felt a series of small, smooth beads being gently inserted into her anus. The added pressure increased her desire yet another notch.

When her lips were held open to their widest point, the massage stopped. Donna looked up to see the man's head move forward, his eyes intent as he watched for her slightest reactions. His breath stirred her pubic hair as he moved closer and closer. Dropping her head back, Donna stared into the darkness, listening to the waterfall, and breathing the musk and her own scent.

The first, faint touch came a moment later, and Donna squeezed her eyelids tightly shut, so as to concentrate all her being on that one sensation. The tip of his tongue began to lightly tickle her along the outside of her labia, followed by delicate nibbles and more intense sucks. As his tongue played with her inner lips, her moans grew deeper and longer. He slipped his tongue inside her and flattened it to lap wetly, like a dog, licking along the most sensitive portion of her labia at the end of each stroke while just missing her aching clitoris by millimeters. Her back arched, and the attendants at her head and breasts finally dropped their heads to her mouth and breasts, sucking and licking and stroking in rhythm with the man below.

After several delicious moments, they pulled back, but the man at the foot of the table immediately inserted three of the fingers of his left hand deep inside her to stroke and massage the walls of her vagina. His other hand dipped below the table to emerge seconds later with a small, self-lubricating vibrator which he applied to her labia and the base of her clitoris, circling the hood but again avoiding her most sensitive spot.

Just when she thought she could take no more, he withdrew his fingers and placed the instrument to the side, but before she could relax, he grabbed her hips firmly, and bent his head once again to her genitals. As the tip of his tongue tenderly brushed her clitoris, screams began to rip from her throat to echo through the room. All the man's efforts were now concentrated in that one small bit of burning flesh, as he nibbled and licked and sucked. The other attendants returned to her mouth and breasts, all four backing off and returning until Donna lost all sense of herself.

Her first orgasm was shattering. A tingling wave of blood surged from the top of her head to the tips of her toes and back again as her genitals tightened in a huge spasm. The man continued to gently coax her clitoris with his tongue while slowly removing the beads from her anus, and the spasms continued with gradually diminishing intensity until he drew away, just before the pleasure gave way to pain. Her clitoris was still engorged, however, so he and the others soon came back, with hands and tongues and vibrator, to bring her to yet another height and yet another orgasm, over and over again until she was spent.

As her body began finally to relax, the table moved downward, and Donna looked to see the man still standing between her legs. His penis was enormous, and his eyes were filled with desire. She looked at him for a long moment and then said one word, "Please." Holding her gaze, he rubbed lubricant on his penis, adjusted the table to the height of his hips, stepped forward, and slid inside, his hands reaching up to pinch his own nipples. The sensation was exquisite against her still-swollen soreness.

Silently, two of the women shed their own robes and began to suck on her bruised nipples while stimulating themselves. Another of the men, also naked, came up behind her and lowered his head to her mouth to gently kiss her swollen lips. The women reached over to fondle his penis and testicles while he reached forward to insert his fingers into their vaginas as they continued to rub their own clitorises with their free hands. In the dark, the attendants who stood by the walls also shed their robes and began to masturbate and fondle each other.

Donna relaxed into the sensations, allowing them to bring her down gently and enjoying the sights and sounds of a roomful of people so excited from witnessing her pleasure. Her vagina pulsed once, twice, three times, and the man inside her uttered a groan as he came. To her surprise and delight, the other attendants joined in a growing chorus of gasps and sighs as, one by one, each of them reached his or her own climax. A moment later, they filed out of the room, leaving her alone in the dark. Her eyes closed, and she drifted to sleep with the sound of the waterfall rushing in her ears.

The gentle return of the rose-colored lights brought Donna slowly back to awareness. Two women entered the room and proceeded to bathe her limp body as though she were a baby. By the time they were finished, she was fully awake. Swinging her legs off the table, she saw a brightly lit recess in which her clothes had been neatly laid out. As she entered the small room, the door shut behind her, blocking her return. A small bathroom opened off to one side, and she took the opportunity to relieve herself and clean off a patch or two of lubricant the attendants had missed.

As she dressed, she looked at herself in the mirror. *I look no different. No one will ever know unless I tell them. Except Irene, of course. I owe her one.* A wide grin spread across her features followed by a blush. *How can I be blushing now!* she thought. Throwing her head back, she shouted, "I would like you to stop now!" and then laughed at the absurdity.

At that moment, a final door opened at the other side of the little room to reveal a quiet side street. Her head held high, joy bubbling through her veins, Donna squared her shoulders and boldly strode forth into the day.

Anchors Aweigh

snakesKin

I DO BELIEVE THAT ONE OF THE MORE UNUSUAL sex toys I've ever shared was a twenty-six-foot sailboat, owned by my boyfriend Tony. One of his claims to fame (at least, in *my* yearbook) was that he was always willing to try something new: a position, a fantasy, a gadget. He once removed the chopstick holding my hair in a French twist and used it to seduce me. But that's another story.

One night we were at the dock, on the boat. We decided to go for a sail, since there was a good breeze and it was very clear out. We headed toward Yerba Buena Island, and the boat was pretty much sailing herself. The Bay Bridge was a beautiful string of lights reflected on the calm waters: purely magical. It was one of those chilly winter nights that makes you appreciate having someone to snuggle with. Tony went below and brought up a blanket, and we were having a great time snuggling, kissing and just guiding the tiller with a light hand.

The boat was heeled over nicely, and the warmth of his kisses was a fire against the cold of the night. Keeping one hand on the helm, he reached under the blanket and began fondling me, then unzipped my jeans and started toying with my clit. I was getting very aroused, but he suddenly started pretending to be preoccupied with sailing the boat. I was getting very hot from his hand down in my pants, and he was acting like everything was "business as usual," discussing sail trim and wind direction. Meantime, I was moaning and writhing around on the seat under the blanket and stretching out so that he could have better access.

Suddenly he jumped up and said, "Here – take the tiller. I have to go make a drink," and he disappeared below. *What!?* I was about to strangle him at that point! I was *really* not in the mood for this to stop when it did, even if he was just tweaking me. I was twitching, I was rubbing my legs together, I was hot and I was bothered – and as I was holding the tiller,

I suddenly had an idea!

I often sail boats standing up, guiding the tiller between my legs so my hands can be free to adjust sheets, etc. This time, I undid my belt, dropped my jeans and panties, did a very thorough check with my hands for splinters, and mounted the tiller. Ooooooh! It felt wonderful. I was so wet at that point that I just slid onto it. There was a large knob at the end, then it followed a slight arc down to the base, where it was hinged so that you could adjust the angle of it up and down . . . and back and forth. All the characteristics of your basic wooden tiller, but suddenly it just didn't look the same to me anymore!

I was holding myself up with one hand, massaging my clit with the other, and sliding up and down that tiller for all I was worth, all the while keeping the boat on course. When Tony turned to come up the companionway, he saw me: naked from the waist down, wailing away on his "stick," my hand spreading my labia and exposing my stiff little clit. First his jaw dropped, then he grinned from ear to ear. He put the drinks down, then reached up, lifted my heavy sweater and turtleneck, unclasped my bra, cupped my breasts and began softly sucking on my nipples just as I exploded and everything went black for a few minutes.

I don't know who was sailing the boat for a while there. I nearly lost consciousness, but I do remember throbbing and moaning for what seemed like a really long time while he continued to nurse on my tits. It was exquisite – the boat gently bobbing from side to side, the background sounds of the Bay Bridge traffic, the city skyline.

I was so weak that he had to help me get my clothes back on before bundling me back up in the football blanket. We just snuggled for awhile, not talking much, and headed back to port. I was one happy little sailorette, lemme tell ya! But the skipper had yet to exact his revenge. . . .

The Twelve Days of Christmas

Dominic Santi

I HAD DECIDED I DIDN'T LIKE CHRISTMAS.

Well, not that I really didn't like Christmas. It was just that I was so horny I thought I was going to die. Jack had walked out on me at Halloween, so this year I hadn't been able to get into the holiday spirit. And I sure as hell wasn't feeling Christmasy.

After a while, even my roommate Perry got sick of listening to me complain. I think the last straw for him had been a couple weeks ago, when he'd said, "You don't look like you're in the Christmas spirit." And I'd told him that blue balls weren't exactly holiday decorations. He'd looked so disgusted that I'd actually hung last year's fuzzy red Christmas stocking on the outside of my bedroom door and said, "Ho, Ho, Ho!" a few times, just to make him happy. I even hung a stocking on his bedroom door – after all, Jack wouldn't be using it this year.

DAY ONE

December 13th. A nice, lucky-sounding day. It was twelve days before Christmas, and hordes of shoppers had descended on the toy store where I worked. My evenings had been kind of quiet of late, and I was getting bored with sulking and watching TV, so I volunteered to take the late shift this season, even closing, so the manager could go home to his wife and kiddies.

I was surprised when I came home that night and saw a bulge in my Christmas stocking. Balancing my soda and mittens in one hand, I reached in and pulled out a large tube of water-based lube – K-Y brand personal lubricant jelly, to be exact. I stood there laughing, looking around and wondering who the hell had put it there. But as far as I could see, nobody else was home, though apparently Perry had left a light on when he'd gone to work. He'd also left a note on my door, written on the back of an envelope in wide green marker.

"My sister sent me some bubble bath for an early Christmas

present. Feel free to use it, dude."

Perry knew I was into taking baths. I'd used up all the hot water more than once. I was still laughing and shaking my head when I sank into the cloud of apple-mint bubbles and let the heat start soaking the stiffness out of my shoulders.

As I soaked, I was thinking about my present. I figured it couldn't be from Perry. Yeah, he'd probably figured out that I was horny, just from how grouchy I'd been. But lube is not the type of present a straight guy gives to his roommate, and I knew Perry was straight. Well, at least as far as I knew, he was. I'd never seen him bring anybody home, but then I'd been so preoccupied with trying to keep Jack happy that I hadn't really noticed Perry much. I'd barely even paid attention when the landlord moved our two other roommates in at the beginning of the month, though I knew they were both named Bill.

To be honest, anybody could have come into the house. One of the advantages of living in a small college town is not having to lock your doors. Hell, I didn't even know if we had keys to the front door. I kept all of my personal stuff in my room.

The thought of that big tube of lube was pretty intriguing, whoever it was from, and I ran my hand over my cock a few times as I relaxed even more, just enjoying the feel of my hand in the warm soapy water as the rest of the tension drained out of my body.

I woke up with a jolt. The bath water was cold, and I must have been sleeping for at least half an hour. Shivering, I let out the bath water as I toweled off fast and climbed into my flannel pj's. Then I dove under the covers to warm up. Before I knew it I was asleep.

DAY TWO

The next day was every bit as busy as the one before. People can be such idiots when they're stressed. I'd thought about the present in my stocking a couple of times during the day, but I'd pretty well forgotten about it by the time I walked in the front door with my burger-and-fries combo meal, until I turned on the hall light and saw the card-like bulge in my stocking.

I looked around, but nobody was home.

I damn near dropped my drink when I saw what was on the card: a pair of nipple clamps. Great. Just what I need, I thought as I tossed the card on the bed and sat down at my desk to eat. Yeah, my nipples are really sensitive, and I love it when somebody plays with them. But in the last few months before we broke up, Jack had decided he liked to snap nipple clamps on me when I wasn't expecting it, just to hear me yelp. They were really tight and they hurt like hell, which he thought was hilarious. The more I thought about it, the more I realized how much of an asshole he really had been.

There was nothing on TV, so as I finished my fries, my eyes wandered back to the nipple clamps again. They looked different from the ones Jack had. I sat down on the edge of the bed, and as I looked at them closely, I realized they had an adjustable screw on them, so the tension could be adjusted.

That got my curiosity. So I wiped my hands on my jeans and opened the package. Set tight, they really pinched my finger. But loose, they just had a nice firm grip. Sort of like somebody's fingers – pinching, but not too hard.

I ran my fingers over the front of my shirt, feeling my nipples harden against my thermals. After a while I yanked my shirt out and lifted it enough to rub my hands over my nips, which made them stand up even harder. They were hungry to be touched, and I was getting even more curious. So finally I put the nipple clamps on – nice and snug, but not enough to really hurt. I was surprised. It felt good! And it was definitely getting the rest of my body interested. Pretty soon I was rubbing the front of my jeans, and every once in a while I'd tug on the chain between the nipple clamps, just to feel the extra pressure.

Well, like I said, I'd been really horny for a long time, so it didn't take long before I'd pulled my cock out of my jeans and gotten it well acquainted with the contents of that big tube of lube from the night before.

Damn, it felt good to come. I didn't even care that I'd come all over my shirt. What the hell, I had to do laundry the next night anyway. I pulled my shirt all the way off and finished wiping up with it, then balled it up and threw it in the general direction of my hamper.

I winced a bit when I took the clamps off. I'd forgotten how the pressure builds up after a while. Still, it felt pretty good, working the feeling back into my skin. But by then I was yawning, so I pulled on my pajamas and went to sleep.

DAY THREE
The lights were on and I could hear Stone Temple Pilots blaring from Perry's stereo when I got home.

For the first time in weeks, I wasn't feeling particularly tired. I'd finally gotten enough sleep the night before. And I knew I had to do a lot of laundry. But I was still shocked when I pulled the cock ring and ball stretcher from my stocking. The label read, "Triple Crown."

Now I have to admit, I was feeling sort of kinky that day. For the first time in my life, I hadn't worn underwear to work. Okay, so I should have done laundry the night before. But it had felt sort of good, letting my cock press against the cotton of my jeans all day. In fact, it felt nice enough that I didn't even get particularly grouchy with the customers. Well, except for the woman who insisted I had hidden the action figures she wanted somewhere back in the storeroom and was just too lazy to get them – I was a bit terse with her. I mean, hey lady, what we have is on the shelves. This is the Christmas season!

Like I said, I was feeling sort of kinky. So I didn't stop to think much once I'd closed the door to my room. I just dropped my pants, slid the leather strap under my balls, and snapped it over the top of my cock. Snug, but not too tight. Well, my cock took interest in that right away! But I resisted the urge to stroke myself – well, okay, just a couple of times. Then I tugged down on my balls and snapped the ball stretcher around them.

Now that felt weird. I mean, any type of pressure on my balls makes me a little nervous. But it didn't hurt. So before I could think about it too much, I pulled the thinnest strap up – the ball separator – and snapped it into place. I stood there really tense for a minute, figuring I could pull the snaps right back open if things started to hurt. But then I realized that the pressure felt pretty good, and my cock was definitely showing its appreciation of my new attire.

I shuffled over to look in the mirror, my jeans down around my ankles. And when I looked in the mirror, I had to nod in approval. I looked pretty hot with my cock jutting out and my balls wrapped in those black leather straps. I watched my cock jump as I ran my finger all the way up the shaft. And then I really shivered as I stroked my fist over myself a few times. Oh, yeah. That felt good.

I was hard enough that it took me a minute to change into my doing-laundry clothes, especially when I had to stuff myself into my old torn-up jeans and get them buttoned. Horny or not, I still had to do laundry if I wanted to have clothes for work the next day. So I took the first load down to the laundry room, and while it was washing I went to the kitchen to get a snack.

Perry was there, pouring himself a glass of milk to drink with the cookies he was eating. He offered me some – they were chocolate chip, my favorite – and poured me a glass of milk, which I figured was pretty cool.

I ate my cookies leaning back nonchalantly against the counter. I was enjoying the way my cock was pressing up, half-hard, against the soft cotton of my jeans.

We both stuffed down about a dozen cookies. And while we ate I noticed, not for the first time, the sizeable basket filling out the front of Perry's sweatpants. His t-shirt was stained dark from his workout – I love the smell of fresh sweat. And his cock was tenting the material out in front of him. Pumping always makes him hard.

He was busy drinking his milk, so I just let myself admire him for a minute. I found myself thinking that I wished my tongue were a drop of sweat running down those tight abs to drip off the end of his cock. Or to soak into what was no doubt a thick mat of hair surrounding those huge balls.

I shook my head and ate another cookie. I was finally over one weird relationship. There was no point in lusting after a straight guy. Though it didn't hurt to admire him.

"Get anything from Santa tonight?" he asked, as he wiped his face on the back of his hand.

"Yeah," I shrugged my shoulders. "A toy." I took another drink of milk, trying not to blush as I thought of the leather ties that were keeping me keenly aware of the state of my cock and balls. "You?"

"A package of cookies," he grinned, holding up the now-empty box. "Can't get much better than that!"

He raised his eyebrows when I blushed and laughed, but I just shook my head and said good night as I went back downstairs to move my clothes to the dryer.

I can't say that I hurried doing my laundry. It felt good walking around trussed up in leather straps. But I had trouble concentrating on my book, and my hands wandered down to stroke myself through the old, soft cotton. More than once I took advantage of the tear where the material had shredded next to the inner seam.

By the time I got into bed that night, I was more than ready to work the lube all over my bright red cock. With all the pressure from the cock ring, it took me a long, long time to come. But damn, it was worth the wait.

DAY FOUR

I couldn't believe it the next night when I pulled the butt plug out of my stocking. I quickly stuffed it back in while I looked around. It had been dark when I'd come in, and there was no sound but the furnace kicking in. I looked down the hall. The two Bills had put stockings on their doors too, and I could see bulges in them. I admit it, I peeked at what the bulges were – all cookies. Obviously I was getting some special attention from Santa, and it was like he knew that with all the jacking off I'd been doing, my asshole was itching for attention.

I must have blushed a thousand shades of red while I hid my present under my jacket and unlocked my door. I threw my mittens and hat on the nightstand, then I stood there shaking my head as I read the package. The Diamond Lil butt plug. Four inches long and one and one-quarter inches in diameter. Designed with diamond-shaped bumps to keep it in place during use so the wearer's hands will be free for other things. Damn, I laughed, shaking my head. Who'd ever think up something like that?

I wasn't going to use it. I mean, I'd never used a butt plug. I only had sex with people, not toys. But it was kind of cute, and even when I closed it in my desk drawer I felt it calling to me. So I finally took it out and started playing with it. It was red, sort of Christmasy, and the diamond-shaped little ripples were fun to play with. I started bopping it back and forth with my finger. It looked kind of like those Jello-brand gelatin snack cubes we used to throw at each other when the scoutmaster wasn't looking. Only firmer. And when I started turning it over in my hand, it got warm from my holding it.

I finally went in and took a shower to distract myself. Not a cold shower – I hate cold showers. Just a long one. So afterwards I was feeling all loose and relaxed. And when I walked out of the bathroom in my towel, there was my cheery little present, sitting on top of my desk. Right next to the lube.

I'm not sure that I ever really decided to put it in. I just set it on the chair at my desk. Pretty soon my room seemed warm enough that I threw my towel over the closet door. I turned on my computer, and when I sat down, well, I just sort of sat on the butt plug. Not fast or anything. I'd squirted quite a bit of lube on it – sort of like putting frosting on top of a 3-D Christmas-tree cookie and watching the icing run down the sides.

It had been so long since I'd been fucked that I was tight as a virgin. But the tip wasn't very big and it felt smooth against my asshole. It just sort of slid in as I sat down. I jumped a little when the first diamond popped in, but it didn't hurt. So eventually I just sat down the rest of the way, over the second diamond, and then the third. I felt my butt touch the cool wood of the chair as my asshole snugged up around the neck of the plug. Like I said, it wasn't too big. I felt pleasantly stretched and full, though it wasn't big enough to reach my prostate. But my cock was definitely starting to pay attention.

Just then my online log-in connected, and pretty soon I was doing my usual e-mail and chatting with my usual friends in the electronics room. A couple of people commented that I sounded like I was in a really good frame of mind. I could feel myself flushing, even though I knew they couldn't see my face.

I even got up and walked around a couple of times. It felt strange, walking with that plug up my butt. But at the same time it felt really good. Especially when I moved it in and out a few times, letting those little diamond bumps pop over my asshole.

After a while I really felt like beating off. I tried to ignore it – I like to use lots of lube, and I didn't want to get my new track ball sticky. But finally I got so horny that I just logged off. I didn't even lie down. I just grabbed my towel off the doorknob, pushed the chair back, and squirted lube all over my dick. It took about two seconds. Then I came so hard the chair thumped against the floor a couple of times.

As I was catching my breath, Perry knocked on my door.

"You all right in there?"

"Yeah." I was surprised that my voice didn't sound quite like me. I guess I'd been even hornier than I thought.

"Well, I heard thumping, and you're usually pretty quiet at night."

"I'm fine. My chair just slipped."

He hesitated a moment. "Well, all right. As long as you're okay."

I heard his footsteps fade off down the hall. *Oh, I'm okay*, I thought. *In fact, I feel great!*

I shivered real hard when I stood up and eased the plug out of my ass, but I made sure the chair stayed flat on the floor. I hadn't even heard Perry come home.

DAY FIVE

The after-hours Christmas party had been pretty rowdy, and I was definitely feeling the effects of the three black-and-tans I'd had with my all-you-can-eat pizza. So I just leaned my head on the door and laughed while I fumbled with the lock, my five-inch vibrating butt plug and two AA batteries in my hand.

It didn't matter that I was a little drunk or that I was alone. I stripped and climbed into bed. And when I shoved that sucker up my ass and turned it on, nothing in the world mattered except the sensations that were vibrating from my ass to my cock. I love getting fucked. I mean I really love getting fucked. And right then my ass felt so good I didn't even care that I was groaning out loud.

I came all over the bed without even touching myself. I was lying on my back and I came so hard I shot over my shoulder. And onto my chest. And my belly. I fell asleep with my cock matted to my pubic hair and my new toy somewhere on the sheet beside me.

DAY SIX

Most of the presents had had weird shapes, but I could tell even before I slipped my hand into the stocking that this one was a video tape. *An Intimate Guide to Male Genital Massage*, to be exact – step by step directions for "the ultimate hand job." I hadn't seen the old version, but this tape claimed to be "new and improved – now expanded to sixty minutes."

I threw my jacket on the chair and sat down on the edge of my bed to watch it. Right away I liked that it was two guys doing the demonstration – "two male lovers," it said on the box. I figured that was cool. And neither one of them looked like Jack.

I know it was an "educational" video, but just watching it made me horny. By ten minutes into it, I had stripped off my jeans and briefs and was lying on the bed, propped up on pillows, with the open tube of lube on a towel next to me and my hands wrapped around my dick, stroking along with the video.

The box said they were demonstrating thirty different techniques, so I counted, holding off until I wanted to come so badly, even my ears burned. I finally let myself shoot during technique number thirty. Since number thirty included inserting a finger in my ass while I beat off, the outcome was pretty much a given. I love having a finger up my ass when I come. I just wish I could reach my prostate with my own fingers. Unfortunately the butt plugs didn't quite reach it either when I was lying on my back, which is my favorite position – ass stuffed and my hands wrapped around my dick.

I jumped when the cable channel blared back on. I'd dozed off and the room was definitely getting a bit nippy. I peeled off my t-shirt and set the alarm while the tape rewound, then I climbed under the covers in just my socks and went to sleep. This time though, instead of holding my cock, I fell asleep with my arms wrapped around my pillow. Damn, I felt good.

DAY SEVEN

I was actually kind of antsy when I got home the next day. My cock was happy, but all this teasing my asshole made me really want to get fucked. I wanted to feel somebody sliding over my prostate while I moaned and thrashed around on the bed.

I was kind of lost in my reverie as I grabbed my mail and started down the hall toward my room. When I looked at my door, at first I was surprised. It looked like there wasn't anything in the stocking. Not that there had to be. I'd just sort of been looking forward to the little surprises each day. In fact, I'd been in such a good frame of mind that even my boss had suggested that maybe I had a new boyfriend. I'd just smiled and looked mysterious. After all, what was I supposed to say, that my new date was my hand? Sheesh!

As I looked at the stocking more closely, I saw that there was a little bulge down in the toe. It felt like a Petrie dish with a lid. And when I drew it out, I saw that it was a string of seven red and green anal beads inside a plastic case. Size large. "For prostatic massage during sex – solo or with a partner." A shiver ran up my spine as I felt the knotted beads through the thin case.

Actually, size large wasn't all that big – at least each individual bead wasn't. They were about three-quarters of an inch in diameter, and when I opened the container and ran my fingers over them, I discovered that they were smooth as glass. Somebody had already filed the seams off the beads. I was starting to wonder who Santa's little helper was. It seemed like I should at least say thank you! Well, yeah, I did have ulterior motives as to how I wanted to thank him.

I hadn't worn underwear that day. I have no idea why – it

was certainly all clean. But I'd woken up late and horny, again. So I'd just grabbed a quick shower and raced out the door, letting my half-hard cock press against the cotton of my jeans all day. As I ran my fingers over the beads, I could feel the front of my jeans getting wet where my cock was leaking. Suddenly, I really wanted to play with my new toy.

I played for a long, long time. I put on some good music – Handel, in honor of the season. Then I lay down on the bed, put a towel under my ass, and got good and comfy. When I started jacking off I alternated my usual fast and jerky motion with some of the massage techniques I'd learned from the video. After a while I greased up my asshole and started massaging it, rubbing first in circles, then slipping my fingers in until I was panting from how good it felt.

Then I started experimenting with the beads. I popped one in, then another, then a third one. I could feel that they were sort of bunched up just inside my asshole. But rather than push them further in, I slowly started to pull them out, just to see what it felt like.

I learned real quick not to pull the string toward the side, when it felt like I was getting a paper cut on my asshole! I stopped for a minute, massaging my poor little pucker and reminding it that I wouldn't do anything to hurt it. The skin wasn't actually cut, but it did sting for a minute. When I was feeling relaxed again, I stroked my cock a few times. Then I very slowly pulled the beads straight out, letting them pop back out of my asshole while I stroked my cock.

I swear every hair on my body stood up as I gasped out loud and my cock filled as hard as a rock.

It took me a minute to catch my breath. My cock was so hard it was damn near sticking straight up at the ceiling. I squirted more lube on the beads – this time on all of them. Then I slowly stuffed them up my asshole while I stroked my cock and tugged on my balls. This time I pushed them a bit further up. And when I pulled them out . . . even my tits tingled as I jerked halfway up on the bed, my body clenching as I squeezed my cock hard to keep from coming.

"Not yet. Not yet," I kept panting to myself as my body

crawled back from the edge. It had been so long since I'd felt
my prostate being massaged that I really wanted to enjoy this
come. Especially now that I had a hint of what it was going to
be like.

I squirted more lube on the beads – I was really glad I'd put
the towel under myself. This time my greedy little asshole
seemed to suck up each one of those hard, slippery beads as I
stuffed them as far up into my ass as my fingers could push. I
could feel the pressure against my prostate. I stuck my index
finger through the ring at the end of the string and started
pressing and tugging on my balls. Then, with my other hand,
I started jacking off. Slowly at first, but I was too far gone for
much finesse. Within a few strokes my fist was jerking hard
and fast over my hard, hot cock. My balls clenched as I began
to come. I pulled slowly on the string, and the smooth, round
balls came rolling over my prostate and popping through my
asshole.

I came so hard I thought my heart would stop. I mean, my
cock and my ass and my nipples – I swear even my earlobes
came! I didn't even realize I'd yelled until afterwards. I was
lying there, curled up in a ball and panting as I came back
down.

Suddenly Perry was knocking on the door and hollering,
"You okay in there?"

"Uh, yeah." I gasped. I was surprised at how detached my
voice sounded. "Why?"

"You just yelled like you'd damn near killed yourself! Are
you hurt?"

"Uh, no," I stammered. I could hardly breathe, much less
think. Finally I just stuttered out, "I'm just watching TV. Ah,
Australian football. Yeah. And somebody just scored." Hell,
who could understand the rules of that game, anyway? I could
feel my vision starting to clear as my breathing slowed down
and my heart rate dropped closer to normal.

"Well, so long as you're okay, bud. Just be careful, okay?"

"Yeah. Yeah, I'm fine."

Damn, I thought to myself as my head fell back onto the
bed. *He has no idea of how fine I feel right now!* I reached up

and flicked a greasy finger over my nipple and my whole body jerked again.

DAY EIGHT

Needless to say, by this time I was seeing a pattern to the gift giving, so I couldn't wait to get home and see what was in my stocking. I was pretty sure it wouldn't be eight ladies dancing. It sure wasn't. Inside the stocking was a sapphire-colored Jelly Jewel dildo, eight inches long and one and a half inches in diameter. That sucker was huge! And I could hardly wait to stuff it up my ass.

In reality, stuffing it up took a bit longer than I'd expected. Between the time I took it out of the wrapper and washed it, and the time I was lying on my back on the bed with a couple of pillows under my hips, that big blue dildo seemed to have grown a couple of inches in length and quite a bit in diameter. I got back up and put the genital massage video in the VCR. As the two male lovers started playing with each other, I started rubbing my dildo date over my cock and balls. Pretty soon I had lube smeared all over myself and the slippery smooth head of the fake cock was kissing my asshole.

I could tell I was tight. Just looking at the size of that thing made me nervous. But my cock was so hard it could probably have cut diamonds. So I just took my time. I mean I *really* took my time. I tipped my hips up to rest my legs on the wall, and played with myself, just enjoying the feelings. As I moved my hand over my cock and balls, I kept a steady pressure on the dildo. Not forcing it in, just pressing enough that as my asshole relaxed and opened, the tip started sliding in, a little bit at a time. It felt so good that I pressed a little harder.

Suddenly the head popped in, and I gasped so hard that even my toes clenched against the wall. Damn, that hurt! Not as much as the first time somebody'd fucked me. But it still hurt a lot. I slipped it back out and felt myself relaxing as I caught my breath. All of my previous dates had been pretty average-sized guys, so I'd never had anything this big up my ass. That was one nice thing about fucking myself, I decided. I didn't have to tell anybody else to back off. I could just pull it out. And before I could change my mind, I popped it right back in.

My toes still curled against the plaster, but this time it didn't hurt as much. I squirted more lube on my sleek new toy, and as I slid it in and out, the dildo gradually started going in further.

Then I got a bonus present. I discovered that I could see myself in the mirror on the closet door. I could see the huge blue jelly cock fucking my hungry asshole. I'd been watching the video out of the corner of my eye, but pretty soon I was concentrating on what was going on in the mirror. And on feeling the huge cock stretch my asshole. And on touching my prostate. I stiffened and moaned each time the dildo slid over it. I didn't have to twist my hips like I used to to align myself with that jerk Jack's cock. I knew just where to put it. In fact, it was almost hard to remember what Jack looked like anymore. I couldn't believe I'd spent so much time trying to make him happy. Well, now I didn't have to think about making anybody happy but myself. And damn, I was making myself feel great!

We were on stroke number twenty-one when I came. My hand slid over my cock as I looked from the video to the mirror and saw the long, sweet, jellied cock sliding full length into my ass. As it slipped over my prostate, I came so hard I started shaking.

That dildo may have had blue balls, but I sure as hell didn't anymore.

DAY NINE

Day Nine's toy was a bit of a surprise. Maybe I hadn't been such a good boy all year, but never before had Santa put a nine-inch leather slapper in my stocking. It wasn't bad looking, as far as paddles go. And it didn't sting all that much when I smacked it against my palm experimentally, although it made a nice thwapping sound.

I'd worn the cock ring and ball stretcher to work. Without underwear again. So I'd pretty much been hard all day. I figured I was in the right frame of mind to experiment. My cock got even harder as I walked into my room and locked the door behind me. I'd never tried spanking before, but as I turned the cool, smooth leather in my hands, I discovered I was more than a little bit intrigued at the thought of feeling that sting across my butt.

I rubbed my hands across my crotch, trying to rearrange myself under my jeans, but the ball stretcher kind of limited my movement. I took off my jacket so I could move a bit more freely. Then I smacked my butt through my jeans a couple of times, just to try out the slapper. It only tingled a little bit, but the sound was enough to make me hot.

I was thinking about having been such a bad boy that Santa had put a paddle in my stocking when I suddenly remembered my present from Day Two. Nipple clamps seemed to go with a spanking, so since I'd figured out how to adjust them, I set the springs just a little bit tighter than I had before and snapped them on, nice and snug. They made my nipples stand up really hard, but they didn't hurt enough to distract me from getting really horny.

I thought Perry was working late that night, but I didn't know for sure. And I didn't want him knocking on the door again if I accidently smacked myself too hard and yelped. So I turned on some loud punk music and started slowly and lightly tapping my butt. Eventually I was whacking myself pretty hard, but it wasn't quite enough.

Finally, I decided that if I was going to be kinky, I might as well be really kinky. So I kicked off my shoes, peeled off my jeans, and started smacking my bare butt. It stung, not a lot, but some. But it was definitely making me hard. When I looked in the mirror, I'm not sure which turned me on more – the sight of my bright red butt or of my hard red cock sticking up out of that cock ring. My balls turned almost purple as the leather bands of the ball stretcher pulled down when my nuts definitely wanted to pull up.

I was going to see if I could come while I was spanking myself, but that was way too distracting. I finally decided this was the type of thing that had to be tried with a partner. My butt felt hot when I laid my palm on it, but it didn't really hurt. So I was surprised when I sat down on my desk chair and got right back up. There was a bit of a burn there! I pulled the chair over in front of the mirror, turning around a bit and looking over my shoulder to admire the color on my butt. Then I carefully sat down again, savoring the feel of the cool wood against my hot skin.

I stretched my legs straight out in front of me, with my ass right on the edge of the chair so I could really see the way my cock and balls were hanging. Then I leaned back, and while my hand stroked lightly over my dick, I tugged gently on the chain that ran between the nipple clamps. That made my nipples ache a bit, but I'd learned the first time I'd used the clamps that the nicest part of the bite was when I took them off.

Well, pervert or not, I liked what I saw in the mirror. So I sat on my hot little butt, playing with myself, until I realized I was getting pretty close. Then I released the nipple clamps, and while I sat there groaning, massaging the feeling back into those sore nubs, I came, my thick sticky cream smearing all over my hands and my pubic hair and that tight leather harness. It was sweet.

It was also the end of the lube.

DAY TEN
December 22. I came home exhausted. John Q. Public goes crazy during the holiday shopping season, and I'd spent too much time on my feet and answered too many questions. "No, Ma'am, I can't get a special order here by Christmas – they're even out at the warehouse." "Yes, Sir, we have that in every color of the rainbow – but not plaid." "I'm sorry, but we're only open until 10:30." I was beat.

I'd meant to stop at the store on the way home and pick up another tube of lube. Instead, I grabbed a drive-through burger and some onion rings. All I could think about was going home and putting my head on my pillow.

I just stood there laughing when I reached into the stocking and pulled out a ten-ounce tube of Astroglide. Maybe Santa had been peeking in my window last night and saw I was out.

I was too tired to use it though. I stripped and climbed under the covers before I had a chance to wonder when I'd started sleeping nude.

DAY ELEVEN

December 23rd. Work was crazy. All the last-minute shoppers were going nuts, and I think the only thing that kept me sane was wondering what Santa might have brought me for Day Eleven.

It had seemed a bit strange when I realized over my morning coffee that although I'd been satisfied quite a bit lately, I was still really horny. But I wasn't feeling frustrated anymore. Instead, it was that kind of horny I sometimes get when I'm having sex a lot, and I feel so turned so much of the time that I've got to come at least once a day. Which is fine by me!

But I damn near fell over when I took the latest toy out of the stocking. It was a Joltin' Jelly battery-powered vibrator, eleven inches by two inches. With a flared base for anal use. That thing would never fit up my ass! But I could feel my cock getting hard at the thought of trying.

I went in and took a long, hot bath to unwind from the day. And I let myself relax completely. The water was so hot and the bubbles so deep that I probably would have fallen asleep if I hadn't been thinking so much about my new toy. I spent a long time leaning back in the water with my head resting on the bath pillow and my knees drawn up while I fingered my ass, making sure it was all loose and relaxed. But I knew it was going to take more preparation than warm water if I was really going to be able to play with my new toy. So as I was toweling myself off, I stuck my slicked-up Diamond Lil butt plug up my ass – I was so relaxed it went in easily. And when it was snugly in place, I brushed my teeth and went back in my room to set up the VCR, putting the remote on the nightstand where I could reach it. It felt strange, walking around with my ass stretched over the slick firm plug. But it made me feel really sexy, too. Like I was really ready to be fucked.

I'd turned up the space heater when I went in the bathroom, so my room was nice and toasty in spite of the snow outside. For a while I just stood there in front of the mirror, running my hands over my body and watching my cock start to get hard while my ass muscles clenched against the plug. Then I got the vibrator and watched how my cock jumped when I turned it on and rubbed it against my skin, especially over the head of my dick. It felt good, but eventually I knew I wanted to feel vibration deep in my ass.

So I pulled down the covers – just let them fall onto the floor. Then I tossed the pillows into the middle of the bed and covered them with towels. (I was really going through a lot of laundry this week!) Then I lay down on the flannel sheets with my butt on the pillows so it was way up in the air and my knees were pretty much over my shoulders. I had a great view of the mirror and the bright red base where the Diamond Lil was plugging my hungry little asshole.

I clicked on the remote and started to play my video. For a while I just lay there watching, while my hands glided over my nipples and gently massaged between my legs. But my fingertips kept wandering back toward my asshole. I moaned a few times as I slid the plug in and out – I couldn't help myself. Pretty soon I'd smeared lube all over myself and was groaning out loud as the vibrator slid over my cock and balls and then the tip hummed against the base of the plug.

Eventually I pulled the plug out and slowly let the head of the vibrator slide over my asshole. It hummed softly as it fuzzed against my relaxed, wide open skin. It felt the way I imagined a good rim job would, though no one had ever done that to me, with the current health considerations and all. But it was soft and wet and it kept pressing and teasing against the mouth of my asshole. Every once in a while I looked at the TV, alternating my stroking, depending on what the guys on the video were doing. But mostly I was looking at the mirror or just closing my eyes and enjoying the feelings.

It was almost a surprise when I felt a little pop and realized the head of the vibrator was in me. I mean, I knew my asshole was now wide open, but I was still a little surprised that the vibrator didn't really hurt. My ass just felt stretched and full in a burning sort of way. As I slid the vibrator back and forth, the burning went away. Then I watched in the mirror as that huge, vibrating fake dick slowly fucked its way into my ass.

It wasn't one of those vibrators that really shakes things up. On low, it barely hummed. But I felt the vibration in my bones. And as that thick, warm rubber sank into me, oh God, I felt it all the way through my joyspot. I didn't even move my hand on my cock much, just a little – just enough, as that huge throbbing dick fucked me like I'd needed to be fucked for so long. I could hear myself crying out as the strokes slid over my prostate, but at that point I didn't care if Perry broke down the fucking door. I think I yelled when I came. Hell, I know I did. My cock shot gobs of spunk down onto my chest while my whole body damn near convulsed from the vibrations.

I had to wait until I'd caught my breath a bit to get the vibrator back out of my ass. It was so big and filled me so tightly that I felt every little bump and vein as it slid back over my hypersensitive asshole and plopped out onto the bed. I reached down and massaged my asshole a bit, enjoying how it felt all loose and puffy and slick.

Perry had to have heard me. I mean I yelled loud enough to drown out the TV when I came, and I knew he was home from work by then. But this time, he didn't knock on the door. I started to wonder why.

DAY TWELVE
Christmas Eve. I'd been thinking about this Santa thing all day as the Christmas shopping season wound down to an end. The two Bills had gone home for the holidays last weekend. Their stockings hadn't bulged since the day they left. In fact, almost everybody I knew was out of town now. I was going to my aunt's the next day for dinner. She'd said I could bring a friend, and I was thinking of asking Perry if he wanted to come with me.

On the way home, I stopped at the store and got him a huge peppermint candy cane. But as I tucked it into his stocking, I was surprised to find it empty. Well, we'd closed early. Maybe Santa hadn't come yet. I dropped the cane in, scratching my balls as I re-situated myself against my jeans for the hundredth time that day. I'd started liking the way the cock ring felt, so I was wearing it again. And again I was free-balling. In fact I'd halfway decided that maybe I didn't want to wear underwear at all anymore. Well, except through airport security systems.

The more I thought about it, the more I realized I was hoping it was Perry who'd been filling my stocking. I'd seen him again this morning, on our way out the door to work. Even though his winter coat had been covering his most obvious assets, I'd still really liked the way he looked. I figured I'd ask him to come with me to my aunt's even if he wasn't Santa.

When I got to my own room, I could see a bulge in my stocking. So I reached in and pulled out a box of one dozen condoms. Ultra-sensitive. Extra large. Mint-flavored. Just like the candy cane.

I had to laugh. Who knows, maybe I'd just surprised Santa in the act! He was probably going to come back to Perry's room later. Well, either way, at least ole Perry'd have his peppermint. I shrugged my shoulders and gave up on trying to figure it out.

The "Twelve Days of Christmas" had been playing on the radio on the way home, so I leaned against the door, my latest gift in my hand, and did a quick mental inventory of my presents. I'd gotten:
one dozen condoms,
an eleven-inch vibrator,
a ten-ounce tube of Astroglide,
a nine-inch slapper,
an eight-inch Jelly Jewel dildo,
a string of seven anal beads,
a sixty-minute video,
a five-inch vibrating butt plug,
a four-inch Diamond Lil plug
a Triple Crown cock ring and ball stretcher,
a pair of nipple clamps,
and a large tube of water-based lube.

Even if I never did figure out who Santa was, it had been one helluva Christmas!

As I put the key in the lock, the doorknob turned, and I froze. The door was unlocked. And I always lock the door to my room.

I hesitated a moment before deciding that, whoever was in my room, I'd take my chances that it was probably Santa. And even if it was a burglar, he'd be in for a surprise, because I was horny as hell, I had a dozen condoms in my hand, and I was coming in that room cock first!

As I opened the door, a laughing voice boomed out, "Ho, Ho, Ho!" And I broke into a grin even before my eyes adjusted to the glow of the candlelight.

There, stretched out naked on my bed, was the best Christmas present of all: Perry, smiling at me, with that huge, hard cock of his pointing up at his belly, and a big red bow tied around his neck.

I climbed up next to him on the bed and kissed him for all I was worth.

Memory Vibrations

Susan St. Aubin

ONE OF THE PLEASURES of age is surprise, because the more you forget, the more the world seems new. You read a wonderful book, then six months later check it out of the library and enjoy it all over again. Halfway through, a vibration begins at the base of your neck and quivers slowly up over your head as you remember that you know these characters, you know what will happen, because you've experienced this book before. The Italian restaurant you found five years ago, the one with glasses full of breadsticks on blue and white tablecloths, can be discovered anew until near the end of the meal when the back of your neck twitches again to tell you that you've been there before.

Sometimes the surprises aren't quite so pleasant. There are pills, for example. The number of pills you take increases exponentially with age. First, there's an alphabet of vitamins: A for eyesight, B for the nervous system, C for protection from cancer and colds, calcium to keep the bones strong, ginkgo for memory (if you can remember to take it) – you add something new every week. Then you move on to the hard drugs: Inderal for an irregular heart beat, estrogen for hot flashes and your bones again, and progesterone to counteract the tendency of estrogen to cause cancer of the uterus.

Your cat is getting older, too – she is eighteen, which is a lot older than you in animal years. Her thyroid is shot and she has high blood pressure and anemia, so now you have to keep track of her pills as well as your own. There's Tapazole to tame the hyperactive thyroid that makes her pace the floors all night, her long claws (a sign of age in a cat) clicking on the floor like a dog's, and Norvasc to keep the blood pressure under control so her eyes don't redden with hemorrhage when you clip her toenails. She also gets a grey-green, cheesy-smelling vitamin pill which the vet cheerfully tells you is flavored with reconstituted mouse DNA. She devours this one with a deep-throated purr, so there's no need to push it down her throat; you save it for last.

You keep charts for all these pills – the cat's Norvasc is every other day, as is your Inderal, while the Tapazole, mouse vitamin, estrogen, progesterone and your vitamins are daily pills. Estrogen is a blue tablet, progesterone is pink, and Tapazole is white, all of them small and round like buttons on doll clothes. At dawn they look the same, so once you accidentally take a Tapazole and give estrogen to the cat. You call the vet because there are certain things your personal physician should never know about you, and the nice young vet laughs as he says, "Oh, once probably won't hurt either one of you, but you really should keep the pills in different rooms so you can't mix them up."

Now the cat's pills go in the kitchen cupboard next to her food, and your estrogen and progesterone go in the bottom drawer of your bedside table, along with lubricants, condoms, latex gloves, and the old diaphragm you keep for sentimental reasons (who knows, maybe wired to a battery pack it could find another life as an internal massager). Also in this drawer are the external vibrators you like to use when you relax after your evening bath.

The bath itself can be a challenge. Lying limp in hot water, it's easy to forget where you are in the process. You start with your face and work your way down with a well soaped sponge: neck, underarms, breasts. Then you sink back in the water to rinse and find your mind drifting like music around the books you've read, the dinner you plan to cook for friends, the woman you saw on the bus who looked like Cleopatra. You slide the sponge over your legs and wonder if you washed your cunt. You can't remember. Did you wash your feet? You scrub them, perhaps for the second time, and rise up on your knees to soap your cunt. You remember doing this already, though maybe it was last night, or the night before.

The sponge is too rough and awkward here, so you use your soapy hand, humming the old feminine hygiene deodorant ad that referred to the cunt as "that most girl part of you." You think of Cleopatra as your hand slips back and forth, soapy fingers entering every fold and crevice, paying particular attention, of course, to the fleshy wattle holding that "most girl" button which should surely be kept very clean. So you run your soapy fingers over it quite a few times, until your knees begin to wobble and you suddenly need to lie back in the water.

After the bath you lie on your bed, wanting more. You wonder how exactly you could wire the diaphragm to make it vibrate, but that's too much trouble to attempt now, and anyway the thought of an introverted massage leaves you cold. You're an extrovert yourself, so you pull open the drawer to the bedside table and feel for the vibrators you know so well by touch you don't need to turn on a light.

That long one with the wheel-shaped head you bought on sale at Long's Drugs years ago is really best for sore backs and legs – it has a name like a truck, the Panabrator IX, and an engine that can reduce any stiff muscle to liquid in seconds. When you turn it on, it jumps all over the bed unless kept under firm control. No, a vibrator that has to be driven is too powerful for your clit.

The shorter one with the smaller, soft head, the Magic Wand, is nice, but like most magic, not enough. The muffled vibrations spread gently from the crotch through the pelvic bone and throughout the body, but without enough intensity for an orgasm, so you end up using your fingers for the last couple of minutes, which defeats the purpose of having a vibrator: that sensation of effortless fulfillment. No, this is the one you use when you've got the flu and want to feel better all over without going to the trouble of actually coming. The effect is more like a close friend rubbing your back.

Then there's the small, boxy Prelude, with the Clitickler tip, not too hard and not too soft, but just right, with vibrations perfectly attuned to the hum of your *kitzler*, as the Germans call it: your tickler. Yes, you pull it out of the drawer by its smooth round handle, like you do every time.

But first the lubricants: Liquid Silk, warmed by your fingers, or slippery Astroglide, lube of the astronauts of erotic space? Astroglide gets sticky, so you choose the Liquid Silk, running it over your body like a scarf, massaging it into your breasts and nipples because it's an excellent body lotion, too; then sliding it down to the cunt, into and over all the folds, into the anus it goes on your forefinger and out again, in and out through the hardening ring of the sphincter.

With well-lubricated fingers, you settle on one spot, the C-spot you call it, because, really, what is this G-spot nonsense, that mythical internal spot of foolproof arousal that no woman you know seems to have? You've searched years for it with fingers and dildos bent to hit the mysterious, ever-moving target; in vain, the poor blind hands and penises of past lovers have probed and stirred inside you. You think that maybe a vibrating diaphragm could hit that spot, but why bother? The C-spot, the clit, the tender button, the stone, the man-in-the-boat, the door-tender, the key, the *kitzler* – this is a sure thing. You slowly tickle it, savoring each pass of your fingers because you have all the time you need now that there's no one but the sleeping cat to disturb you.

Your fingers are trapped in a rhythm of self-pleasure, your mind lost to it; your clit, and then your whole body, begins to hum. But something is missing. After a while, your hand begins to get numb, and you think, this is taking a very long time. What's wrong? You move your fingers faster, but that's not it. A vibration starts at the back of your neck, but the constant, pre-explosive hum of your clit overpowers it. Soon, soon. But you stay on that humming plateau while your poor, numb fingertips stumble along.

You stop, shake your hand, flex the fingers, and pick up again right where you left off because your clit has waited for you, humming, not yet, not yet. All right, when? This is all very nice, but you feel that strange twitch at the base of your neck that means something's missing. The pulsation climbs up the back of your head until a flash of memory comes to you with the best surprise of all: There's an amazing invention, the vibrator, a machine that will match the man-in-the-boat hum for hum to bring you over the top of that wave of pleasure you've been riding too long.

There it is on the pillow beside your head, plugged in and ready for work. You grab the smooth plastic handle of the Prelude, rubbing it over your sensitive palm; you push the switch and put the Clitickler knob firmly on the left side of your own knob, the easy and obvious C-spot, and soon your whole body is buzzing in time with the vibrator and your clit is humming as you ride the wave up and over the top where hum matches buzz on the long slide to shore.

What else could hit you like *that* revelation, the re-invention of the vibrator? Perhaps the day will come when you won't even remember you have a cunt or a clit, until one evening when you'll step into the bath and wash yourself with the sponge a bit roughly before switching to your hand and find – oh, yes, like a child again – that if you stroke there, press there, on the little nose between your legs, a warm sensation will creep up your spine, warmer than the water, and your toes and breasts will tingle, and it won't even be a memory any more because you're beyond that; it'll be the real thing, the final surprise, new every time it happens.

Tea for Three

Francisco Hulse

IT WAS ONE OF THOSE RARE occasions when her waking hadn't woken me; and she remembered, bless her heart, to rouse me from slumber in a way I had always dreamed of. Her warm, soft lips pressed against the back of my neck just as I became conscious. I didn't let on that I was awake. I wanted to see what else she would do. Her lips retreated from my neck, and I felt her hot breath on the damp line that her tongue was tracing down my shoulder blades and over my spine.

I had to groan slightly from the pleasure, then. She laughed her velvety laugh and, without stopping her love bites, started humming Uncle Bonsai's "Boys Want Sex in the Morning." Against the explicit advice of my chiropractor, I had rolled over some time during the night, so that I was now face down, making all this possible. "Hmm, not much sustenance there," she mumbled to no one in particular as she stopped chewing on my back. "Where else can a gal get some breakfast?" And suddenly her legs were straddling my ass, her nipples grazing my shoulders as her lips engulfed my left earlobe.

"Kayla, you're going to be the death of me!"

"Why, 'cause I give you what you want even before you're conscious?"

"Yes. My brain will melt down from a pleasure overload. If I'm ... ah ... conscious, at least I – oooh! – can brace myself. . . ." She was outlining my ear with the tip of her tongue, and kept this up throughout our conversation, pausing only when she spoke.

"At least you'll die happy!"

"True . . . but I don't want to die before Gwen gets back from Seattle!"

"Okay," she whispered, "I'll stop." She kept talking quietly right into my ear. "I want you very much alive and fully . . . operational when she gets back today with her harness. . . ." Kayla pulled my left shoulder back and neatly rolled me over without my assistance. She is much stronger than she looks.

Now face to face, we looked into each other's eyes. "Good morning, Gorgeous," she said.

"Same to you, Handsome." We kissed. Not the first-morning-kiss-through-a-grimace you see on the mouthwash commercials, either. I stopped suddenly, because I realized what she had just said. "Gwen's flying back *today*?"

"Well, I wouldn't call it proof of the existence of God, but it does give an atheist a moment of pause, doesn't it?"

I squeezed Kayla to me for the joy of that news, holding onto the small of her back and pulling her down to kiss her again. My erection slipped between her thigh and her vulva. Delightfully, she mistook this for urgency, crying, "Hang on! Let me get you a jimmy, Tiger."

She swiped frantically at the bedside and came up with a Gold Coin. We had the foil off and the condom on in record time. Then, carefully, she started rubbing the head of my cock between her nether lips, cooing, "Faustino, you're going to feel sooo good sliding into me . . . I'm nice and wet already. I was 'reading Braille' before I started in on you." Now she had a couple of inches worked in, and she pushed forward, drowning the rest of me. Usually Kayla and I have to work a little harder for me to fit, since she's not a big girl, but the anticipation of Gwen being back a whole day early got both our motors running quickly.

It was a delicious morning quickie.

Faustino rushed off to his first interpreting appointment that morning after minimal primping – not characteristic of him. As for me, I had the day off. I could have followed our quickie with a couple more quick orgasms with my favorite vibrator, but I decided not to. We were picking up Gwen from the airport about three, and I wanted to be fresh for her. I distracted myself by running a few errands, practicing the drums, and shopping for dinner. Then I called the airline to check that the flight would be on time. Of course, that got me thinking about Gwen again, so I ended up wearing my June Cleaver-gone-bad dress, the tight little '50s number, over my velvet bra, garter belt and stockings – no underwear, naturally – to meet her at the airport.

So there we were at the gate, waiting for Gwen. Faustino had on his tightest black jeans, a billowing white shirt, and one of his flashy vests. She strode up the ramp to the gate, red curly hair cascading past her lopsided smirk as she caught sight of us, then dove into our arms. We extracted two or three hugs apiece from her, and then sandwiched her between us, Faustino in front, and me behind. "You naughty girl!" Faustino clucked, then to me: "She's packing!"

I moved one of my hands down from her breasts (which I had been discreetly cupping through her shirt, since Faustino's body covered them from public scrutiny), and felt a cylindrical bulge in her pants. "How did you get this past airport security? Didn't the ring in the harness bring guards crashing down on you?"

"I changed in the airplane bathroom."

"By yourself, or did you have company?" I leered.

"By myself . . . although I wish you'd both been there."

Faustino laughed. "We tried that once, remember?"

I remembered it vividly. On the red-eye back from the March on Washington, we tried expanding on a popular fantasy. It was difficult enough to get two people into an airplane bathroom, and three proved impossible, so we took turns, while the third person distracted the flight attendants.

We retrieved Gwen's luggage from the carousel, and headed out to my van in section C-5 of the parking garage. She rambled on about the software developers' conference she had just been to, but when she saw that I had brought my van instead of her car, she stopped mid-sentence, and hooted. "I'm assuming you brought the futon, then?"

I assured her that we had, as we climbed in and pulled all the drapes. I took one of Gwen's arms and unbuttoned the cuff of her shirt, as Faustino unbuttoned the other. Gwen pulled my head toward hers and kissed me, a friendly hello-kiss, and followed this with a few where-have-you-been-all-my-life kisses. Meanwhile, Faustino was re-acquainting himself with the taste of Gwen's neck, and sliding her shirt off her shoulders.

Gwen put a hand behind each of our heads and pulled them

to her breasts. We each pulled a bra strap down and fell to kissing, sucking and biting her erect nipples. "My sweet babies," she cooed, in a distinctly non-maternal fashion. She was leaning back against the wheel well, her hands clutching the edge of the futon, beginning to sweat, her breath catching. She often comes this way, damn her, without any pressure on her clit, when both of us are at her breasts. (I should be so lucky.) This time was no exception.

Momentarily satisfied, she pushed my dress up and oohed and ahhed at my stockings and absent underwear. Her tongue made a beeline for my hot, wet clit. Faustino joined her in fondling my breasts in the velvet bra, all the while kissing my neck, and nibbling my earlobes. He and I kissed again and again as Gwen slipped two long fingers inside me, wiggling them against my G-spot, the way I like. "Oh, I know what I want," I announced abruptly, "Gwen, you get to fuck my cunt, and Faustino, you . . . "

But they didn't let me finish. They had me on all fours in no time, and as Gwen slipped superb silicone into my cunt from behind, I unbuckled Faustino's jeans and slipped out his erection.

They know me pretty well.

Faustino's rod was hard and sweetly musky, and I wrapped my tongue around the head. My cunt felt absolutely full as Gwen started alternating hard, fast strokes with grinding motions. Her thighs slapped my ass on the hard strokes, and when she would start to grind, her hands took over the spanking. Faustino leaned over me to kiss Gwen and fondle her breasts, moaning all the while as I sucked his cock. This constellation of gyrations and rotations got me very, very hot. I was close to coming when Gwen pulled out and whispered urgently to me, "Turn over."

I did. She plowed that nice bionic boner back into me. Now my head was between Faustino's legs, and my lips brushed his hirsute orbs. Naturally, I started licking them. She started in on his cock where I had left off, all the while grinding against my mons, between my stocking-clad legs. Faustino's breath got faster. I could feel his balls start to quiver, and pull into his body, away from my mouth. Gwen's head bobbed slightly, as she was taken off guard by his orgasm, but she didn't miss a stroke, either on his cock, or with the skillful doppelganger she was using on me. She leaned back, raising her body with her hands, to lick Faustino's nipples, as he tried not to collapse. In so doing, she drove the wicked wand just a little further than before and sent me over the edge. I came hard.

There are orgasms, and there are orgasms. For my money, it's hard to beat the kind I have with the kink and intimacy of nice toys operated by good lovers who are great loves.

Once Kayla and Faustino and I had thoroughly debauched ourselves in the van, I took the harness off, and we headed back to slightly more private quarters. I had been away for a week due to the conference, so we got got caught up on each other's news as we prepared dinner and sat down to eat, serenaded by the CD player shuffling between Laura Love, Elvis Costello, Dire Straits, Gentle Giant, and Liszt's "Hungarian Rhapsodies."

After dinner, we all cleared away the dishes and Faustino started to wash them. I put some water on to boil and looked through the teas, to see if one would suit everybody's mood. For three people who are so compatible in the sack, it's surprising that we have such a hard time coming up with consensus on tea. Still, if there has to be incompatibility, I'm glad it's in that area, rather than the sexual realm.

When I turned around to suggest an apricot blend, it was only to see Kayla on the edge of the dining-room table, her legs crossed, her dress hiked up, the tops of her stockings showing, and a come-hither smile on her face.

I forgot all about the tea. I walked over to the table, and kissed Kayla's cheeks, her eyebrows, her forehead, the tip of her nose, the tip of her chin, and finally, her sweet lips. Faustino noticed that we had gotten very quiet, and looked over his shoulder, from where he was still washing the dishes. He smiled, with equal parts compassion – at seeing the two loves of his life in love with one another – and simple voyeurism. And then he went back to washing the dishes. He's an odd duck and a good egg.

Meanwhile, Kayla's kisses drew me back to the here-and-now. I pushed her down, laying her across the table. She smiled, having guessed my intentions, raised her eyebrows, and queried in her most innocent voice, "Would the lady care for dessert?"

"The lady is going to have her fill!" I hiked up her dress, and dove into her short black pubes. She squirmed out of her dress, and kept squirming as I kept my tongue humming over her clit. Suddenly, Faustino was back — back behind me. I couldn't see him, but I felt two cocks between my legs. I reached back to feel, and just as I suspected, he had a harness around his waist, and it wasn't empty.

Kayla, as usual, was not shy about asking for what she wanted. "Gwen, lie on top of me. Faustino, you know what we planned for tonight." I lay on top of Kayla, since I was dying to be fucked from behind. Faustino's latex-sheathed cock slid nicely into Kayla, as did the dildo into my cunt.

Yes, dear reader, the motions were difficult to coordinate. And worth every ounce of concentration exerted, I might add. A general groaning and moaning filled the air, along with copious profanity and exhortations to a god we don't believe in, yet can't help calling out to as we deliver our viscous corporal love to each other.

We lay in a heap afterwards, utterly satisfied. Then the tea kettle reached its own climax, whistling its head off.

"So — apricot tea all right with everybody?"

The Punishment Stick

Debbie Ann Wertheim

WHAT I REALLY LIKE about the punishment stick is that it delivers maximum effect for minimum effort. The wood is so dense, and in such a concentrated area – eighteen inches long, two inches wide – that sometimes a mere ten strokes given hard and fast on Debbie Ann's bare bottom will bring tears to her eyes.

I like to look into those eyes and say, "Crying from just ten strokes? I thought you said you were a masochist." If I say it just right, I'll get a flare of anger. Then I'll say, "Angry? Are you angry? You must need more," and then I'll give her ten more. Hard. Fast. And when I look in her eyes again, I find even more anger, edged in frustration. I like to watch the emotions motivate her. She's so easy to push. Out of the anger and frustration she'll start yelling that she hates me. I like taking her to that place.

I calmly give her ten more. The more upset she gets, the calmer I am. The punishment stick makes it so easy. No chance of strands going astray, no pinpoint accuracy needed – just a strong arm and the determination to cause a whole lot of pain. Other paddles may be louder, or wider, or thicker, but none is more effective than the punishment stick.

The punishment stick is beautiful, not just in craftsmanship, but in its perfect simplicity. It has a range from enjoyable to hateful, and I delight in showing off its versatility, as Debbie Ann knows full well. When I'm not pushing her through a rollercoaster of emotions, I can actually make her wiggle with delight just by using the punishment stick in an entirely different way.

If I could take only one toy to a Debbie Ann island, I'd take the punishment stick and I know she'd be content.

Secret Santa

Sue Raymond

EVERY YEAR, OUR OFFICE has a secret Santa. Names are pulled anonymously and no one knows who their gift will come from unless the buyer wishes to be known. It's always been fun. I remember getting boring things like a coffee warmer from one of the guys in Engineering and, once, a set of inflatable boobs from the head of Purchasing.

We laugh, we joke, but I never expected the froth of red silk and black lace that fell from the box I opened. A chorus of catcalls rose from my fellow workers. I scanned the room, hoping to catch a slight flush of cheeks, an intimate smile, something to indicate who would offer a beautiful teddy, but there were no takers. The blush rose to my cheeks instead as I wondered. Was it Dave in Marketing? Rob in Sales?

Quitting time had come and gone, darkness falling outside the glass windows as champagne flowed and humor abounded. I circled the room, curious as to who could have offered me such a personal gift. No hints. No intimations. No sign that the one who'd drawn my name had even stayed long enough to see my reaction.

Finally giving up the hope of finding my secret admirer, I went to my office to get my things. Family waited at my mother's; gifts still needed to be wrapped.

As I leaned over my desk to retrieve my purse from the bottom drawer, someone closed my office door. I reached for the light near my computer when a voice whispered in my ear, "It's crotchless."

An immediate warmth replied, pulsing wet staining my underwear. I didn't recognize the voice and that made it so much better. Did I want to know?

Hands traced my shoulders, ran down along my arms and reached under to find my breasts. Imagining a tall, hard body, I lost all desire for light. I didn't want to know. I wanted Santa to remain a secret, to fulfill the fantasy of a faceless fuck.

Hands kneaded, measuring and weighing my breasts, hips pressed into mine with the promise of long, hard flesh. Then one hand dropped to the junction between my thighs, slowly drawing my skirt up until he discovered my wet panties.

"I've dreamed of you in that teddy ever since I bought it."

I refused to concentrate on the voice, afraid I'd recognize him. I didn't want to know. That brought complications, the possibility of a relationship I didn't want. I was comfortable with my life as it was and didn't want to change it. But my smile grew. Nothing wrong with a long, hot fuck with a stranger. No commitments. No complications. Just what I needed to make my holiday.

Toying with my panties, pushing and tugging, until long fingers were buried in my steaming labia. A few quick strokes across my clitoris and I was flying, ready to come without the usual long, involved foreplay.

"Not yet, my sweet."

Pressure on my back caused me to bend over my desk and I felt the body behind me slide down to his knees as he raised my skirt, running his hands along my garters and stockings. I always wore my panties over my garter belt. It made it easier on bathroom trips. He liked it too as he swept my underwear down to my ankles, gently lifting my feet to make the panties disappear.

My juices flowed with the ultimate turn-on. Though it was too dark to see, I knew my pussy lay inches away from his mouth, a taunt, waiting for him to ease his tongue inside and relieve me of the pressure that had built within my belly.

One long swipe of his expert tongue was all it took and I exploded, come dripping as he teased my lips, sucking and licking, throwing me into a second orgasm before I could recover from the first.

Then he rose, grabbing my hips in his strong hands, and shoved himself inside me, bringing me to a complete halt. That prick wasn't real.

"Jesus Christ!" I pushed, shoving the dark form back, and whirled around.

Annie Muldoon from Engineering smiled in the dark, her

features barely visible in the shadows. Her large hands found my breasts again and she moved between my legs.

"If it's cock you want, I can give you that, but only a woman knows how to suck a pussy properly."

As her long fingers found my clit again, I capitulated, hoping Santa would keep this secret . . . for now.

You Sent Me Flowers

Leslie Gardner

YOU SENT ME FLOWERS. At work. Three perfect, long-stemmed roses. One red: "With love," the card said; one white: "respect," read the next line; one yellow: "and passion," completed the brief message. Before any of my colleagues could ask to see it, I slipped the card into the pocket of my shirt, the one right over my heart. But I'm getting ahead of myself. . . .

You'd been gone for two weeks on an extended business trip. It was the longest we'd been apart during the year and a half we'd been living together. Then finally, the day of your return arrived.

6:58 AM: You phone me, just as I'm waking up, to let me know you'll be home by the time I return from work. You tell me how much you've missed me, how much you want me.

11:07 AM: The roses are delivered.

3:00 PM: I return to my desk after a meeting and collect my voice mail. Message number four holds your soft and sexy voice announcing you've arrived at the airport and I should get home as soon as I can. I struggle to concentrate on the work I need to finish.

4:30 PM: The phone rings. It's you. You say you've been fantasizing for two weeks about making love to me and that you're at home waiting for me now. I turn my face away from my co-workers for fear they will read the lust in my expression. You tell me you love me. Click.

4:32 PM: Mumbling some lame excuse for leaving early, I make a mad dash for the door, move swiftly to my car, and head for the highway. I find the shoulder harness annoying; my nipples are extremely sensitive and it keeps brushing against them. I have the convertible top down and the music blaring. The bass is turned up full blast adding to the vibration of the car. I find myself squeezing my thighs together and rocking my pelvis gently as I speed down the road.

5:14 PM: I park the car and dash up the back stairs. The door

157

is ajar. I enter the kitchen and glance toward the table – it is strewn with yellow rose petals . . . passion. I stand in front of the table to read the note propped up there, "With all my Love, Respect, and Passion." At that moment, all the clocks stop.

Suddenly, I feel you standing close behind me, your arms encircling my torso. I try to turn but you tighten your embrace, keeping me where I am. Your hands make their way to my breasts, finding my nipples swollen and taut. You knead the fleshy roundness of my breasts before moving to pinch and flick the sensitive points between your fingers and thumbs. I feel your hot breath on my neck, your moist tongue in my ear. I can barely hear you over the pounding of my heart when you breathe into my ear, "I want you . . . now." Feeling weak in the knees, I lean back into you. It's then that I feel the unanticipated hardness pressing into my butt from between your legs. It's then that I know you're going to fuck me.

I push myself back into the fly of your jeans, letting you know I want it. We work together to quickly remove my clothes, you stripping my trousers and panties to the floor while I pull my sweater and bra over my head. Your hands return to my nipples, tugging and pulling them just a little roughly. I widen my stance, letting you know I'm ready. You slip one hand down over the smooth globe of my ass and onto the thatch of wiry hair covering my pulsating heat. You don't even need to part my labia, my clitoris is so swollen it is extended well beyond my lips. A sweet, soulful groan escapes your lips as you feel my slipperiness smear on your palm and you realize you've brought the woman you love to this passionate and ready state.

You bend me forward at the waist and I brace myself with my arms extended down to the table. I hear the rustle of fabric as you quickly open the buttons on your jeans and pry the dildo out of the tight denim. I hear the tearing of cellophane and know you're rolling a condom onto the instrument of my pleasure. Next, the familiar sound of the lube; I imagine its cool slickness slathered on the silicone rod poised alert and ready behind me. Then you move up against me, the shaft wedged smartly up against my pussy lips. I bend down a little further, displaying my swollen, dripping, maddeningly empty hole.

You lean against me, your breasts crushed against my bare back. You slide your hand the length of my arm and place your hand firmly over mine. "Don't move," you say, as I rock my hips with desire. "*Don't* move, baby, stay perfectly still. I want you to feel every inch as I slide it into you, now stay very still."

With great effort, I still myself and every nerve seems to be focused on the entrance to my vagina. You press the head of the dildo against my opening and I moan. You slip the tip in, I gasp and move my hips. It always feels so big when you first put it inside of me. You grab my hips and begin to introduce more of the stiff shaft into my cunt. It feels a little rough, textured. I can feel every movement as you slowly slide it further into my dripping canal.

Glancing over my shoulder, I can see you're watching the thickness and length of the strap-on as you work it expertly in and out of my cunt. It excites me to know you're watching yourself fuck me. I push back against you as you slide the length of the thick dildo between my sodden outer lips and bury it deep in the smooth passage of my vagina.

Finally, with the entire shaft slick with my juices, you fall into a rhythm of stroking deep and strong. I can feel the ribs on the condom gently rasping against the walls of my cunt with each thrust. You reach around my hips, your fingers seeking out my clitoris. It is swollen and throbbing. It's so sensitive that your touch is like a shock. I bolt backward suddenly, taking the dildo deeper into me. Then I dive forward again, struggling to rub my aching clit against your fingers.

You ride me that way, fingering my little erection while you pound into my cunt and I hump my needy pussy against your skillful hand. I feel the orgasm rising up in me. I can tell by your movements that you're about to come too. As my cunt starts grabbing the dildo with the contractions of a heaving orgasm, you piston the shaft in and out of my grasping pussy and rub your clit against the dildo's base, carrying yourself through your own shattering peak. Finally, with one last thrust, you bury it deep inside of me and press your hand firmly against my clit as I continue to rock and grind against you. Thrashing about in my climax, I notice a shower of yellow rose petals floating from the table to the floor.

As my orgasm subsides, you gently run your hands up and down my back and tangle your fingers in my hair. When I've been quiet for a minute or two you start to withdraw from inside of me. I ask you to wait, my smooth muscles are still "ticking" involuntarily and it's so nice to feel stretched and full. I hear you working deftly at the buckles of the black leather harness which has been holding the rod of silicone firmly against your mound. You manage to remove the harness, leaving the dildo resting deep in the center of my pleasure.

You gather me into your arms and carry me to the bedroom. You lay me on the crisp sheets, freshly littered with red and white rose petals . . . love and respect. You lay down with me, enfolding me in your strong, loving arms. We lie there entwined, me with the dyke cock still gripped tightly deep within me, exactly where you left it, next to my heart.

There Was a Young Man from Racine ...

Ray Glass

MORNING. SATURDAY. What was that dream? Women wanting me, smiling, showing me their wet pants. A cave on the beach; there were other copulating couples there. And then I was back in a wooden schoolhouse and there was a teacher I hated. . . .

Morning hard-on. It makes it hard to turn over. Fantasizing about lewd phone conversations with an old kiss-and-tell girl-friend, who spun half-real stories presented as true, sparking off her obsessions or leading her into new ones. "So then me and her decided to check out the porno theater. You know they're all just gay cruising joints now? So this guy sits down next to her. I figure she can take care of herself. His thing was the size of a beer can, she said later, but I couldn't see in the dark, y'know. So she leans over and says 'he wants me to tell you. . .'"

I could keep pulling my pud and shoot off into the covers here, but I'd like to make it more interesting. Most jack-off acts are as uneventful as brushing your teeth: you gotta do it for mental hygiene. But once in a while the soul gets horny and needs more exquisite satisfaction. How about just calling someone up, saying "fulfill my needs!"? It's communication, but ultimately augmented jack-off. Cruise the nude beach? Probably just go home with visual material to jack off to. Ditto for going to a porno theater or bookstore. What I want to do is *make* something today, turn this dick-vector energy into a lasting thing, say hello to my special creativity, pat myself on the back, spend a special day with myself and get a unique present at the end. It's project time!

I wear these jeans for grungy work, but they show my basket and emphasize wet spots from snake tears, which happen frequently now that I'm fantasizing all the time, handling myself in the car and all. This is what I get for not coming when I need to, but it makes for an exciting balancing act between diligent work on the technical project at hand, and spewing my load at the slightest provocation. First stop: surplus electronics.

It's like going grocery shopping when you're hungry. Bins and bins and piles and piles of juicy, cheap electro-junk. The old nerds come here, telling stories of ancient projects and failed designs, initiating their sons into the priesthood of techno-magic. Laying hands on the metal and plastic, they invoke intuition gained from living for years within a unique view of the material world, enabling them to see into machines' inner lives. There's a rarity: a genuine female technophile, talking electronics jargon as glibly as anyone, in that clipped, rapid, nasal tone that drives me wild with desire. Oh, nerd girl with your tied-back hair and chunky ass, do you know how hot you are to the man with the wet spots in his jeans, who could put all his know-how to work to make you come? I feel these power-supply capacitors, big and round and heavy in my hand.

Lookit all these motors, some actually for vibrators. Here's some high-voltage transistors, ripe for an electro-stimulation creation. Last time I tried that, it just made my ass hurt, and I worried I'd burn out the nerves that activate my hard-on. That's the kind of "oh shit" I can do without.

Some pneumatics here . . . Oooh! Solenoid valves! Hot damn! With these, some of those solid-state relays over there, and my old air pump, I can make something that'll suck my dick till Sunday!

Next stop: hardware store. By this time, jizz pressure buildup has caused semen backup into the cranium, resulting in distorted perceptions of every potential sex object as abnormally attractive. I look past the screws and bolts to the suburban housewives in cut-offs and t-shirts. . . . The shirt doesn't touch her belly because it hangs off her protruding breasts, you see? Hey, I'll improve your home, honey. With me around, you won't have to do-it-yourself. Let's say I attached six-inch straps of soft silk onto a slow-moving variable-speed drill; would your clit stand up and say, "hey, me first!"? Or how about a juicy dildo in place of the blade on a reciprocating saw, would that get the job done?

No, I'd better stop this, or I'll buy armloads of expensive stuff, sucked into consumerism by sexual frustration in a way that no one had ever anticipated. A plywood board and some L-brackets will have to do.

In the garage, it's work-a-little, wank-a-little, work-a-little, wank-a-little. It doesn't help that that box of magazines hasn't been absorbed into the porno file cabinet. This woman's ad in the swinger mag reads "CUM IN ME. NX-11467. Passionate, bi-minded, married lady (must be discreet). Unsatisfied, hungry, compulsive masturbator. Wish to hear from couples, women, men, who can travel here. I'm a compulsive come freak. Need hot sex. Need you to come inside me. All answered. Hurry! KOKOMO, IN."

Come come in. There she is in black-and-white, pushing the wand vibrator hard underneath her protruding clit, eyes closed, mouth open, building up to another one. She probably wrote this in the same state of horniness-induced insanity in which I now find myself, connecting heart-to-heart with her little poem, seeing her tensing body as the materialization of my own inner "compulsive come freak," an androgynous demon.

"Hi."

"Hello?"

"I saw your ad. I . . . I'm in the same state you're in."

"You mean Indiana?"

Ohhh no, not yet. No satisfaction until the project is done and it can do it for me. Put that thing away and get to work.

I'll use the latex sucking sleeve from one of those oversold, underdesigned, overpriced sex toys I took apart. . . . See, the problem with pneumatic masturbation machines to date is that they depend on penis parameters for proper pistoning. A motor pushes a bellows or diaphragm back and forth, and this is connected by a hose to the cylindrical sleeve part that thus goes up and down on your wiener. My new invention will not only fit all sizes, but stroke length will be variable, and it will never work its way off, but stay on with leech-like tenacity. The secret: an ultrasonic sensor to monitor how deep your dick is into the suck sleeve. Ha! Plus a continuous air pump that could handle a horse. Line 'em up, guys!

The exciting moment has arrived: the union of man-meat and machine. Spreading the lube around in the soft receptacle using my pud probe proves to be so stimulating the experiment almost ends, but I control myself in the interest of science. In the first powered test, I find that in "suck" mode my machine works like a vacuum pump, making my member so hard it threatens to explode sideways. This added benefit should definitely be included in the sales brochure: "Press the 'rigidify' button and the machine produces an instant rock-hard erection, the throbbing subject of its orgasmic ministrations."

Starting up the electronics, there's always reversed connections, tweaking to do on timing circuits. The sleeve starts rhythmic excursions on my boner, pausing occasionally as I move a wire or replace a resistor. My own resistance is being worn away as I adjust circuit voltages to make the piston slide just over the head of my cock, testing its ability to stay on. My staying ability is being tested as I tweak the timing to increase stroke speed, and watch the pump pressure needle.

How would you like to watch this, Kokomo come freak, suburban housewife, fast-talking nerd girl? Would the sight of my reddening face and overwhelmed penis turn you from engineering grad student into wanton fuckpig? Stand there with your thick thighs spread wide, dripping onto the sawdust. Mouth open, staring, washed over by a flash flood in the stream of consciousness: "She always tucked them in, or else the nipples . . . And he stayed hard? Wow, how many times? . . . They saw us, but couldn't stop, I guess . . . Just do it in my mouth. I know a way we can both . . . Just the tip, just the tip – you're large! . . . soaked right through and the outside was slick. The one with the big dimensions, it just kept coming and coming. Oh yeah, I never forgot. . . ."

Yikes! Jizz is getting vacuumed into the solenoid valve, making a sound like a gurgling baby eating a pinball machine, and fucking up the air pressure. Turn the thing off, before it gets into the filter! Instantly my mind attacks the problem and comes up with a solution: put a jar with two hoses in the top into the line. Catch the jism. My mind is so clear now.

Insight floods the cranial space where the come used to be. A relevant fragment of limerick comes to mind: "There was a young man something something, who invented a fucking machine. Both concave and convex, it fit either sex, and was perfectly simple to clean." Now *there* was an engineer.

A Jewel of a Woman

Mary Anne Mohanraj

YOU EVER WONDER WHAT women think about when they're grabbing the goatee? I bet you hope they think about you – about
the smell of you, or the taste of your salty come, or how much
they want a nice, thick cock slamming into them right about
now . . . well, sorry to disappoint you, but I don't think about
men when I'm jilling off. Maybe other women do, but I'm a
little strange. You know what I think about?

Jewels. That's right. When I'm fluffin' the muffin, buffing
the beaver, airing the orchid – you know exactly what I mean
– I'm thinking about rubies. Rubies and diamonds. Rubies and
diamonds and emeralds and sapphires and I'm getting wet
just thinking about it. Here, let me get more comfortable –
undo this silly bra and spread my legs so I have some room to
work with – ah, that's better.

So as I was saying, I don't know what other girls do when
they're dousing the digits, but me, I get myself off with gem-
stones on my mind. Before I even start, I open up my jewel
case and adorn myself with some pretty or another – not that
I can afford real jewels, but at least I can pretend. Sometimes
I wrap imitation pearls around my waist, or put a string of
bangles on my naked arm. I've thought about getting my
nipples pierced, so I could hang earrings from them – wouldn't
that look cute? And at Christmas, I could dangle little orna-
ments there.

I once tried that trick you read about, where you stuff a
bunch of pearls deep into your pussy and then pull the strand
out slowly, one by one. It felt so good, so fucking good as they
came out, grinding against my clit one by one, but it totally
ruined those imitation pearls. I need real ones, baby . . . real
strands of pearls. And topazes, and opals, and amethysts, and
garnets – I'm not picky – I'll even take semi-precious if it's
the best I can get.

Mmm . . . just thinking about it makes me want to fuck. And

since you're not here, I'll have to do the best I can myself. Let my fingers do the walking, from my hard nipples down to pet the pussy, oh yeah. Uh huh. Just a little tickle here, then a little jab there . . . pull those labia apart so I can really get to strumming the clitar, oh yes. I left my vibrator at the office – silly me – but hey, I've had years of getting off without it. Just takes a bit more work. Just thinking about diamonds, diamonds in my hair and ears and around my smooth white neck – a diamond in my belly button and another in my pubic hair. They say that back in olden times, ladies used to grow their pubic hair extra long so they could tie ribbons in it. I'd dangle diamonds from each ribbon.

Maybe I'd just stuff a handful of rubies up my pussy. Oh, yeah. Nice, big, goose-egg rubies, cold and hard at first, then warming up inside me. I could walk to work with all those rubies jangling around in my pussy, and strange men would look at me in the street, wondering where that knocking noise was coming from. And I would smile. . . .

God, I'm soaking now, at the thought of all those rubies inside me. I wish I did have something inside me, something big and hard. Rubies would be best, but I wouldn't complain at a cock right now, no I wouldn't. My fingers are getting wrinkled, and it would be nice to have someone else take over thumbing the button, waxing the saddle. You could buy me jewels – the kind of jewels I can't afford earning $7.75 an hour as an Arthur Andersen file clerk.

How about that for a deal, huh? Buy me rubies and pearls, black onyxes and opals, and I'll deck myself out in jewels from head to toe, like those exotic harem girls over in Arabia. Hell, I'll wear an opal in my ass. And you can lick me all over, lick right around and over and under all those pretties, and take 'em off one by one to leave a clear path for you to fuck me. Oh yeah, oh yeah, oh yeah – wrap your fingers in my hair and pull me down to the bed naked and wet beneath you. Just leave me my pearls, my string of pearls wrapped twice around my waist, and I will fuck you like you've never been fucked before. Oh boy, oh God, yes – I will fuck you until you scream.

The Fishing Show

Mel Harris

"OH BABY . . . OH BABY! Wheeee, here we goooo. Would you look at the *size* of that thing! Oh – oh – oh!" Bone Wrinkelman's raspy voice filled the den. For a moment the only sound was a soft wheezing, then: "Oh, noooo! Here we go again." More wheezing. "Come on, baby. Come on. Come to Daddy – oh yeah. . . ."

Laybee Wrinkelman reached over, picked up the remote, and snapped off the VCR. She'd had enough of "The Fishing Show with Bone Wrinkelman." She tossed the remote back on the coffee table.

"Ha! I'd like to see him get half that excited when we make love," she muttered, getting up from the couch and heading for the kitchen.

She glared at the huge muskie, mounted in an upward leap, affixed to the rustic wooden beam above the doorway to the kitchen. "And I *know* you got more foreplay than I've had in the last three months!" she said to it, as she walked past.

Laybee opened the refrigerator door, hunting for the pasta salad she'd made yesterday, but all she saw was six-packs of beer, logs of cold cuts, cartons of dip and six dozen eggs.

Great, she thought. Bone was going on location again, and she wouldn't see him for another two weeks. She wouldn't get near him tonight either: one of Bone's ridiculous superstitions. "Honey, I *gotta* reserve my strength for the big game," he'd say, whenever she tried to snuggle up to him before one of his trips.

She shoved a huge jar of mustard to the side and found the salad. Grabbing one of the beers, because it would irritate Bone, she slammed the door shut with her hip, picked up a fork and returned to the den. She flopped down on the couch and turned this week's show back on. Bone liked her to watch it every week before it aired: another one of his superstitions.

"Yeah, yeah, oh *yeah*!" Bone's breathing was quite heavy

now as he skillfully brought a nice largemouth bass close to his boat.

"You're just going to wet yourself, aren't you?" Laybee said, taking a long swig of beer. She watched as Bone leaned over and lifted the hefty bass out of the water and held it up for his viewers to admire.

"There's just *nothing* that compares to the feeling of landing one of these beauties!" Bone gently stroked the glistening side of the wriggling fish.

"That's not what you used to tell me," Laybee mumbled, swallowing another gulp of beer. She remembered the way Bone had been during the first years of their marriage, coming back from his trips all eager and excited, testosterone raging.

They'd jump in the shower and he'd wave his Ugly Stick (Laybee's pet name for it) at her, talking like he did on the show, "Come on baby, soap up the rudder, baby. Make it nice and clean so it can slip through your wake." He'd made her laugh. And after she'd gotten it squeaky clean, she'd drop to her knees in the shower and ummm, ummm, ummm.

Laybee sighed. Now he just came home exhausted and hung over. She took another swig of beer and sank back into the soft cushions on the couch. She'd just have to resort to "Paddling the Pink Canoe," as Bone called it. She reached down and slid out of her jeans. She was already so wet.

Laybee finished her third beer and was on her way to the kitchen for a fourth when she noticed the clock. Oh boy, Bone would be home any minute to pack and he'd want his snack before he laid down for his ritual pre-trip nap.

Rifling through the cupboards, she took out some crackers and peanut butter, then retrieved an apple from the refrigerator. "Damn superstitions," she muttered, as she cut the apple into wedges. Bone claimed protein built up his endurance and the crackers settled his stomach for the flight. Laybee added the apple so he wouldn't die from scurvy.

She'd just finished spreading the last cracker when Bone walked through the door, hefting several large bags onto the counter. "Hi, hon," he said, walking over to the refrigerator to find room for the six pounds of bacon he'd bought. Laybee busied herself cleaning up from the snack, trying not to move too quickly as the beer had made her a little woozy.

"Hon?" Bone said, his head in the refrigerator. "What have you done to my supplies?"

She looked up to see him dangling the half-consumed six-pack by one of the plastic rings.

"You *know* I have to have all this stuff accounted for. It's all on the expense records."

"Relax, Bone," she said, not hiding her irritation. "It's just a couple beers. It's not like I sold all your tackle in a garage sale."

"*Lay*! Don't even *think* that!" The veins on his neck bulged.

"Sit down and have your snack before you have a stroke," Laybee said, pushing the plate of crackers toward him. She picked up the bags on the counter. "I'll take this stuff up to the bedroom."

Bone threw her a hurt look, but said nothing as he took the snack to the den and flipped on the VCR to watch his show.

Laybee heard him mumble, "Mmmm – yeah. Oh that was great!" through mouthfuls of cracker as she climbed the stairs to the bedroom.

The master bedroom was the second biggest room in the house, after the den, specially built so Bone could view the many trophies, awards and mounted game he'd gotten over the years. The large four-poster water bed occupied the center of the room. At the end of the bed sat a huge aquarium filled with Bone's favorite species of freshwater fish.

Laybee threw the bag on the bed and flopped down. She'd always found the fish gliding back and forth through the water soothing and sensual. The lighted tank threw a romantic glow on the bed. They'd spent many a night with the fish watching them make some waves in the water bed. She reached down and slid her hand inside her panties, still wet from her episode on the couch.

Since turning forty, two years ago, she'd found herself thinking about, and wanting, lovemaking nearly every day. It was worse than being a teenager. She'd been letting "her fingers do the walking" quite a bit more lately, but Bone's fingers were the ones she wanted, and his tongue, and his lips. . . .

She sighed again. If only he didn't have this damn trip tonight. The shoot wouldn't even start for another three days, but Bone liked to get there early and check everything out. And, as if he didn't get enough on the shoots, he did some fishing just for pleasure.

Maybe she could talk him out of leaving tonight. He could catch the first flight out in the morning and still arrive in plenty of time for the shoot. Laybee rolled over on her side and propped herself up on her elbow to stare at the fish. Nope, Bone would never go for that. His location shoots were like religious rituals. She looked around the room at the dozen or so boxes of tackle, fishing line and artificial bait that would be soon packed for the trip. She reached over and picked up a bag of glitter-infused, fluorescent-yellow night crawlers. They felt cool and enticing through the package.

Suddenly, Laybee dropped the bag back into the box and started searching through the rest of the boxes. Leaders, lures, floats, weights. She sat back down on the bed, a wide grin on her face.

Laybee heard the muffled thumps of Bone's slow, steady footsteps on the carpeted stairs as he headed for their bedroom. She hurried to finish brushing her hair and straighten her robe. She hoped she had returned every thing to its proper box so as not to arouse suspicion.

"I'm going to go downstairs and read so you can have some peace and quiet for your nap," she said to him as he entered the bedroom.

"Thanks, hon," he said, his hair tousled, eyelids heavy. "I really am tired. Will you be sure to wake me in an hour so I'll have plenty of time to pack?"

"Sure," she replied, looking at her watch. "One hour. Sweet dreams."

"Thanks, Lay," he said, pulling off his flannel shirt and hanging it over the back of the stuffed bobcat poised next to the bed. Clad only in his underwear and socks, he settled comfortably into the bed.

She flipped off the light and went downstairs to the den to put the finishing touches on her plan.

Laybee moved quietly through the darkened bedroom and stood next to the bed watching Bone sleep, sprawled out on his back. She shivered. She'd spent the past twenty minutes pacing the carpet in the den, finalizing her plans and waiting to make sure Bone was fast asleep. He slept like a rock, but still she moved cautiously. She had to have everything in place before he awoke, or it was never going to work.

Spying the large box she was looking for next to the bed, she reached over and gently removed four hinged rod holders, a manufacturer's gift given to Bone to promote on the show. She unfastened the hinges, trying to control her breathing. Her hands trembled as she opened each of the cuff-shaped rod holders. The holders were lined with a soft polyurethane foam, designed to prevent scratching and nicking expensive fishing rods.

Laybee snapped two hundred-pound test leaders to the ring on the outside of each rod holder, then looped the leaders around each of the four bedposts and fastened them on the ring. Very cautiously, she slid one of the holders around Bone's wrist; fastening it securely to form a cuff, she quickly repeated the process on his other wrist, and then on each of his ankles.

Opening another box, she found a large round cork float and set it on the edge of the bed. She also found one of the red bandannas Bone wore around his neck, a trademark of his show.

As she was double-checking the rod holders to make sure they were fastened securely, Bone began to stir. He opened his mouth in a wide yawn, obviously not yet aware of his predicament. Laybee stood back to admire her work and to see if the contraption would hold.

Suddenly Bone's eyes grew huge.

"Ah," she said with obvious satisfaction. "I see you're awake now."

"Laybee?" he said, still not fully comprehending. "What's goin' on?"

He tried to sit up, but when he realized he couldn't, he looked over at his wrists, and then his feet. The look of surprise quickly turned to panic.

"Don't get yourself all worked up, Bone." Her voice was oddly calm.

Bone's panic did not subside, however, and he began pulling his arms and legs, frantically trying to free himself. He only succeeded in pulling the rod holders more tightly around his wrists and ankles, the edges cutting into his flesh. Finally he gave up and lay panting on the bed.

He raised his head and looked at her in puzzlement. His eyes narrowed. "You've been watchin' them talk shows again, haven't you?"

Laybee said nothing.

Bone finally dropped his head back down on the bed. "C'mon Laybee, you've had your fun. Now, I've *got* to get ready. . . ."

"I don't think so," she interrupted, walking around to the end of the bed. "I watched your show today, Bone. It was real good. Just like it always is with all your hootin' and hollerin' and all those sweet words for the damn fish. You get so excited, I bet you come over the edge of the boat after the camera stops rolling."

"No, Laybee, that's *not* what happens – well okay, maybe once. But just that time in Minnesota when I landed that big muskie. Uh – and that time on Lake Michigan when the drag was set just right and . . . "

"Shut up, Bone!" she snapped. Laybee was pacing now.

Bone lay back silent for a moment, nervously flexing his hands. He looked at her again.

"Laybee, honey, *please.* I'm *so* sorry you feel ignored, but I have to go on this trip." His voice was pleading, feigning sweetness. "Is it PMS, hon? Is it – *that time?*"

She'd heard enough. Moving quickly now, Laybee dropped the float in Bone's open mouth and tied it in place with the bandanna.

"Munggrahhh?" Bone mumbled behind the cork.

"Ah, ah, ah!" Laybee said, shaking her finger at him, as she straddled his chest. "You're going to gag yourself."

"Aaragganth, bblanth, aahh garratsh . . . " He was waving his hands and jerking his head toward the boxes and suitcases next to the bed. "Mmrrrunggah!!" he growled again and started to cough.

"Oh, you're not going anywhere, Bone Wrinkelman," she said with a satisfied smile. "I've been waiting for a moment like this for a long time." Her nostrils flared. "I've spent the last two years waiting for you to stay home long enough to remind you what being with a woman is like. I've barely gotten enough time to watch you milk your monkey."

Bone grew strangely quiet. In Laybee's heated discussion, her arm-flailing had caused her robe to fall open, revealing the tight leather teddy she'd slipped into earlier. She stopped for a moment, watching Bone stare at her heaving breasts. He looked nervous. She knew he could feel her wet heat spreading across his chest. A smile returned to her tempting lips.

Laybee slid off him, stood next to the bed and removed her robe, letting it fall to the floor. Bone made some sort of gurgling sound deep in his throat. His eyes were glued to her.

"Ah, you like my new outfit?" She turned around, allowing him full visual advantage. "I got it last year while you were on location in Canada."

"And look at these neat little accessories," she said, peeling off the cups of the bra, revealing her full nipples. Another groan arose from Bone.

Laybee returned to the edge of the bed. Bone's boxer shorts were beginning to crease at an odd angle. She reached over, lifted the elastic waist band and took a peek. "Mmm, it's true. Graphite rods *do* have the best action," she said, slipping her hand inside. The boxers turned and tugged like a squirrel had gotten loose in them.

She removed her hand from Bone's shorts, letting the elastic band snap. Bone whimpered softly, his eyes pleading. Laybee turned again to search in one of the boxes. She came across a small, zippered case. Smiling, she opened it.

Bone could see she held something in her hand as she turned to face him again, but it wasn't until she sat the camcorder on the corner of the aquarium and was carefully focusing it on him, that he realized what she was doing.

"We're going to make our own little show, Bone Wrinkelman." Laybee pushed the record button.

Still searching, she reached into a nearby box, pulling out a multi-purpose pocket tool. She fiddled with it and found it had a pliers, screwdriver, corkscrew, and several knife blades, all in one. "Hmmm. *The Leatherman.* This is *very* interesting," she said. Bone's eyes widened.

"This should do it," she said, and pulling out the longest of the knife blades, she ran it lightly up the inside of Bone's thigh, lifting at the leg of his boxers.

He squirmed and whimpered, trying to get away from the cool, sharp, blade.

"Relax, Bone," she said. "I'm horny, not stupid."

She grasped the shorts in one hand and cut through the material with several deft strokes, the tattered remains falling back on the bed. Bone inhaled sharply. Before he could recover enough to take another breath, she repeated the process on his t-shirt, exposing his heaving chest and splendid erection.

Bone looked at his erection, then at Laybee, then back at his erection. His eyes begged.

Just then, the phone beside the bed rang. Laybee jumped and Bone whimpered. She picked up the phone. "Hello?" She put on her best housewife voice.

"Hey, Laybee. This is Rog Sparks. We're waiting for Bone down here so we can load up the plane. Is he there?"

"Hi Rog," her voice sweeter than Berkely's Liquid Fish Attractant. "I'm so sorry, but Bone can't come to the phone. He's all tied up right now – some special research or something."

Bone was waving his hands and making strained grunting noises. Laybee leaned over and pressed the exposed blade of the Leatherman firmly into his flesh, just below his navel. It immediately silenced him.

"Well, is he going to make the flight, Laybee? He knows we leave in half an hour."

"Mmm, well. I wouldn't count on it, Rog. I think he said

something about catching up with you guys tomorrow on location."

The silence hung for a long moment.

"Well, I, ah, guess we'd better go on ahead. . . ."

"Yes, Rog, I think that's wise."

"Okay then. Bye."

Laybee hung up the phone. Bone's breathing had slowed, his erection flagging.

"Now, back to business." She leaned over. He felt her heated breath. "We'll fix Mr. Wiggley," she murmured, taking all of him into her mouth.

Slowly, keeping a firm suction with her mouth, she pulled back. Bone's breathing quickened as she withdrew, his hips bucking forward in an attempt to thrust himself further into her mouth. Laybee took his wrinkled pouch in her hand and gently, but firmly, drew his swollen jewels toward his thighs. Letting him slide out of her mouth, she admired him for a moment, glistening and pulsating in the light of the aquarium.

The muscles of his abdomen tightened, and Laybee noticed the escalating bucking and pitching of his shaft. Bone's eyes rolled back in his head and he let out a deep gurgling moan. She reached over and frantically rummaged through the boxes. She recognized that motion; Bone Wrinkelman was about to spill.

"Oh no you don't," she said, taking one of the glittery neon jelly worms and tightening it firmly around the base of his penis.

The artificial bait did the trick – his erection finally stopped its lurching and stood tall and proud. Bone was now making slow, steady grunting noises.

Laybee returned to pacing beside the bed. Then, snapping her fingers, she rifled through the boxes again. Bone's erection rose and fell, following Laybee's movements, as if watching her.

She found a large aerosol can. "BANG! Fish Attractant," she read. She popped the cap off and sprayed a little of the contents into the lid and sniffed it.

"Whew," she said, coughing and waving her hand. "That

smells like Rog. No wonder he never has a date." She tossed the can back into the pile.

Holding up a package, she discovered a long carolina leader: a weight and two glowing red beads threaded onto a length of wire and finished on the ends with two snap swivels. She took it out of the package and fastened it around his neck, linking the swivels together.

"There," she said, arranging it. "Now you're dressed for the occasion."

She held up several more packages and read their contents out loud: "Pearl White Lizards, six-inch size. Shaky Tail Worm in June-bug and watermelonseed colors. Four-inch Meatheads, and the ten-inch *Old Monster?*"

She looked at him, "Jeez Bone, what do you guys *do* with this stuff?"

Bone shrugged.

"I might have to keep some of these for myself." She picked out the six-inch Pearl White Lizards and the ten-inch Old Monster in watermelonseed color and walked over to her dresser, depositing them in her underwear drawer.

Returning to the bed, she opened a couple of packages and pulled out their contents. The smooth, rubbery jelly baits wiggled and danced in her hands. They felt sensual, almost alive. Too good to put on a hook, she thought. Selecting a couple of glimmer-blue Split Tail Trailers, she draped them over her nipples and turned to Bone.

"Do I attract you now, Bone?" She shook her shoulders briefly, the shivers causing the Split Tail Trailers to dance erotically. Then she picked up a bait that looked like a giant red and black rubber caterpillar.

"Oohh – a Bush Hogg," she started to moan. "I know *just* where I want you." She slipped aside the leg of her teddy and rubbed the trembling lure along the inner edge of her recent trim. Her head fell back and she savored the prickly texture, beginning a steady rocking motion as she maneuvered the jelly bait. The Split Tail Trailers flipped onto Bone's chest.

He stared at them. He had forgotten to breathe, and he was turning a deep cinnamon red. Suddenly, he took a huge breath.

Laybee looked at him. "We can't have you passing out for lack of air now, can we?" she said, putting down the now-wet lure and opening a big box. She took out a bait aerator, an apparatus that looked like a small aquarium pump, attached a long plastic tube to it, and then plugged it into the wall. It made a quiet hum.

Setting the pump down next to the bed, she inserted the end of the tube under the bandanna tied around Bone's mouth, alongside the cork float. A more normal color soon returned to Bone's face.

"There we go," she said, slapping him gently on the cheek. "Now you'll have plenty of air."

Bone gave her a look that said he knew she had completely and utterly lost her mind. But then he gave another pleading look, nodding toward his penis.

Laybee pressed a finger to the top of his penis and watched it twitch. "Don't worry, Bone. I have big plans for the Ugly Stick." She slid her finger around the edge of his purple helmet.

Picking up the Bush Hogg again, she resumed her exploration, only now she propped one leg on the edge of the bed facing Bone as she worked. Laybee was thoroughly enjoying herself, finding the texture and sensation of the soft bait exquisite. But she was also keeping a close eye on Bone. His nostrils flared with each breath, his eyes transfixed by the action of the lure.

"Now don't you wish you were Mr. Bush Hogg here, Bone?" she cooed as she slipped the tail of the bait further inside.

Bone had resumed his quiet steady grunting, fascinated with the steady motions Laybee was making with her hands and the lure.

Laybee had to be careful. This lure was very effective, and she felt herself teetering on the edge of an unstoppable freefall. She slipped out the Bush Hogg and climbed on the bed. Kneeling next to Bone's hips, she began rubbing the wet, tensile bait along the length of his shaft.

"Aaaggrrrl," Bone growled, his toes curling up.

She leaned over and followed the motion of the lure with

her tongue, causing his erection to make short jerking strokes in her mouth.

"Mmm," she murmured, without stopping.

Bone began thrusting his hips forward again, increasing the motion of her mouth.

Laybee sat up for a moment, but Bone continued his thrusting, moaning in protest.

"Hold on boy," she said breathlessly. "We're gonna take care of that for you right now."

Laybee carefully straddled his hips. She gripped his erection in both hands and, poised above him, she began her descent. Bone, urgent and shaking, saw her hover briefly above him before plunging downward. It was only at the last moment he saw the split in her teddy, allowing an unencumbered splashdown.

Bone's crescendo was drowned out by Laybee's own ululating. She'd found the Bush Hogg again and was rubbing it on the front side of his shaft, both of them sharing in the pleasure. Laybee rose and fell on Bone like the waves of the sea.

Finally she could wait no longer, and she reached around and tugged at the jelly worm still tied around Bone's erection, releasing him. Laybee leaned forward and gripped Bone's shoulders, increasing her rocking as together they rode the wild wave.

"C'mon baby . . . that's it. C'mon home to me now. That's it!" Bone's grunting filled the den. Laybee giggled.

They snuggled together on the couch, watching his latest show.

She looked at him and he grinned as he patted her gently on the thigh. It had been a wonderful week since he'd been home from the shoot. Bone hadn't left the house since he'd been back, except for beer and food.

She watched him pull up a gorgeous walleye on the video. "Wow! Did you come after that one?" she teased.

"Naw," he blushed. "I saved my bait just for you, baby."

Laybee giggled again.

Bone traced the outline of her left breast with his finger. "I

think I found a new pre-trip ritual, too." He grinned again.
"Mmm, and I have the video to prove it," Laybee said, snuggling into his shoulder.
"Watch this," Bone said, picking up the remote to turn up the volume.

The last few minutes of the show was coming up.

The camera zoomed in on a very relaxed, slightly sunburned Bone standing on the edge of a dock next to a boat. He was wearing the leader "necklace."

"Remember folks, the key to a successful fishing trip is being prepared." He propped one foot on the edge of the boat. "The right bait, the right lures, and the right equipment for the right moment." Grinning, Bone patted the rod holders, now mounted on the boat.

"But most of all, remember that everything in life is better when you share it with the one you love. Bye now, and cast your line with a friend!" On the video, Bone waved and the credits began to roll.

Girls, Boys and All of Our Toys

M. Christian

SHE'S SMALL AND IMMACULATE: skin like scrubbed china, body like a precisely painted doll's. She doesn't look her size until you're standing next to her – then you realize her scale. I don't know what I expected her to like, but when I found out, when she shared this information with me and the others in my tight little circle, I do admit to being delightfully surprised.

Considering, it makes sense: her little vibrating dildo looks like a toy, a child's plastic gizmo. It's made of blue plastic and smells like the beach toys she had as a kid – a kind of tart but fruity smell. The Japanese have either laws or a cultural thing against calling a dick a dick, so the shaft of her Japanese toy is the body of an Eskimo maiden. At the base of this totem pole that happens to look very much like every cock I've ever seen sits a slender polar bear whose tongue, with a flick of a switch, starts to flutter rather . . . excitedly. Flick a second switch and it starts to hum, vibrate and oscillate like a snake charmed by a slow dance-tune.

I admit a gentle desire to see her with her favorite. Not because I have the hots for her (though she is definitely hot), but rather for the punch-line, the sweet conclusion. After enjoying her toy, she often, she admits with a sly smile, falls asleep with it still inside. Hearing this for the first time, two things came to mind: the precious image of this beautiful girl, all fine china and elegant poise, lying back on a futon, legs spread, toy humming in a slow-dance, its polar bear tongue fluttering while she dozes content and spent, a blissful smile on her perfect face.

The other thing that struck me was how, like people and their pets, all the special people in my life resemble their toys.

She's a teacher. What she teaches is near and dear to all of our . . . well, let's just say that what she teaches is near and dear. Like her students, she thinks a lot about sex, about what she likes and what she doesn't. It's that honesty that I find so endearing. No apologies, no embarrassments. Just an "if it's fun, and it doesn't hurt anyone, then do it" attitude. I was over at her place for a talk, having dinner, and the subject just sort of came up.

Like her, it's big and black. Fat would be a good word – and one she'd agree with. Picturing her with her toy, I can just about imagine her chat with her students: "I like the sensation of being filled. I've tried vibrators, but I'm too sensitive. I like to come very slowly, and my hand's best for that. But I do like being filled. It took a long time to find the right one. I know some women like theirs 'realistic' and others prefer them simple, streamlined. I don't really care – I chose mine because it was big and fat, something that I could ease into myself, slowly, as I rubbed my clit."

I have an image of her: sitting like a black Buddha, a big, beaming grin on her face, her favorite toy in her lap – proudly displaying the source of her pleasure, and demonstrating what she loves to teach us: "don't be embarrassed if it gives you pleasure!"

He's a big burly bear of a man. That's right – and so is his toy. When you look at him, you see what he proudly proclaims: "I'm a grizzly!" From his great furry beard to his warm furry belly, he is someone you could easily see rubbing his back on some tree in the forest. Sometimes, when you look at him just right – say under the cold blue glare of a setting moon – you could swear that he really was a beast of the forest: barely trained to walk upright and eat with a fork.

His toy, his special plaything, is what you'd think it would be: strong and manly. I never heard him talk about it, unlike some of my other friends. But one day I dropped in on his . . . excuse me, I was about to say his house. But he is a beast and beasts don't have houses, do they? One day I stopped by his cave, his lair, and there it was: plastic as pink as his tongue, as pink as his asshole (well, naturally). I've seen butt plugs before and since, of course, but this one was the beast of butt plugs. Looking at it sideways you could see it, too, lurk-

ing in the forest, waiting for the right asshole to walk by
before . . .

Unorthodox as she is, they are perfect for her. I've known her
a long while, and while others see chaos and a Mistress of
Flake, I see a spirit too free to be hemmed in by outside con-
vention or even fundamental laws. She is as wild and untamed
as her hair — a rusty metal halo around her freckled face and
green eyes. Always in motion, always half-way somewhere,
she darts around in her slender, peaches-and-cream body —
never quite in place.

For some she is a source of frustration, wild and unkempt,
but she manages to make it work for her. Things that, for the
rest of us tamed people, would never work in a thousand years
just seem to click, clack, klunk into place for this certain red-
head.

The same goes for her toys. I've never known anyone who
could make those stupid little eggs work. No one I know has
ever gotten off on Ben Wa balls.

Except for her — and knowing her luck, the very first time.
Now they are a staple of hers. That and her rocking chair that
always squeaks. Many times I visit, wondering as she rocks
back and forth in that squeaky chair, if the smile on her ani-
mated face is because a friend has dropped by or because of
those uncertain, unpredictable, metal eggs rolling around inside her.

Me? I have to continue this hypothesis, I guess. Like my toy, I
am long and thin. It's strange how you suddenly have a favorite. I've tried many toys over the years: things that oscillate
and hum, buzz and expand, plastic and rubber, wood and metal.
But then I found the one, and it's been on my night stand ever
since.

Long and thin, yes. For certain. Long and thin and leathery.
Well, I ain't *that* old — so maybe we can supplant "leathery"
(and all its tired, worldly connotations) with tough but flexible.
I've tried other kinds, the rubber rings (watch out for pubic
hair!), the steel ones (hard to get off but fun), and the velcro

ones (but they get loose), so mine has snaps.

Now for the personal details: I like the sensation when I loop it around the shaft of my cock and my balls. I like the constriction, the strength it gives me when I'm hard. I like the way it also changes how I feel – suddenly my skin feels less sensitive, like my cock belongs to someone else. I enjoy it – a lot.

So I guess I'm like my cock ring. We both exist for fun. Lots and lots and lots of fun.

Tool Time

Dave Sommers

I WAS OUT IN MY WOODSHOP doing some finish sanding with my quarter-sheet Makita Palm sander. The sandpaper that I was using just plain wore out, so I took the sheet off. The pad beneath the paper is rather soft, and I knew that the sander really had some serious vibrating power. I looked around to make sure I didn't have an audience, and just for kicks, I touched the pad to the crotch of my jeans and turned the sander on.

The sensation startled me at first. After pulling away for a second, I decided to try again. I pressed the pad against my pants, grabbed the sander with both hands and held it still for about two minutes. The sensation was incredible. I had a full erection at this point and was climbing toward extreme arousal. The thought that I ought to stop before I made a mess in my pants quickly gave way to impending orgasm.

I was sweating and holding that sander tight to my penis – my knees started to get weak, but I was able to remain standing. The feeling was almost too intense. I knew I was at the point of no return and when the spasms started, they just kept coming. I couldn't believe that I could keep coming for that long! It was probably only about three minutes, but it felt like ten.

When I finally turned the sander off, I was shaking from head to toe, and my whole genital region was tingling. I couldn't remember when I'd had an orgasm of that intensity.

I now have a whole new outlook on finish sanding.

Two Toy Tales

T.L. Robertson

I WAS EMPLOYED in the motion picture and TV production industry for twelve years as a Teamster. I drove people and equipment from motorcycles to eighteen-wheelers, and I was outnumbered by the men in the business at least ten to one. We were preparing to go to San Bernardino for a three-day location shoot, and I loaded my bag with everyone else's in the luggage compartment of the crew bus. I drove a motor home to location and then went to recover my bag from the crew bus. Too late, I realized that I had the distinct "honor" of having the only bag that was faintly humming as it was offloaded. Of course, the man who handed me my bag pointed this out to everyone. For days after that, the sound men and prop makers were offering me "C" cells in case my vibrator ran down. . . . Of course, I took the batteries. It always pays to be prepared.

My daughters, who were teenagers at the time but spooked by being in the house without me at night, became frightened by a loud noise emanating from my bedroom, which was in the back of the house. They called the landlord because they were scared to go into the room to find out what the noise was. I'm grateful he wasn't home. Next, they called our neighbor and long-time friend who lived downstairs. Bonnie agreed to come upstairs and investigate. As they opened the door to my dark room and followed the sound – you guessed it – my vibrator was on and vibrating against a loose drawer, making an awful racket for such a small thing! They all had a good laugh then and the many times afterward that they told the story at my expense.

Sneak Attack of the Sex Toys

John Alden

WE ARE IN BED, in our bedroom. I sit upright in bed, a pillow on
my knees. My wife of thirty-five years kneels on the bed, her
head on the pillow. With my left hand, I caress her hair, the
back of her neck, her back, her arms. With my right hand, I
gently rub her pussy and her clitoris. Because she is kneeling,
her ass in the air, her clitoris is fully exposed to my fingers. I
put my right thumb into her pussy, while circling her clitoris
with my right index finger. Sometimes I put a thick dildo in her
pussy, pushing it in and out while my other hand excites her
clitoris. Her face is turned away from me on the pillow, and she
doesn't speak. All our communication is through the movements
of her body, which are exquisitely picked up by my hands, and
especially my fingers. When she reaches orgasm, her pussy
contracts strongly on my thumb or the dildo. A little Astroglide,
and we can go on like this for twenty minutes.

It wasn't always like this. My wife was raised a Catholic,
taught that fucking was for the sole purpose of conceiving
children. No "decent Catholic wife" wanted sex just for the
pure pleasure of it. I may have taken the girl out of the Church,
but I can't completely get the Church out of the girl. Her approach is to try to make me climax as quickly as she does. But
I value foreplay at least as much as climax. I enjoy creating
good sexual experiences for my wife; it's like the pleasure of
creating a good meal. From a variety of ingredients you select
a combination that will create a uniquely satisfying experience. So there has always been some sexual tension between
us – she reaches orgasm quickly, with a minimum of foreplay, and wants me to be similarly quick; I want to play for
twenty or thirty minutes, bringing her to repeated climaxes.

I don't think this tension will ever be fully resolved, but sex
toys have played a role in helping to reduce it. Through trial
and error, I discovered that my wife's Catholic ethics can be
circumvented if she has the opportunity to relinquish control.

For example, her favorite fucking position is lying on her stomach while I enter her from the rear. Since I am pressing down
on her, she can't move and so has no responsibility for her
own or for my orgasms. I can reach under her and finger her
clit while I stroke her pussy, and bring her to climax as frequently as I wish.

I had noted that her favorite "guilty pleasure" reading was
the sort of romance novel where the innocent virgin is carried off by the pirates and ravaged against her will, only to
discover that she actually enjoys the ravishment. Putting together these observations, I conceived the idea of introducing
sex toys. The priests may have taught her that sex with one's
husband is for procreation, but sex with a toy obviously hasn't
any purpose at all . . . except pleasure.

I began with a campaign of stealth and treachery. My wife
enjoys soaking in the tub. At four o'clock one afternoon, I ran
her bath water, added her favorite bubbles, and put some wine
and cheese on the table next to the tub. I turned on her favorite music and left her to soak. Every ten minutes I came in,
kissed her, and checked on her status. After half an hour, I
came in with an Aquassager, a little, hand-held waterproof massager. Concealing the Aquassager in my right hand, I knelt
beside the tub, leaned her head back, and kissed her deeply.
When she began to moan, I gently inserted the Aquassager
between her legs. The combination of the warm water and
the wine had so relaxed her that the Aquassager quickly found
its target and she just as quickly found her climax. I moved
the Aquassager to her face and neck for a while, and then
began to kiss her deeply again while returning the Aquassager
to her pussy and clitoris. This time her climax was so explo-
sive, she sloshed water out of the tub.

In short, my theory had worked: reduce her defenses with
hot water and wine and music, then enlist a toy as an aid, and
don't give her any choices to make. Since that first success,
we've enjoyed other sex toys together. Some things don't
change: once I enter her, she wants me to climax quickly. But
the preliminary use of sex toys lets us prolong lovemaking,
and enjoy a variety of pleasures. I suppose you could rail

against the shame injected into an innocent child by the Church and fight to eradicate these deeply held beliefs. But I have found that a little stealth and cunning, coupled with sex toys, works pretty well instead.

Turnabout Is Fair Play

Hanna Levin

UP UNTIL LAST YEAR I had never even seen a sex toy. I wouldn't have said that my sex life was boring, but after ten years of marriage, my husband Paul and I had developed a regular routine. Twice a week Paul would eat my pussy until I was wet enough to fuck and then fuck me in the missionary position until I came. Then he would turn me over and fuck me in the doggy position until he came. Elapsed time: thirteen minutes give or take thirty seconds.

I'd heard about "sensuous massage" and how it could add spice to your sex life, but it took me quite a while to get up the courage to order the massage oil and how-to guide from the intimate-products catalog. When the package arrived I opened it with anticipation. Imagine my surprise when I found, not the items that I had ordered, but a vibrating dildo, a sleek leather harness and a full set of restraints!

At first I thought that this was some sort of a practical joke. As I said, I'd never owned a sex toy before in my life and these were hardly the sort of items I would have started with. But when I looked more carefully at the label I saw that the package had been addressed to Anna Levin. My name is Hanna Levin. I smiled as I imagined Anna, wherever she lived, opening the package meant for me. I hoped she wasn't too disappointed.

For my part, I was intrigued. The dildo was made of firm, flexible rubber and was quite realistic in appearance. It was also huge: nine inches long and two inches around at its widest. Trying to convince myself that I was only satisfying an academic curiosity about how such an item actually functioned, I got some batteries and K-Y Jelly and headed for the bedroom.

I slipped out of my jeans and lay on my back. Then I turned the vibrating dildo on and began, tentatively at first, to rub my pussy through my underwear. The sensation was, if you'll

pardon the pun, quite electrifying. In fact, I'd never felt anything so good in my life. I got wet almost immediately and it
wasn't long before I was naked and had the dildo inside me.
The massive size of the thing held my pussy lips wide apart,
exposing my clit to its humming surface.

Something about satisfying myself with a dildo gave me a
feeling of being in charge and made me want to be on top. I
turned over and began humping my new "friend," tilting my
pelvis so that my tingling clit rubbed all the way down the
pulsating shaft with every stroke. I was really getting excited
now, but as I humped harder, I was having trouble preventing
the dildo from moving around. All of a sudden it occurred to
me that I had the means to fix that little problem. I slid off the
dildo, slipped it through the harness, and then cinched the
harness firmly around two pillows. Feeling very much like
"woman the tool-maker," I remounted the dildo and went back
to work.

There was a faint rustle from the living room, but in my
excitement I assumed it was only the cats playing and never
missed a stroke. Just as I was nearing the point where an orgasm was inevitable, I heard a distinctly human sigh from the
bedroom doorway and turned to see my husband, Paul, home
early from work. He couldn't have been watching for more
than a few minutes, but if I could judge from the smile on his
face and the bulge in the front of his pants, he'd had plenty of
time to get very excited! He crossed the room and began massaging my ass with one hand and undressing himself with the
other. "Don't stop on my account," he said in a husky voice.
(As if I had any intention of stopping!)

Naked now, Paul got on the bed behind me and began rubbing his very erect cock against my ass as I humped the dildo.
At first I thought he was going to try to get his cock in my
pussy too. I was about to point out that, considering the huge
size of the dildo, there wasn't any more room, when Paul
grabbed the K-Y Jelly and started massaging it into my ass. I
couldn't believe it. Was my husband, mister only-twice-a-week
and always in the same position, really about to stick his cock
up my ass? I was intrigued and excited but, frankly, a bit con-

cerned as well. Would I enjoy it? What if I didn't? What if I did?

I didn't have to wait long for the answers to these questions. Paul leaned forward, pressing his cock firmly against my asshole. At first it seemed like I was too tight and he'd never get in. But all at once I relaxed and the tip of his cock slipped inside.

Once Paul had his cock inside my ass, he began humping me, gently at first and then with increasing determination. Every time he pushed into me, it forced my clit down against the humming base of the dildo. The sensation of getting fucked up the ass was so intense that I could hardly concentrate on what was going on in my pussy. My orgasm, when it came, almost caught me by surprise. I must have tensed as I approached orgasm and clamped down even tighter on Paul's cock, because right in the middle of my climax I heard Paul cry out with pleasure and felt him come too. I could feel each individual spasm of his cock and each spurt of his ejaculation. A new position and simultaneous orgasms, I thought through the afterglow. Not bad for a couple of old married folks. I headed to the bathroom to wash up.

In the weeks that followed, both the frequency and variety of my sex life with Paul improved dramatically. Our new toys had opened up so many possibilities that we hardly had time to explore them all. One thing did bother me, however: sometimes it seemed as if Paul took the extraordinary change for granted.

The matter came to a head (so to speak) one evening when we went to bed early to fool around. I had used the restraints to strap Paul's wrists and ankles firmly to the bed frame and was in the process of giving him a blow job. My intention was to suck Paul's cock until he was close to a climax, to mount him and ride him until I came, and then to finish him off with a few quick licks. However, Paul seemed to have other plans for the evening. "Why don't you untie me and turn around so we can do something a little special?" he asked.

I knew what Paul wanted, he wanted to fuck me up the ass. And frankly, I was a bit offended. Please don't misunderstand

— I enjoy anal sex. However, my definition of "something a little special" is a blow job on the couch before dinner. When I let a man fuck me up the ass that's something very big and very special! I stopped in mid-suck. I really felt the need to explain this difference in our perceptions to Paul. After all, honesty and openness are the cornerstones of our relationship. However, I just couldn't think of the right words. Then it occurred to me that a demonstration might succeed where an explanation would fail. "I think a little turnabout is an excellent idea," I replied.

I undid one of Paul's ankle restraints. Then, just when he thought I was about to undo the other, I reached under him with both arms, rolled him onto his stomach, and quickly retied his free ankle. I stood by the head of the bed, where Paul could see me, and removed the dildo and harness from the drawer. Paul's eyes grew wide as I slipped the dildo into the harness and tightened the harness firmly around my legs and waist. The huge cock stood out at attention. I tested the batteries — full power.

"You're not really going to fuck me with that thing?" Paul asked, a note of genuine trepidation in his voice.

"Why not?" I replied. "We both enjoy it when you fuck me up the ass. I'm sure that it won't be any different when I do it to you." Of course, I knew that this was different. For one thing, my dildo was half again longer than Paul's cock and close to twice as big around. I patted his ass to reassure him, then jumped onto the bed, placed my knees against the inside of his thighs and pushed his legs far apart.

I squeezed a generous amount of lubricant onto Paul's ass and then touched the massive vibrating head of the dildo to him. His sphincter puckered in response, and I waited patiently until he relaxed before I tried again. This time he managed to stay relaxed. I applied gentle pressure until the head of my dildo entered him. Then I advanced the dildo, and Paul responded with appreciative moans. When I gained full entry, I shifted my position so that my clit rested against the humming base of the dildo and began to fuck Paul with slow smooth strokes.

The combination of the dildo vibrating directly against my clit and seeing Paul in this extraordinary position was bringing me close to orgasm, but I was amazed to see that Paul was getting very excited as well. He began by rotating his ass in slow circles and soon was pushing himself up into me with every stroke. I almost couldn't believe that he was enjoying himself so much, until I reached under him and grasped his rock-hard cock. He was ready to come.

Paul's excitement was the last straw for me. I came so long and so loud that the cats arrived from the kitchen to make sure I was all right. My climax brought Paul along too. I heard him cry out and felt the throbbing contractions of his cock as he came. I waited until Paul's erection faded before I slowly switched the dildo off and gently withdrew. Then I untied Paul. "You go wash up," I suggested. "I'll change the sheets."

That evening seems to have produced an understanding between Paul and me. We still use all of our sex toys. In fact, we've bought a few more. However, Paul is now very careful about anal sex. Usually he waits for me to offer. But even when his excitement gets the better of him, Paul is sure to ask respectfully if it's okay with me before he jumps to any conclusions. I guess he's learned that turnabout is fair play!

The Contributors

Blake C. Aarens published her first story at the age of nine. She lives in Oakland with the Queen of the Universe (currently in feline form). Her first novel, *Cowards of Conscience*, is with her agent in New York. She is hard at work on the second one.

Rebecca C. Abbott is a missionary kid who used to design and make sex toys for a living. She has always wanted to be a writer, but she hopes her mother doesn't read this, her first published story.

John Alden is sixty years old, married, with four children. An executive with a Fortune 500 company, he enjoys a variety of sexual activities with his spouse, and has found monogamy to be extremely rewarding.

Lyn Chevli, addicted to the benevolent weather in Southern California, whiles away her time devising new ways to subvert conventional culture. She also tends to her garden, a mix of asparagus, peaches and hollyhocks.

M. Christian's stories have appeared in many books, magazines and anthologies, including *Best American Erotica 1994*, *Best American Erotica 1997*, *The Mammoth Book of International Erotica*, *First Person Sexual* and *Sex Spoken Here*. He is also the editor of the anthologies *Eros Ex Machina* and *Midsummer Night's Dreams*. Many of his friends oscillate, gyrate, and vibrate.

P.D. Curry has been told her imagination is a little too "colorful" for her academic and business colleagues. She finds that middle age has made matters worse but has also made her care less than ever. She lives in the Midwest with a kind, good-humored man, two serious-minded cats, and two computers.

Leslie Gardner lives in San Francisco and is anxiously waiting for someone to send her flowers.

Marlo Gayle, a disgruntled engineer from Ohio, moved to the San Francisco Bay Area to continue exploring his own sexuality and the sexual underground. He hopes to move back eventually, and try to open a few minds. He currently is happily working for a San Francisco fetish clothing manufacturer.

Ray Glass is a porno artist with a scientific bent. He has worked with other San Francisco Bay Area sex explorers, shooting and editing artistic and experimental video erotica. Years of lecturing about pornography to sexuality classes at San Francisco State University have taught him enough to fill a book, which is his current project.

Mel Harris is a forty-one-year-old mother of two who lives on the Gulf of Mexico in northern Florida. She is currently working on a novel about a woman in her spiritual journey. "The Fishing Show" is her first published short story. She has only recently begun to write erotica and is enjoying it thoroughly. The bumper sticker on her car reads: "I tried to contain myself – but I escaped."

Jacob Hugart, between sporadic bouts of writing, wastes time on the Internet, works on a computer helpdesk, hangs out with jugglers and magicians, tries to relax, and lives with his wife in Minnesota . . . but not necessarily in that order.

Francisco Hulse, guitarist, drummer and composer, lives in San Francisco, interpreting and translating Spanish and English. This is his first published work of fiction (not autobiographical, sadly), and is dedicated to all his lovers past, present, and future, even the ones who would say, "oh, blech!" if they read this.

Hank Hyena is the author of a short story collection entitled *Miracles of the Flesh* and an upcoming spoken word CD, *The Whole World Lives In My Bedroom.* He frequently performs his monologues, slide shows, puppet shows, and poems at San Francisco sex readings.

Joel King is the pseudonym of a Seattle attorney who believes in constant vigilance to prevent encroachments on our First Amendment rights to free speech.

Hanna Levin lives in central Maine with her partner and cats. She teaches biology at a small college. "Turnabout is Fair Play" will not appear with her scientific and pedagogical publications in her upcoming application for tenure.

Adam McCabe's erotic mystery stories have appeared in a number of erotic magazines and anthologies. The thirty-something author lives in Cincinnati with his lover and muse.

Mary Anne Mohanraj has lived in Sri Lanka, Connecticut, Chicago, Philadelphia and the Bay Area. Her poetry and prose have appeared in a variety of forums, including her book, *Torn Shapes of Desire: Internet Erotica.* She moderates the Internet Erotica Writers' Workshop; see http://www. iam.com/maryanne/ for details and more juicy tidbits.

Anne Moon lives in rural Illinois with her partner of ten years and their two cats. She has a Ph.D. in Journalism, works in higher education, and writes erotica for pleasure. This is her first published piece.

Frank Paine actually did study electrical engineering in college but then discovered that filmmaking and writing were a lot more fun. He is the author of the audio book *Motel 69,* humorous tales of sexual misadventures.

Sue Raymond lives in Connecticut with her husband and two children. Her goal as an erotic author and aspiring romance writer is to bring the best elements of both genres together. Without the encouragement and support of her fellow writers on Compuserve, she wouldn't have attempted to succeed.

Loren Rhoads is the editor of *Morbid Curiosity* magazine. Her essays have appeared in *Travelers' Tales San Francisco* and *Paris.* She'd like to thank her dear friend Christine for giving her the Oster as a birthday present and Ann Marie for returning *Macho Sluts.* Such good friends are a blessing!

T.L. Robertson resides in Santa Fe, New Mexico.

Dominic Santi is a Los Angeles-based freelancer who writes sexy stories because they're such great fun. Using the online moniker "Cady," Dominic is section leader for Alternative Eros in Compuserve's Erotica forum. Partnered for many years, the author shares a home office with a dog and two opinionated cats.

Lawrence Schimel wrote *The Drag Queen of Elfland*, co-edited *Switch Hitters, PoMosexuals, Two Hearts Desire* and edited *The Mammoth Book of Gay Erotica*, among other anthologies.

Karen A. Selz is an Assistant Professor at a top-ranked medical school, where she applies the conceptual and computational tools of mathematical physics to the study of brains and behavior. She lives happily with her most wonderful husband, Arnold, their dog, Senator Alvin Barkley, and their cat, Miss Goo.

Anne Semans is happy she finally got to work out her Cinderella complex. She lives with her beautiful young daughter and her much-loved partner.

snakesKin says, "My higher power is Murphy's Law; and chocolate is my destiny." A San Francisco Bay Area resident for twenty-five years, she is a professional musician whose passions include sailing, cooking, raising reptiles, travel and erotic adventures. This is her first published erotic writing, but not, she vows, her last.

Dave Sommers is thirty-four with two young children and a lovely wife. He has many different hobbies and a strong desire to learn new things. One of his favorite subjects is female sexuality. His best sources of information are Good Vibrations, Carol Queen and Betty Dodson.

Susan St. Aubin's erotic writing has appeared in every volume of the *Herotica®* series, as well as in *Best American Erotica 1995, Yellow Silk: Erotic Arts and Letters,* and *Fever.* She lives with her husband and their twenty-year-old cat, Georgia.

Michael Stamp is a New Jersey-based author who works a boring day job for a paycheck, and writes erotica for satisfaction, hoping one day to turn that satisfaction into a career. Stamp is currently single, and shares hearth and home with an overweight feline named Sam Beckett.

Diane Stevens is the pseudonym of a writer who lives and works in the San Francisco Bay Area. "Beauty Shop" is her first published erotic story.

Alison Tyler is a shy girl with a dirty mind. Her erotic novels include *Dial "L" for Loveless, Dark Room, Venus Online, The Virgin,* and *The Blue Rose.* She edited the compilation of short stories *Girls on the Go.* Listen for her on the audio versions of *Heroticas 2* and *3.*

R. Jay Waldinger, an artificial intelligence researcher on the San Francisco peninsula, practices aikido, yoga and meditation, and makes bread, cookies and good coffee, but is new to erotic fiction.

Debbie Ann Wertheim would like to thank all the wonderful people who have used the punishment stick on her. She is sure this is the source of much inspiration. Her work also appears in *Sex Spoken Here* and can occasionally be found online in soc.sexuality.spanking.

The Editors

Anne Semans and **Cathy Winks** enjoyed selling sex toys for over ten years at Good Vibrations in San Francisco. They are the authors of *The New Good Vibrations Guide to Sex* and a forthcoming book about sex on the World Wide Web.

To Order Down There Press Books:

_____ **Sex Toy Tales,** *Anne Semans & Cathy Winks, editors.*	$12.50
_____ **Good Vibrations Guide: The G-Spot,** *Cathy Winks.* Demystifying what some consider the ultimate pleasure spot.	$7.00
_____ **Good Vibrations Guide: Adult Videos,** *Cathy Winks.* Everything you wanted to know about selecting and watching X-rated flicks.	$7.00
_____ **Good Vibrations: The Complete Guide to Vibrators,** *Joani Blank.* "...explicit, entertaining....encouraging self-awareness and pleasure." *Los Angeles Times*	$6.50
_____ **Sex Spoken Here,** *Carol Queen & Jack Davis, editors.* Cutting edge erotic prose and a sprinkling of verse from Good Vibrations.	$14.50
_____ **Exhibitionism for the Shy,** *Carol Queen.* "A sexual travel guide...." *(Libido)* to discovering your erotic inner persona.	$12.50
_____ **Herotica®: A Collection of Women's Erotic Fiction,** *Susie Bright, editor.* Lesbian, bi, and straight short stories that sizzle and satisfy.	$10.50
_____ **I Am My Lover,** *Joani Blank, editor.* Twelve women celebrate self-sexuality in over 100 exquisitely explicit duotone photos.	$25.00
_____ **First Person Sexual,** *Joani Blank, editor.* Women and men describe their masturbation experiences in forthright anecdotes and essays.	$14.50
_____ **Femalia,** *Joani Blank, editor.* Thirty-two stunning color portraits of women's genitals, demystifying what is so often hidden.	$14.50
_____ **Anal Pleasure & Health, revised.** *Jack Morin, Ph.D.* Comprehensive guidelines for AIDS risk reduction and safe, healthy anal sex for men, women and couples. Completely updated for the '90s.	$18.00
_____ **The Playbook for Women About Sex,** *Joani Blank.*	$4.50
_____ **The Playbook for Men About Sex,** *Joani Blank.* Activities to enhance sexual self-awareness and consciousness.	$4.50
_____ **Sex Information, May I Help You?,** *Isadora Alman.* An "...excellent model on how to speak directly about sex." *S.F Chronicle*	$9.50
_____ **Erotic by Nature,** *David Steinberg, editor.* Luscious prose, poetry and duotone photos in an elegantly designed cloth edition.	$45.00

Catalogs — free with purchase of any book, else send $2

_____ **Good Vibrations Mail Order.** Many of the sex toys described in this book, as well as massage oils, safe sex supplies and videos.

_____ **The Sexuality Library.** Over 300 sexual self-help and enhancement books, videos, audiobooks and CDs.

Buy these books from your local bookstore, call toll-free at **1-800-289-8423,** or use this coupon to order directly:

Down There Press, 938 Howard Street, San Francisco CA 94103

Include $4.50 shipping for the first book ordered and $1.00 for each additional book. California residents please add sales tax. We ship UPS whenever possible; please give us your street address.

Name _____

UPS Street Address _____

_____ ZIP _____